How to Improve Your Bridge

Also by H. W. Kelsey

*

MATCH-POINT BRIDGE
ADVANCED PLAY AT BRIDGE
KILLING DEFENCE AT BRIDGE
MORE KILLING DEFENCE AT BRIDGE
LOGICAL BRIDGE PLAY
TEST YOUR MATCH PLAY
THE TOUGH GAME

HOW TO IMPROVE YOUR BRIDGE

H. W. KELSEY

First published in 1971
by Faber and Faber Limited
3 Queen Square London WC1N 3AU
Reprinted in 1973
This paperback edition first published in 1979
Reprinted 1982, 1985 and 1991

Printed in England by Clays Ltd, St Ives plc

A CIP record for this book is
available from the British Library

ISBN 0-571-11438-5

# *Acknowledgements*

I AM indebted to the Editor of *P.A. Features* for permission to include some material that first appeared in my syndicated column.

My thanks are also due once again to Denis Young and Tom Culbertson for making a critical examination of my script and combing out a number of analytical errors.

H.W.K.

Contents

Introduction

WHEN people ask me how they can improve their game my stock answer, 'Cut down your errors', is not always received with favour. To players keen to embark on some dynamic course of action the suggestion seems altogether too obvious and too tame. And yet cutting down on errors is not merely the best way to improve; it is just about the only way.

Technique in bidding and play can carry you only part of the way towards success at bridge. Once a certain level has been reached the scope for improvement narrows and the rate of progress automatically slows down. A law of diminishing returns sets in, each further small advance in technique being won only at the cost of an agonizing effort.

Most of you will not be prepared to make this effort, and you are quite right. You play bridge for fun, and there is not much fun in burning the midnight oil over obscure squeeze matrices which you may never encounter at the table. Besides, if your technique is no more than adequate you are good enough to be the biggest money-winner in your club. For that matter you are good enough to win a World Championship if only you can learn to cut out the wholly unnecessary errors that you make.

A study of the records of championship matches shows time and time again that the winners are not the players with the sharpest technique but those who commit the fewest blunders in simple situations. A good example is the 1969 Bermuda Bowl contest in which a star-studded U.S.A. team was beaten into third place by a little-known team representing Nationalist China. The Chinese would not claim to be wizards of technique, but they played up to their own standards by keeping their errors to an absolute minimum and this enabled them to defeat a technically superior team.

After a good session a player will sometimes claim to have played flawless bridge. Don't you believe it. What he really means is that his mistakes passed unnoticed because they escaped punishment on this occasion. The truth is that all players make a number of mistakes in every session of bridge that they play. Good players make fewer than beginners, of course. The very best players may make no more than two or three errors per session, but there is no doubt that they make them.

Unfortunately, most players are over-sensitive about their mistakes. The better your standard the less happy you will be about admitting a mistake to others, for this involves some loss of face. Well, there is no need to parade your mistakes in public. You needn't even confess them to me. But you must admit them to yourself, for without that admission there can be no improvement.

Human nature is such that we tend to remember our successes and forget our failures. The memory of recent blunders is acutely embarrassing and the natural reflex is to banish the unhappy experience from our minds. Those who wish to improve, however, must put up with the embarrassment and take a long, hard look at every disaster that overtakes them. Each mistake we make (or at least each mistake that we recognize as such) should be set up under the microscope for a detailed and critical analysis. Only thus can we hope to learn from our mistakes and prevent a repetition.

For tournament players this should be a partnership exercise, particularly where bidding misunderstandings and defensive slips are concerned. Make a practice of getting together after the session and trying to root out the cause of every bad result on your score-card. Don't neglect the good boards either, for there may be concealed errors on a number of these. No doubt you could have done better still on some hands and were lucky to escape with your skin on others.

This willingness to face up to your mistakes and learn from

them is the real secret of success at any form of bridge. As soon as a player begins to feel that he has no more to learn he is on the way down.

In this book my aim has been to set out under rough headings some of the constantly recurring errors I have noticed in myself and in those with whom I play. To keep the book compact I have refrained from casting my net too wide. Bridge is a game of infinite variety and it would take several large volumes to cover the whole spectrum of error, but I believe that what I offer is quite a representative selection of common failings. Writing about them has certainly helped my game and I hope that reading about them will help yours. If you can manage to avoid just a few of these mistakes in future you will be a winner in any circle.

1

Abuse of Conventions

THERE are those who insist that bridge would be a better game if all conventions except the opening two-bid were barred. This is a minority view, however, and its exponents might just as well argue that the game of golf should be played with only one club.

After all, the right kind of convention is designed to make the game easier for us. If it does not always achieve this purpose the fault lies in ourselves, not in the convention. We are apt to overuse our favourites, putting them to work on the wrong hands or at the wrong time. Using a number two wood from a bad lie in the rough is unlikely to give a satisfactory result.

There may be some difficulty in deciding which conventions to adopt. So many have come on the market recently that players are faced with a bewildering choice. Of the new conventions that appear each year some are good, some of dubious value, and some so monstrous that they can be loved only by their creators.

For the beginner my advice is to keep it simple. Stick to Stayman and Blackwood and one or two others that have stood the test of time. This is all that is needed to play an effective game. Later, when you have gained some experience, you can add further conventions as you feel the need. But you should still be highly selective and avoid taking on more than you can carry. Young players often make the mistake of trying to play every second convention they hear about. They stagger round the course with their overloaded bags and wonder why their results are disappointing. The reason is that half the time they are using defective clubs, and even when they succeed in choosing the right club they are too weary or too confused to use it properly. Each additional convention you adopt places a small extra load on your memory and increases the risk of a fiasco.

Apply this three-fold test to determine the value of any convention you may be thinking of adopting.

1. Is it really effective on the hands for which it was designed?
2. Does it fully compensate for the loss of the natural bid it displaces?
3. Has it a reasonable frequency of occurrence?

The last point is often overlooked. There is no profit in carrying an extra club if you have a chance to use it only once a year. All such dead wood should be thrown out.

Having chosen your conventions you are still left with the problem of how and when to use them. This is where the mistakes creep in. When players adopt a convention they hate to keep it idle and are often tempted to give it an airing on a completely unsuitable occasion.

They say that ninety-five players out of every hundred use Blackwood, and I'm prepared to wager that ninety of them would be better off if they had never heard of the convention. Blackwood lends itself particularly easily to abuse. Like all conventions that trigger off a series of automatic responses, it seems to exercise a peculiar fascination over its followers. At the first hint of slam possibilities players rush to press the Blackwood button for the pleasure of seeing the wheels go round.

What they forget is that Blackwood was not designed as a slam-bidding device. Its sole purpose is to keep the user out of slams when two aces are missing, and it should never be used unless it is certain that the two hands have the values for a slam between them. Hands that are suitable for Blackwood—where the number of aces held is the only information required—do not come up very often. Nine out of ten slams ought to be bid without the aid of any four no trump convention, but to many people a slam without Blackwood is as unthinkable as champagne without bubbles.

This is the sort of thing that is apt to happen when there is a Blackwood addict at the table.

Abuse of Conventions

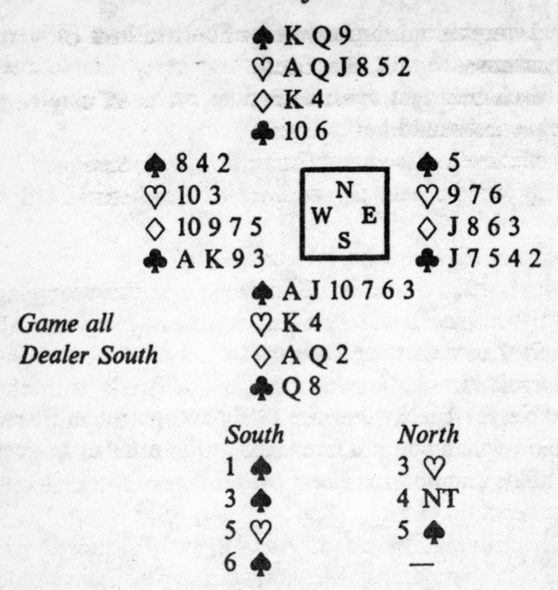

West naturally has no difficulty in cashing the top clubs to defeat the slam.

North champs his cigar and glares across the table.

'When I sign off at the five-level after using Blackwood that's the finish,' he snarls.

In a sense he is right, of course, but my sympathies are entirely with South. It was hard for South to imagine any hand on which his partner could force and follow up with Blackwood that would offer no play for a slam.

North was the main culprit. His four no trump bid was reckless, for North was not in a position to underwrite a five-level contract if his partner had only one ace. It was also futile, because North had no way of telling if a slam was on when his partner showed two aces. Interchange South's minor suit holdings, for instance, and the slam is cold.

North bid the full value of his hand when he forced and he should content himself with a raise to four spades on the second round. It is South who must start the slam investigation on this hand, but Blackwood is not the answer for South either. To learn that North has one ace will be of little use here. Simple cue-bidding will reach the right spot, as it does on most hands. A reasonable sequence would be:

South	*North*
1 ♠	3 ♡
3 ♠	4 ♠
5 ◇	5 ♡
5 ♠	—

Both partners know that the club control is missing and the slam is easily avoided.

Hands suitable for Blackwood are easily recognizable. These are the hands on which you are interested in the number of aces your partner holds and nothing else.

♠ K Q 6 4
♡ K Q J 5 4 2
◇ 8
♣ K 2

South	*North*
1 ♣	1 ♡
3 ♡	?

Nothing could be more apt than a Blackwood four no trump bid from North on the second round. In the unlikely event of South having only two aces North can pass the five heart response. Otherwise he can place the contract safely at the six- or seven-level.

Transfer bids of all kinds are enjoying a bit of a vogue. I don't care for them myself, mainly because I am lazy and shrink from learning a number of new sequences with subtle shades of meaning.

One of the advantages claimed for transfer bids is that the weak hand normally goes down on the table while the strong hand remains concealed. But is this always a good thing?

Abuse of Conventions

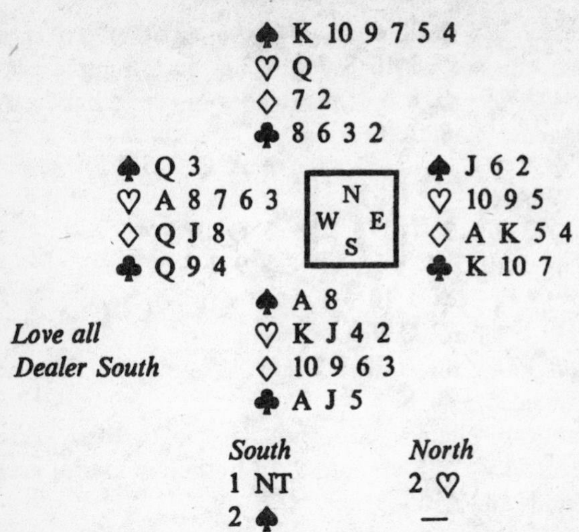

North's two hearts was a transfer bid demanding conversion to spades. Luckily South remembered the convention.

The queen of diamonds held the first trick and West, viewing that dummy, could see that the defence would need club tricks to defeat the contract. He therefore switched to the four of clubs and East played the king.

South won and led a heart, but West took the ace, led a diamond to his partner's king and won two club tricks on the return. The defenders still had to make a trump trick and the contract went one down.

What would happen if North bid a direct two spades? East would start with a top diamond, but it would not be easy for him to find the killing club switch. He might well lead a heart and allow the contract to be made.

The lesson emerges that it is often the weak distributional hand rather than the strong hand that needs to be concealed.

If you must have transfers, try to use them with discrimination. The misuse of a transfer bid cost a vulnerable game on the following hand.

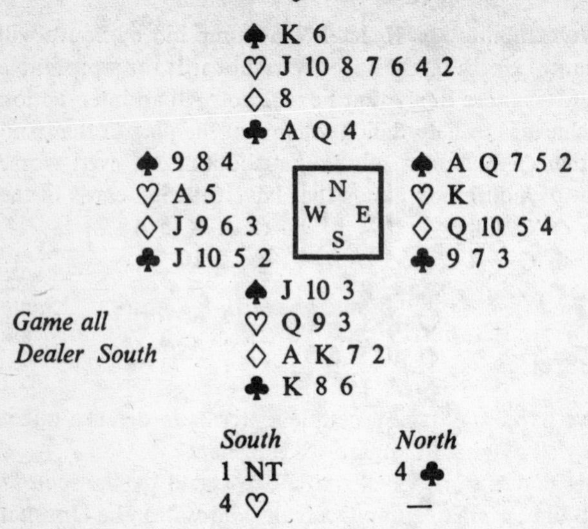

North was committed to South African Texas and could not resist the urge to give it an airing. The four club response demanded conversion to four hearts, and South duly obliged.

The idea of this transfer is to enable the no trump opener to play the hand and have the lead come up to his tenaces. But on this particular hand it is North's tenaces that need protection from the opening lead. If his desire to play with his toy had not overcome his judgement, North would have bid four hearts himself.

Justice was served when West found the spade lead to defeat the normally unbeatable contract.

The Unusual No Trump is a convention that seems to exercise a fatal fascination over many players. This gadget enables one to show a shapely hand with length in the unbid suits. A common mistake is to trot out the Unusual No Trump whenever the distribution is right.

♠ 10 2
♡ 7
◇ K 9 6 5 3
♣ A 10 8 7 3

West	*North*	*East*	*South*
1 ♠	—	2 ♡	?

At any vulnerability an Unusual No Trump bid by South will lose on balance. North might have the right cards for a profitable sacrifice but it is more likely that he will not. All an intervention will then achieve is to help the opponents in the play of the hand by giving them a blueprint of the distribution. An even worse habit is that of bidding on hands that have the high cards in the short suits.

	West	*North*	*East*	*South*
♠ A				
♡ K J				
◇ 10 9 7 6 4	1 ♠	—	2 ♡	?
♣ J 9 8 4 2				

The above hand may take a couple of tricks in defence but it will not do well playing in a minor. Keep silent.

Like other conventions which show two-suited hands, such as Tartan Two Bids, Roman Jump Overcalls and Astro, the Unusual No Trump is effective only when used to indicate good playing strength in the long suits. To make it worth while competing there must be a real chance of your side being able to buy the contract. The following hand is ideal.

	West	*North*	*East*	*South*
♠ 6				
♡ 9				
◇ Q J 10 8 7 3	1 ♠	—	2 ♡	2 NT
♣ A J 10 9 3				

The Gambling Three No Trumps comes in for its share of misuse. This convention shows a solid six- or seven-card minor suit with not more than a king outside. For those who have no use for a natural opening of three no trumps this is a good way of employing the idle bid. It is highly pre-emptive and yet retains the chance of playing in three no trumps if partner has a suitable hand.

Abuse occurs when the opener has more than seven cards in his solid suit or when he has support for a major suit.

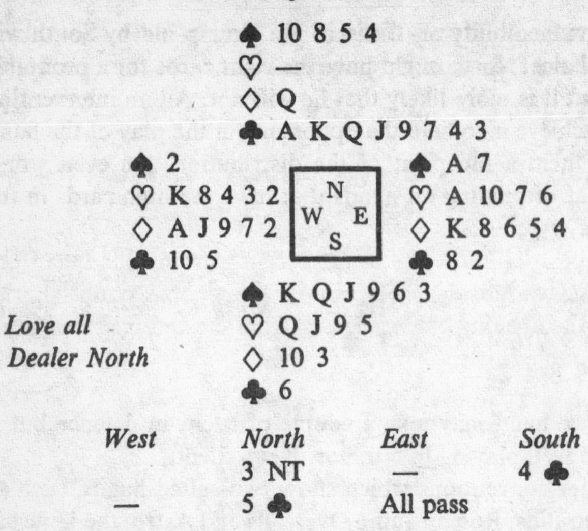

When his partner took out into four clubs North decided to press on to game, but it was the wrong game. After cashing the ace of diamonds, West led the spade to his partner's ace and obtained a spade ruff to defeat the contract.

A three no trump opening is seldom satisfactory when the minor suit is longer than seven cards. With very unbalanced distribution such as North has here it is not necessary to pre-empt, since the other suits are sure to be breaking badly. The sensible bid on the North hand is one club, after which the spade game should be reached without trouble.

Weak Two Bids have never gained in Britain the popularity that they have achieved in the United States. This is not so much because they clash with the concept of the Acol Two Bid, for that difficulty can be overcome by the use of the Benjamin Convention. It is more a fear of the bad results so often associated with the Weak Two.

Yet the treatment is not without merit. Weak Two Bids can be very effective when properly used. It is misuse that produces the bad results.

The Weak Two Bid should show a six-card suit with good

playing strength and very little in the way of defensive values. Hands like the following are suitable.

(*a*)	(*b*)	(*c*)
♠ Q J 10 9 6 3	♠ K 4 3	♠ 5
♡ 10 4	♡ K Q 10 9 7 2	♡ 8 7
◇ A 9 2	◇ 8 5 4	◇ A J 10 8 6 5
♣ 6 2	♣ 2	♣ Q J 9 5

If your partner knows he can expect a hand of this type from your Weak Two Bids the partnership will not come to much harm. It is when the opening bidder departs from the accepted standards that the trouble starts.

(*d*)	(*e*)
♠ Q 10 9 7 4 3	♠ J 9
♡ A Q 9	♡ J 9 6 5 4 3
◇ 4	◇ A Q 7
♣ Q J 6	♣ 6 4

Hand (*d*) contains too much defensive potential for an opening two spade bid, which could induce partner to take a phantom sacrifice. The hand is a one spade opening for any player with red blood in his veins. In hand (*e*) the suit is altogether too weak to stand a pre-emptive raise from partner on a doubleton honour. You just don't have the playing tricks for a Weak Two, so pass and await developments.

A convention of fairly recent origin is the Competitive Double, used as a forward-going move when both sides have found a fit at a low level.

West	*North*	*East*	*South*
1 ♠	2 ♡	2 ♠	3 ♡
Double			

The double shows the sort of hand on which West would have made a game try if space had been available. It is left to East to take the appropriate action.

The Competitive Double is best reserved for semi-balanced hands in the 15–16 point range. Here is an example of abuse from a B.B.L. International Trial.

Abuse of Conventions

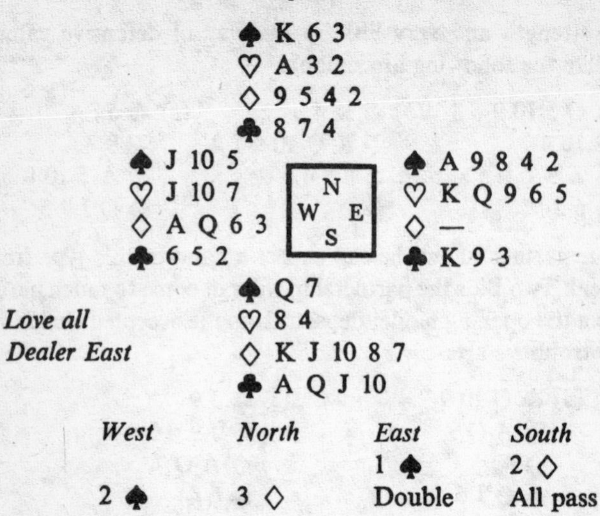

West	*North*	*East*	*South*
		1 ♠	2 ♢
2 ♠	3 ♢	Double	All pass

The lead of the knave of spades ran to the queen, South returned the king of diamonds, and West made the mistake of winning. He was subsequently unable to deny a trump entry to dummy, and the contract was made by finessing twice in clubs.

East's Competitive Double was unwise, since his strength was mainly distributional. A normal trial bid in hearts—or even a jump to game—would have worked better. Four spades was made on a diamond lead at a number of tables.

More widely accepted is the Responsive Double, used in situations like the following.

West	*North*	*East*	*South*
1 ♠	Double	2 ♠	Double

South's double is Responsive, showing 7–10 points and a desire to contest over two spades. It is logical to ascribe a conventional meaning to this double, since opportunities of doubling for penalties are rare.

Besides showing values, however, the double should deny the ability to describe the hand with a natural bid. Look at what can happen when this principle is ignored.

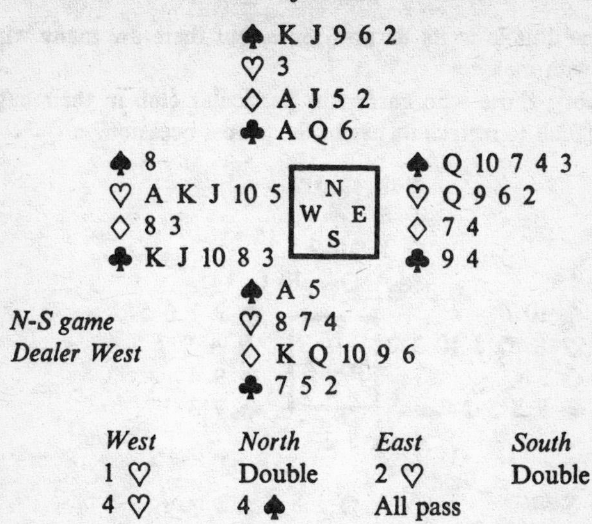

North managed to hold the loss to 100 but, with five diamonds on ice, that represented a swing of 700 points.

South thought his strength was about right for a Responsive Double. So it was, but he overlooked the fact that a clear-cut natural bid was available. If South had made the obvious bid of four diamonds over two hearts the partnership would have had no trouble in reaching the correct game contract.

Closely related to the Responsive Double and gaining ground in tournament circles is the Negative Double. This convention can solve the responder's problems on those awkward 7–10 point hands when enemy interference makes life difficult.

♠ A 7
♡ 8 7 3
◇ K 9 4 3
♣ Q 7 6 4

South	West	North	East
1 ♠	2 ♡	?	

It is certainly convenient if North can double in a negative sense to show some values and support for the unbid suits. Personally I do not think the advantage fully compensates for the loss of the double in its natural sense, but there are many who disagree with me.

Inevitably, those who carry this particular club in their bags find it difficult to restrict its use to the proper occasion.

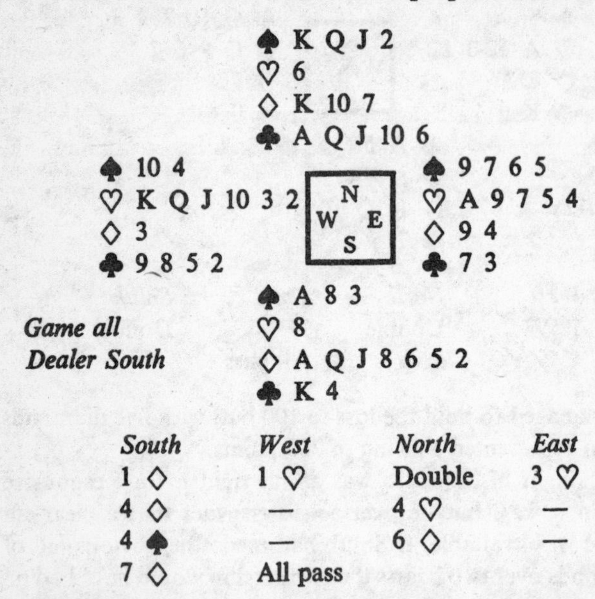

North: ♠ K Q J 2 ♡ 6 ◇ K 10 7 ♣ A Q J 10 6

West: ♠ 10 4 ♡ K Q J 10 3 2 ◇ 3 ♣ 9 8 5 2

East: ♠ 9 7 6 5 ♡ A 9 7 5 4 ◇ 9 4 ♣ 7 3

South: ♠ A 8 3 ♡ 8 ◇ A Q J 8 6 5 2 ♣ K 4

Game all
Dealer South

South	*West*	*North*	*East*
1 ◇	1 ♡	Double	3 ♡
4 ◇	—	4 ♡	—
4 ♠	—	6 ◇	—
7 ◇	All pass		

The bidding no doubt went astray at several points, but the main cause of the disaster was North's fatuous use of the Negative Double. Still stuck for a bid on the second round, North marked time with a false cue-bid in the enemy suit and South could not thereafter be persuaded that there was a heart loser.

Over the intervention of one heart an obvious natural force was available. North should have bid three clubs and saved the Negative Double for a more suitable occasion.

Perhaps you would as soon use a double negative as a Negative Double, but you are likely to have some pet convention of your own. If your favourite has not been mentioned do not assume that it is any less susceptible to abuse. In this chapter I have picked out a number of conventions at random to illustrate improper use, but all conventions suffer in the same way. You name it and players will butcher it, a thousand times a day and in fifty different languages.

The lesson is that the best of conventions is beneficial only when it is used with discretion. Keep those of your choice in your bag until the right moment comes along. And above all do not accept a strait-jacket of conventions as a substitute for thinking.

If you can acquire the right perspective, treating conventions as slaves rather than masters, it will be worth a lot of points in the course of a year.

2

Mistiming

In ball games the vital factor that makes the difference between success and failure is a sense of timing. This is the secret behind the booming serve, the flashing drive through the covers, the long tee-shot down the middle, and the header that leaves the goalkeeper standing. A fine co-ordination of eye and muscle results in the striking of the ball at precisely the right moment for maximum effect. It is the same story in boxing, wrestling, fencing, athletics, or any sport you care to name—the time element is of prime importance. This is also the case in spheres quite unconnected with sport, such as business, politics, drama and stock market speculation. The concept of timing is universal and can be applied to every form of human activity. Bridge is no exception.

The force of the time factor in the play of the cards is seen most clearly in those no trump contracts that develop into a race between the declarer and the defenders to establish long suits. The play of such hands is normally a simple matter, but the loss of a tempo through attacking the wrong suit will usually prove fatal. At the other end of the scale are the difficult hands involving end-plays, coups and squeezes. In all such advanced plays success is dependent upon precise timing.

Between the two extremes lie a multitude of ordinary hands which are neither easy nor difficult. These are the hands on which the declarer or the defender has a number of jobs to do. The order in which these jobs are tackled will very often decide the fate of the hand. It is in this intermediate range that most of the common errors in timing are made. Here is an example.

Mistiming

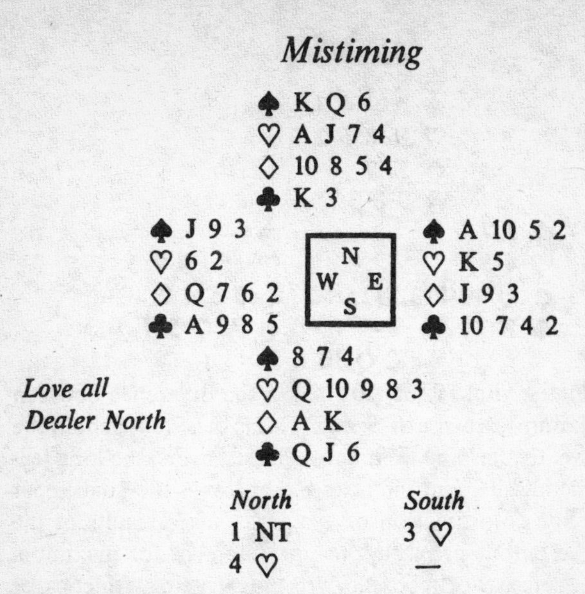

West led the two of diamonds to the nine and ace, and at the second trick South led the ten of hearts for a losing finesse. East reasoned that since the defence appeared to have no diamond trick they would need two spades and a club to defeat the contract. Accordingly he returned a low spade and the nine forced out dummy's queen. The declarer drew the outstanding trumps and then returned his attention to clubs, but it was too late. West took the ace of clubs and shot back the knave of spades to defeat the contract.

South's sense of timing was at fault here. He should have realized that there was no need for haste in the trump suit. His first task should have been to establish the clubs for a spade discard in dummy, thus ensuring ten tricks even when the trump finesse was wrong.

South was fortunate that West failed to find the initial spade lead that defeats the contract out of hand. When you receive the gift of a tempo from the opponents it is a pity to hand it straight back.

In the next hand the declarer's mistake is less glaringly obvious.

Mistiming

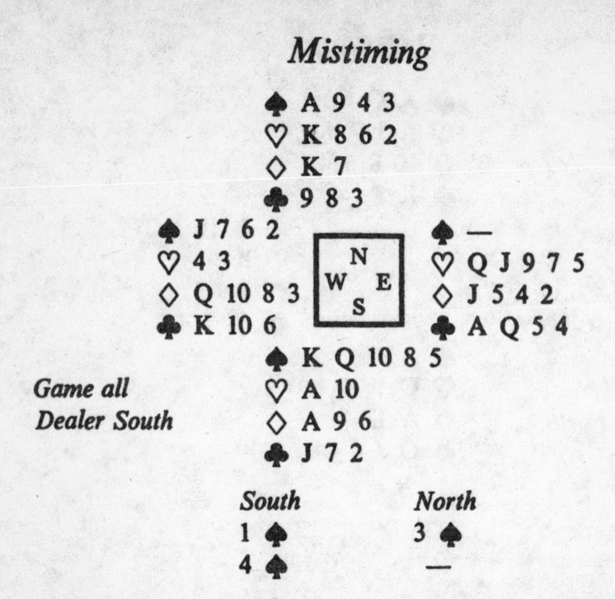

West led the four of hearts and South captured the knave with his king. The declarer saw that his contract was in no danger unless the trumps broke 4–0, so at trick two he led the king of spades from hand.

That is the correct safety-play to cater for four trumps in either hand, but it didn't do much good in this case. When East showed out South continued by finessing the nine of trumps, then cashed the king and ace of diamonds and ruffed the third diamond in dummy. After cashing the ace of spades, however, South was unable to return to hand to draw the remaining trump. He did his best by playing the king and another heart and discarding a club from hand, but West also discarded a club and eventually scored his knave of spades *en passant*.

The declarer's timing was at fault once again and the slip occurred, as it often does, at the first trick. South should realize that he will be short of entries in his own hand if East is void in trumps. He should therefore win the first trick with the king of hearts in dummy and lead a trump to his king.

On many hands the declarer must refuse to allow the defenders to gain the lead until the right moment.

Mistiming

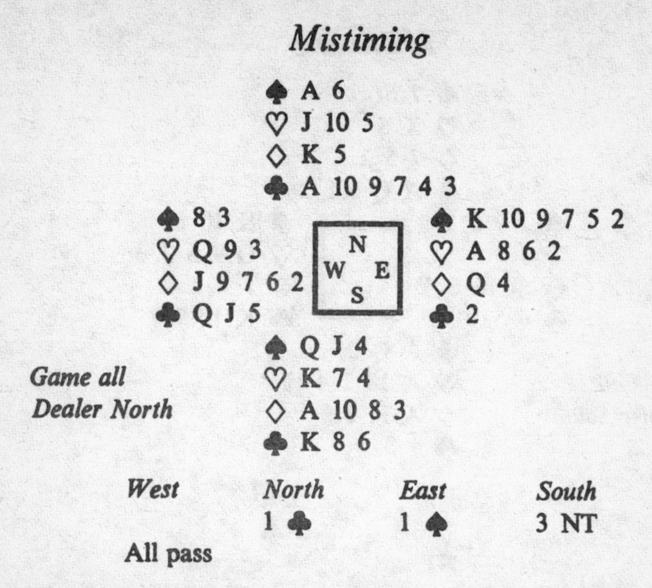

West led the eight of spades in response to his partner's overcall, and the declarer played low from dummy, reasoning that if East took the king that would establish the ninth trick in spades.

So it did, in a sense, but South had failed to consider his potential losers. East won the king of spades and, seeing little future in continuing the suit, switched to the two of hearts. The declarer played low permitting the queen to score and East ducked the second round of hearts. When West regained the lead in clubs he was able to lead a heart to give his partner two further tricks in the suit.

Better timing makes a certainty of the contract. South should play the ace of spades on the first trick and set about establishing the club suit. No matter what West returns South will always be able to score a ninth trick either in spades or in hearts.

Slips in defensive timing are common, but very often a defensive slip is balanced by an error on declarer's part. The par result is thus achieved in spite of the worst efforts of both sides.

Mistiming

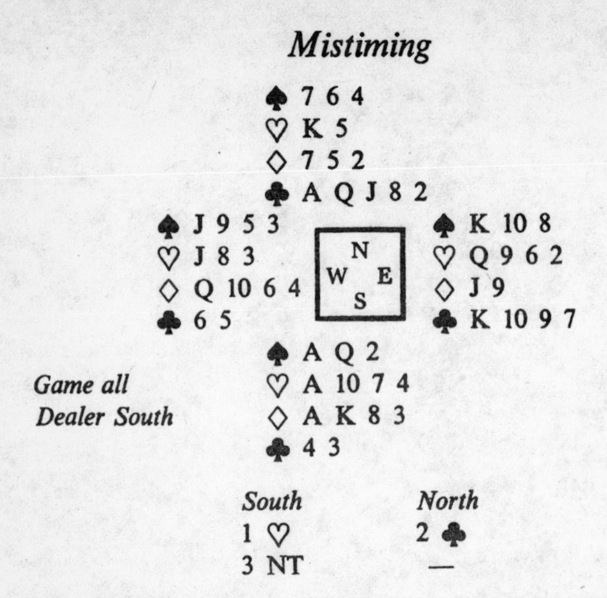

South	*North*
1 ♡	2 ♣
3 NT	—

West led the three of spades to the king and ace, and the declarer tackled the clubs. The finesse of the knave lost to the king, and East returned the ten of spades. Winning with the queen, South played out the clubs. He had to concede another trick in the suit, but made his contract comfortably with three clubs and two tricks in each of the other suits.

Better timing by East could have defeated the game. If East withholds his king on the first round of clubs the declarer will lack the entries to dummy to establish the suit. Failure to hold up in such situations is a defensive error which is duplicated a hundred times a year in every bridge club in the country.

The defence would have had no chance, however, if the declarer had shown a better sense of timing. Since he can afford to lose two club tricks he should play the eight, not the knave, from dummy on the first round. This forces the defenders to use up one of their stoppers at a time when dummy still retains an entry card in the suit.

Here is another case where both sides erred.

Mistiming

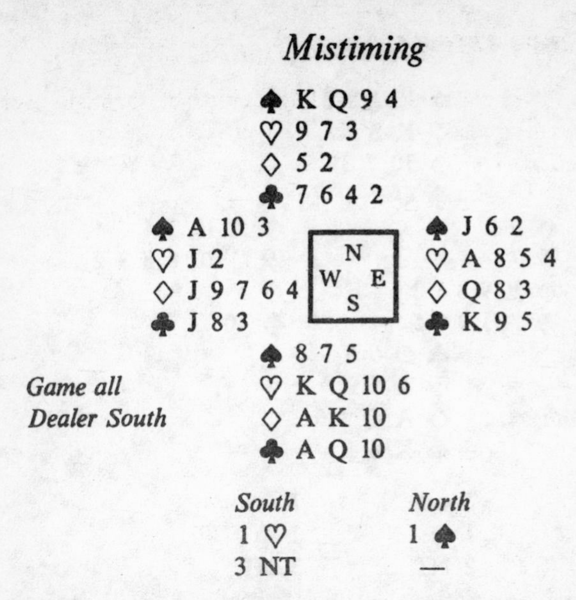

Let me say at once that I don't endorse the above bidding. Against this hair-raising contract West led the six of diamonds and the queen forced the king. South led a spade to dummy's queen and returned a heart which he won in hand with the king. He continued with a second spade to dummy's king, finessed the queen of clubs successfully, and then led the queen of hearts from hand. When the knave appeared South made cackling noises and nine tricks.

East was at fault, of course, in ducking the first round of hearts. In such situations it usually pays to go up at the first opportunity and return partner's suit. Had East done this the defenders would have scored three diamond tricks plus their two aces.

But South's timing was not as precise as he thought it to be. His first lead from dummy should have been a club for a finesse of the queen. When in dummy with the second spade he can lead a heart and thus come to nine tricks against any defence.

A common instance of faulty timing by the declarer is the knocking out of enemy stoppers in the wrong order.

Mistiming

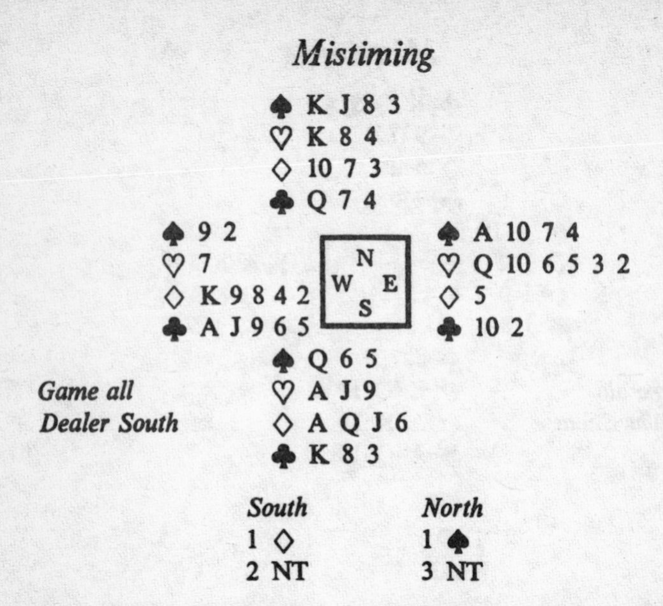

West led the six of clubs and East's ten was taken by the king. When South attacked spades by leading a low card to the knave East won immediately and returned his second club. West won with the ace and continued with a third round of clubs.

South still needed to establish some diamond tricks, but when he took the finesse West produced the king and cashed two clubs to defeat the contract.

The opening lead marks West with the long clubs and the contract is clearly impossible if West has both the ace of spades and the king of diamonds as entries. South can always succeed when West has only one of those cards, however, provided that he tackles the diamonds first. At the second trick South should enter dummy with the king of hearts in order to take the diamond finesse.

This play knocks out the entry to the dangerous hand in good time and the club suit can never be established.

Faulty timing can rob the declarer of one of his options, as happened on the following hand.

Mistiming

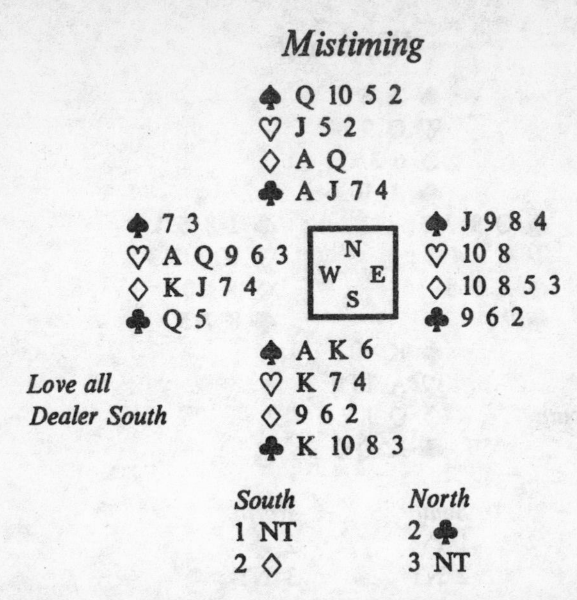

The opening lead was the six of hearts and the declarer put up the knave from the table. Clearly South could not afford to risk East gaining the lead and shooting a heart through, so he took the club finesse the other way, first cashing the ace and then finessing the ten to West's queen.

West returned the seven of diamonds, which placed South in a nasty dilemma. He had to make an immediate choice between risking the diamond finesse and playing for an even break or a doubleton knave in spades. Inevitably he guessed wrong by going up with the ace of diamonds. When the knave of spades subsequently failed to drop the contract had to go one down.

The problem was of the declarer's own making, and the way to avoid it is simple in the extreme. Before finessing in clubs South should play off the three top spades in order to clarify the position. Then he will know how many diamond tricks he needs for his contract if the club finesse loses.

Mistiming

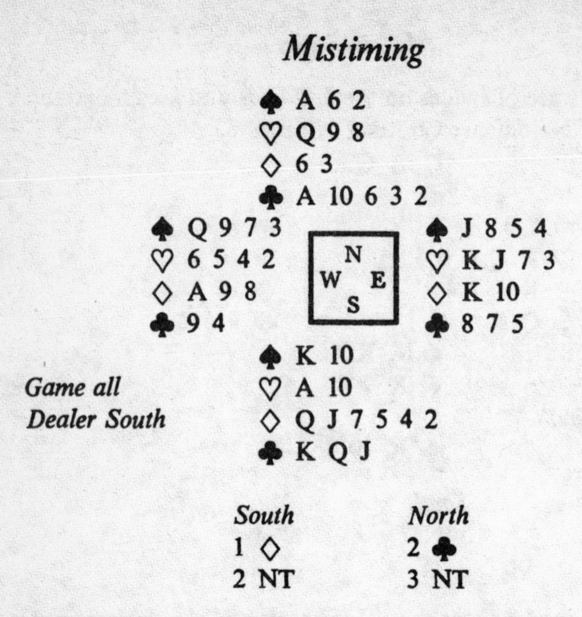

West led the three of spades and South assessed his chances. Since the spades appeared to be 4–4 he correctly decided that diamonds offered the best chance of the ninth trick.

Just in case West had led from the queen and knave, South played low from dummy on the first trick. The knave of spades forced the king, and South played clubs, overtaking in dummy on the third round to run the suit. On the long clubs East discarded the four of spades and the three of hearts, South two diamonds, and West the nine of diamonds and the four and two of hearts.

When a diamond was led from the table East stepped in with the king and shot back the seven of hearts. South saw that he could not afford to play low if West had the king, for a spade would come back and the defence would make five tricks. He therefore decided to abandon diamonds and try for a second heart instead. South played the ace of hearts and continued with the ten to dummy's queen, but when East produced both heart honours and returned a spade that was the end.

South was unlucky to encounter such a hot defence, but his troubles were all of his own making. To get the timing right he must play dummy's ace of spades on the first trick and lead a diamond immediately. No defence can then defeat him.

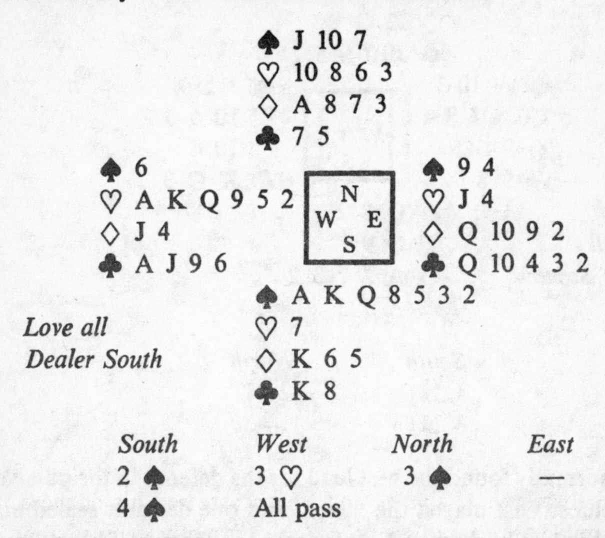

South	*West*	*North*	*East*
2 ♠	3 ♡	3 ♠	—
4 ♠	All pass		

West started with two top hearts and the declarer paused to consider. He saw that he could make the contract if the diamonds broke 3–3 provided that he could keep East off lead. Accordingly, instead of ruffing the second heart he discarded the five of diamonds from hand. Unfortunately the diamonds turned out to be 4–2, and with the ace of clubs offside the contract had to go one down.

South was thinking along the right lines, but his timing was imperfect. The proper play is to ruff the second heart and draw trumps with the ace and knave. Another heart ruff is followed by the play of the king and ace of diamonds. Dummy's last heart is led and now is the time to discard the small diamond from hand. After winning this trick West must either open up the club suit or lead a heart, conceding a ruff and discard.

This line of play ensures the contract whenever West has fewer than four diamonds.

When the following hand turned up in a pairs event most of the declarers got the timing wrong.

Mistiming

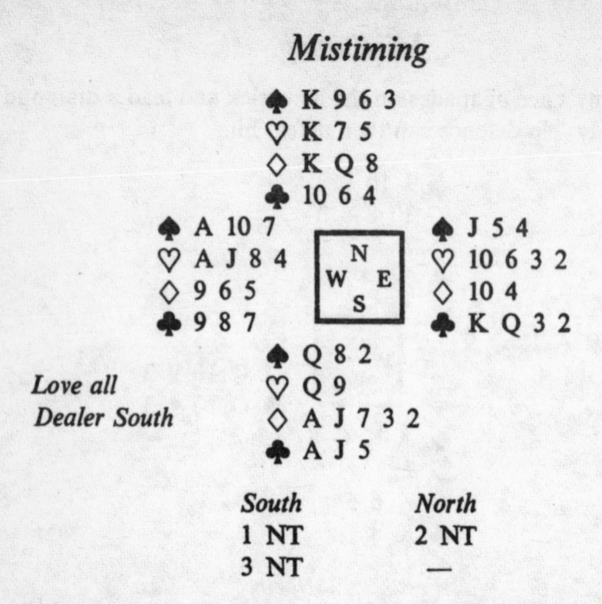

South	*North*
1 NT	2 NT
3 NT	—

West normally found the best lead for the defence in the passive nine of clubs. East played the queen, and one declarer sealed his fate swiftly when he ducked. East switched to the two of hearts and the defenders eventually made three hearts, a club and the ace of spades.

Another declarer won the first trick, led a spade to the king, and returned a club. Again the timing was imperfect and East took advantage by ducking the club lead. After making his diamonds South had to allow the defence to score the ace of hearts, two clubs and two spades.

It is surprising how many players underrate the value of running the long suit in such circumstances. South can have no certainty of making this contract, but to give himself a chance he must win the first trick and run the diamonds immediately. This forces West to weaken his hand in some way, and if South reads the discards correctly he can always make nine tricks.

A slight error in timing cost a vulnerable grand slam on the following hand.

Mistiming

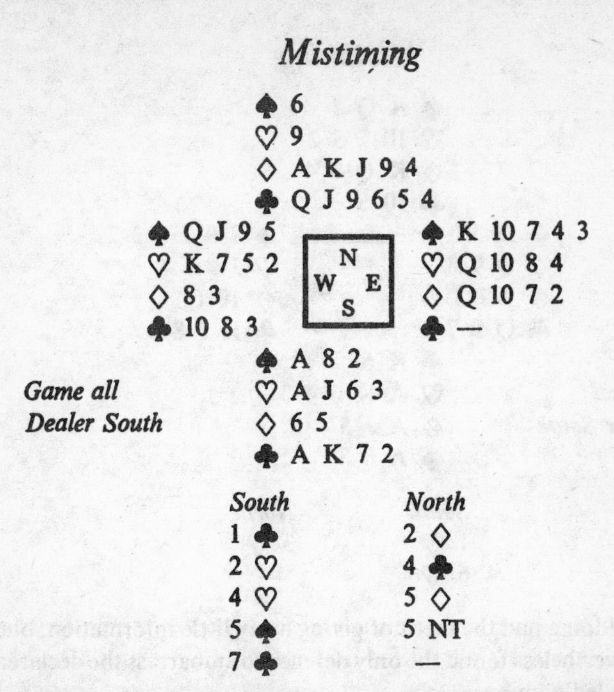

The opening lead of the queen of spades was won by South's ace. Without giving sufficient thought to the hand the declarer cashed the ace of clubs at the second trick. Nine times out of ten he might have got away with it, but this was the tenth case and it was no longer possible to make the slam.

South should realize that if the diamonds are 4–2, as is most likely, he will need to ruff diamonds twice in his hand, and he should therefore give a little thought to the possibility of a bad trump break. If East has all three trumps there will be no danger, but if West has three trumps South will need to retain his high trumps for ruffing diamonds. The first round of trumps must therefore be won on the table.

Faulty timing in the side suits was responsible for the loss of a slam on the next hand.

Mistiming

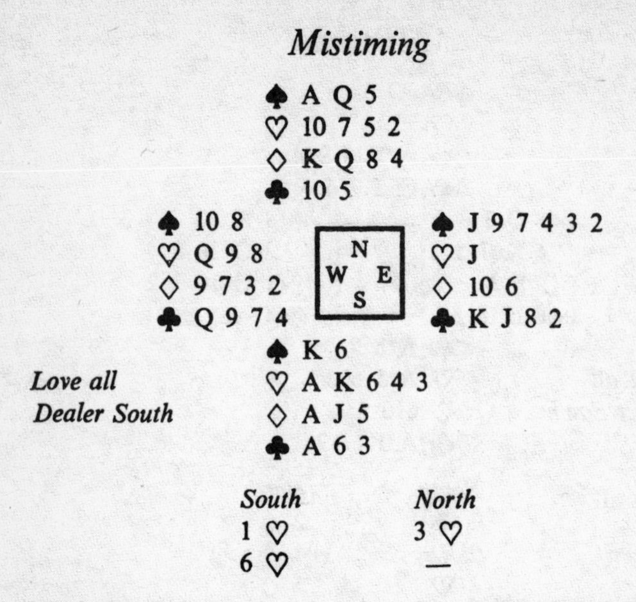

The bidding had the merit of giving away little information, but West nevertheless found the only defence to embarrass the declarer when he led a club.

South captured the king of clubs with his ace and played off the ace and king of hearts. East's spade discard revealed a sure trump loser and South realized that he would have to get rid of his losing clubs without delay. He played three rounds of spades and discarded a club from his hand, but West ruffed the third spade and cashed the queen of clubs to defeat the slam.

It seems natural to play the shorter side-suit first, but South overlooked the fact that the slam could not be made unless West had at least three diamonds. That being so, he should have tested the diamonds first. When East shows out on the third round, a club can safely be discarded on dummy's fourth diamond. The second club loser then goes away on the third round of spades and it does not matter whether West ruffs or not.

Allowing the defenders to make an early trick may be all that is needed to tighten up a squeeze position. In this deal the declarer failed to get the timing right but the defenders made no mistake.

Mistiming

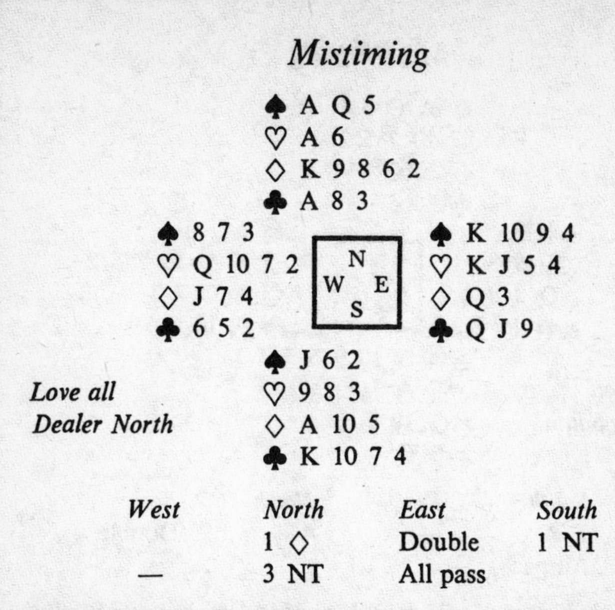

West	*North*	*East*	*South*
	1 ◇	Double	1 NT
—	3 NT	All pass	

West led the two of hearts, dummy's ace was played, and East contributed the knave. South led a diamond to his ace and ran the ten of diamonds on the way back.

If East had cashed the king of hearts after winning his queen of diamonds there would have been no further defence. But East led the four of hearts to his partner's ten and West found the spade switch.

South went up with the ace of spades and ran the diamond winners, but East was in no pain. He discarded two spades and the king of hearts, retaining the small heart in his hand. South could then do no better than cash his top clubs and concede one down.

The defence was certainly very good, but the declarer missed his chance at trick one. If he had ducked the first heart the timing would have been different and East would have been unable to escape the black-suit squeeze.

After making his contract on the next hand the declarer fished for compliments, but none was forthcoming and indeed none was deserved.

Mistiming

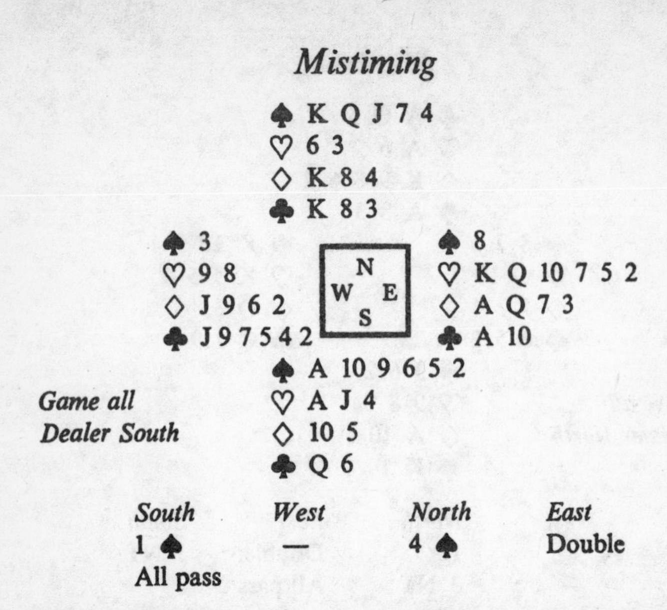

East's double was a wild gamble and his partner could hardly be blamed for failing to find the killing diamond lead. Instead, West led the nine of hearts to the queen and ace. A spade to the king drew the outstanding trumps and a second heart was led from the table.

East won with the king and returned the suit. South had no useful discard to make on the knave of hearts, so he ruffed it on the table and led a small club. When East played the ten the queen won, and South ducked on the way back in the hope that East's ace was now bare. It was his lucky day.

After the heart lead the contract should be made no matter how many clubs East has. The first lead from dummy ought to be a club. When the queen wins, dummy is re-entered with a trump and the heart led. East will take the king and return a heart as before, but now the timing is right for an elimination play. Dummy's small club is discarded on the knave of hearts and a second round of clubs is played. On winning the trick, East must either open up the diamond suit or concede a ruff and discard.

A declarer can occasionally create an extra option by delaying his choice of discard until a time convenient to himself.

Mistiming

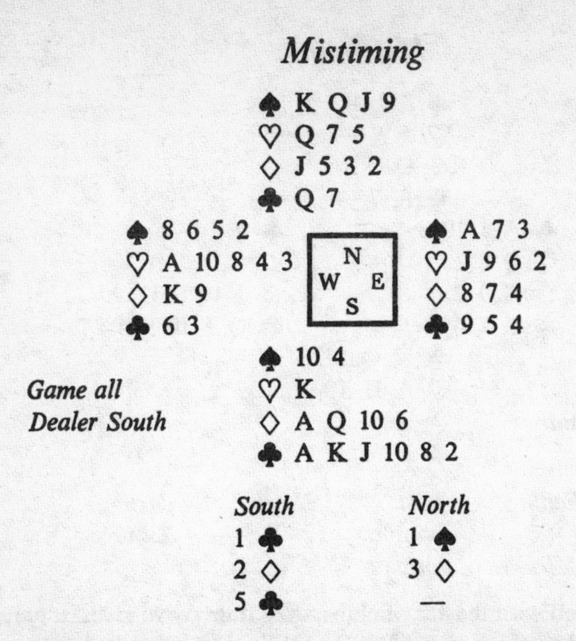

West gave the declarer a chance when he began with the ace and another heart, but South quickly messed up the hand by discarding a small diamond on the queen of hearts. After drawing trumps he led the ten of spades and overtook with dummy's knave, but East noted his partner's eight of spades and held up his ace. South had therefore to resort to the diamond finesse and the contract went one down.

South should, of course, have ruffed the second round of hearts, preserving the queen in dummy. After drawing trumps he could then proceed as before, leading the ten of spades and overtaking with the knave. The difference is that East cannot now afford to hold up his ace lest South discard his remaining spade on the queen of hearts. So East wins the ace of spades and returns a diamond, but South plays the ace and has three winners in dummy to take care of his losing diamonds.

Defenders sometimes have the opportunity to ruin the declarer's timing on similar hands containing the elements of avoidance play.

Mistiming

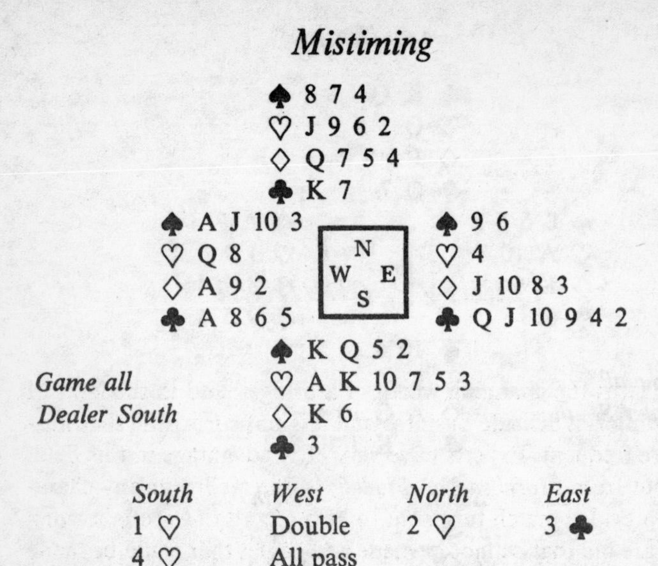

South	*West*	*North*	*East*
1 ♡	Double	2 ♡	3 ♣
4 ♡	All pass		

West started with the ace of clubs, eyed dummy with disfavour, and switched to the knave of spades in the hope that his partner could provide some help.

South won the queen of spades, drew trumps and led the six of diamonds. West could not play the ace without establishing two winners in the suit and allowing South eventually to get two losing spades away. He therefore played low, but when dummy's queen won the trick South was able to discard his king of diamonds on the king of clubs and concede two spade tricks.

A simple club continuation at trick two is enough to defeat the contract. This forces the declarer to take his discard on the king of clubs at an inconvenient time, and the defence must come to four tricks.

3

Faulty Valuation

ESTIMATING the changing worth of a bridge hand in the light of the bidding is a delicate business and it is not surprising that mistakes are frequent. Experts have very little advantage in this field. To quote from *Morehead on Bidding*—'The record of any championship bridge match turns out to be a record of experts' errors. Games are bid that cannot be made and games that could be made are not bid.'

Over the years many methods of hand valuation have been tried. All have something to be said for them but none is perfect, and inevitably a great deal is left to the judgment of the individual. This opens the door to error.

The Culbertson Honour Trick Table will evoke for many players memories of their first steps in bridge. This remains the most accurate means of measuring the defensive trick-taking potential of a hand. For estimating the number of tricks the combined hands will produce in a trump contract, however, there is nothing to beat the Losing Trick Count. Culbertson's count of playing tricks is almost equally effective for this purpose. After his partner has given a single raise in a major suit, a player will not go far wrong if he makes a game try with six playing tricks and jumps to game with seven.

Various point-count methods of evaluation have had a vogue. These assigned graded values to the honour cards—7–5–3–2–1, 6–4–3–2–1, 3–2–1–½ and so on. Today the Milton Work Count of 4–3–2–1, although not the most accurate, has gained universal acceptance because of its simplicity.

The point count is at its most reliable in assessing the prospects of no trump contracts. For suit contracts its value is less certain, since what matters at the higher levels is distribution and controls.

Until a player acquires some experience he is unaware of the importance of the distributional factor, and for this reason bridge writers and teachers usually insist that the beginner should add on points for long suits or shortages as well as counting the high-card points in a hand. This is a good thing, for it forces the beginner to take account of distributional values and thus enables him to bid better at an early stage in his education.

A rule of thumb cannot take the place of judgment for all time, however. Good players do not consciously add on points for distribution in calculating the worth of a hand. They total the high-card points to give them a rough yardstick, and rely on experience to value their distribution and correct the imperfections of the point count.

Here is a situation in which players often go astray.

	Game all. Dealer South	
	South	*North*
♠ J 10 8 5 3		
♡ A 7		
◇ K 4	1 ♠	3 ♠
♣ A 10 8 5	?	

South opens one spade and his partner gives a limit raise to three spades. Slaves of the point-count will add up once more, reach the same rock-bottom figure of twelve and pass quickly, hoping they are not already too high.

That is entirely the wrong attitude. In borderline decisions what should sway the issue is not the presence or absence of a few extra points but the quality of the honour cards. For the purposes of high-level suit contracts aces and kings are undervalued by the point-count. This hand, with first-round control in two of the side suits and second-round control in the third, is by no means a minimum and South should bid four spades automatically. Furthermore, if West doubles in the hope that his trump honours are well placed South might redouble to teach him a lesson.

When the problem arose in a pairs contest the full hand was:

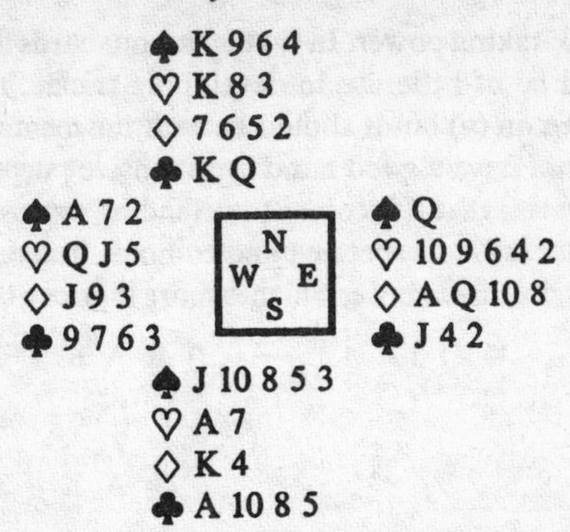

The game depended on the favourable position of either the ace of diamonds or the queen of spades—a comfortable 75 per cent chance.

On the other side of the medal, after a double raise from partner it may well be wise to pass certain hands which contain a higher point count.

	Love all. Dealer South	
	South	*North*
♠ K Q J 10 5		
♡ Q J	1 ♠	3 ♠
◇ J 9 3	?	
♣ K J 5		

There is a lack of quality about the above 14-point hand—too much wastage in the trump suit, too few controls, too many queens and knaves which will not play their full part in a high-level suit contract—and a pass could easily be the right answer.

Honour cards are at their most effective when they are situated in your long suits, for they can then fulfil their proper function of promoting your small cards into winners. Consider the following hands.

(*a*)	(*b*)
♠ A Q	♠ 6 4
♡ J 9 6 4 2	♡ A Q J 9 2
◇ 10 7 6 2	◇ K Q 10 2
♣ K Q	♣ 7 6

Both hands have the same point-count, but (*b*) is far superior in offensive trick-taking power. In (*a*) the honour cards in the doubleton suits will be of little use in developing tricks. You may still decide to open on (*a*) but it should be with the mental reservation that you do not have a good hand for offensive purposes.

Note, however, that if it comes to defending against a high-level spade contract (*a*) is the better hand to hold. It is certain to take two or three tricks in defence, which is more than can be said for (*b*).

(*c*)		(*d*)	
♠	A K Q J 7 3	♠	A K Q J 7 3
♡	K Q	♡	6 5
♢	A	♢	9
♣	9 6 5 3	♣	A K 4 3

Each of the above hands qualifies for an Acol opening bid of two spades, but the experienced player will make the bid with reluctance on (*c*) and with a song in his heart on (*d*). With hand (*d*) you require no more than the queen of clubs from partner to give you a play for game, while with hand (*c*) you need considerably more. Yet to dedicated point-counters (*c*) is the better hand.

Pay serious attention to the location of your high cards, therefore, and discount to some extent singleton and doubleton honours. Beginners should do this consciously by deducting one point from the value of each honour card in a singleton or doubleton setting. Experienced players should not need a conscious effort to discount such holdings and modify their bidding accordingly.

Another important factor in assessing the value of a hand is the presence or absence of 'body'—intermediate cards such as tens and nines and even eights. Such cards are easily promoted into tricks, and the experienced player allows their presence to influence him in borderline decisions.

(*a*)		(*b*)	
♠	A 10 9	♠	A 6 5
♡	Q J 9 4	♡	Q J 5 4
♢	J 10 6	♢	J 7 3
♣	K J 8	♣	K J 2

Each of the above hands has a point-count of twelve, but what a difference there is in trick-taking potential. It is enough to make (*a*) a sound weak no trump opening, while (*b*) is no more than a maximum pass.

(*c*)	♠ K 10	(*d*)	♠ Q 6 5 2
	♡ Q 10 7		♡ K Q 3
	◇ A J 9		◇ Q J
	♣ K J 10 8 3		♣ A J 5 4

Playing a 15–17 point no trump, a good many players would make the mistake of opening one club on (*c*) and one no trump on (*d*). In fact it should be the other way round. Hand (*c*) counts to only fourteen points but the good five-card suit and the abundance of intermediate cards make it worth a no trump opening. Hand (*d*) on the contrary is a very barren 15-count. The doubleton queen and knave in diamonds and the total absence of body make it advisable to demote the hand and open one club.

In general, hands containing good intermediates and secondary stoppers will play best in no trumps, while hands rich in controls are more useful in suit play.

The ace, however, has a unique value in both suit and no trump contracts. Not only is it the most flexible of stoppers but it also represents the quickest of quick tricks. No establishment is needed; the ace is ready to be cashed whenever it may be convenient. This is of great practical value in the play of the hand, and the ace is normally worth rather more than the four points assigned to it in the Milton Work count.

Most authorities recommend that a point be deducted for an aceless hand. It can certainly be difficult to make game if there is a shortage of aces, no matter how many playing tricks the combined hands may have. This is particularly true in no trump contracts when the opponents are known to have a long suit. In such cases a severe downward adjustment of the point-count should be made to take account of the lack of aces.

♠ K 5
♡ Q J 3
◇ A Q 10 6 2
♣ K Q 7

Game all. Dealer South

South	*West*	*North*	*East*
1 ◇	1 ♡	1 ♠	—
?			

Faulty Valuation

A common error is to assume that the above holding is worth a rebid of two no trumps. True, you have seventeen points and a good five-card suit, which would normally be enough for two no trumps on the second round. But in this case the opponents are known to have a long suit and you are short of aces. Even if partner can contribute eight or nine points you are unlikely to be able to develop nine tricks in time. With the advantage of the opening lead, the opponents will be able to establish and cash their heart suit first.

If you rebid two no trumps North will be justified in raising to three on either of the following hands.

(*a*)	(*b*)
♠ A 9 8 6 2	♠ A Q J 9 4
♡ 8 4	♡ 8 4
◇ K 7 3	◇ 7 3
♣ J 6 5	♣ J 9 6 5

On a heart attack you will have little chance of making three no trumps with either of these hands as dummy. It follows that your hand, for all its seventeen points, is worth no more than one no trump on the second round. If partner cannot advance over this there will be no game.

Note the difference if we alter the hand slightly.

♠ K 5
♡ Q J 3
◇ A Q 10 6 2
♣ A 10 7

Game all. Dealer South

South	*West*	*North*	*East*
1 ◇	1 ♡	1 ♠	—
?			

Superficially the hand is slightly weaker, but the ace of clubs, representing a fast trick as well as a stopper, is worth a great deal more than the king and queen in such a setting. This hand fully warrants a rebid of two no trumps. Opposite hand (*a*) you can practically underwrite nine tricks, while with hand (*b*) as dummy there will at least be a play for the game.

Aces pull their full weight, however, only when your hand contains some distributional feature. Possession of the aces buys you time in which to develop your long suit. Barren aces in a flat hand may actually be worth less than the four points accorded them by the Milton Work scale.

Faulty Valuation

To achieve good results it is desirable to recognize the importance of this factor in the bidding.

♠ A 10 3
♡ K Q J 7 4
◇ A J 3
♣ A 5

South	*North*
1 ♡	1 NT
?	

The above hand is full value for a raise to three no trumps. You can provide seven playing tricks and it is reasonable to expect partner to contribute two.

♠ A 6 5
♡ A Q 8 3
◇ A J
♣ A 7 4 3

South	*North*
1 ♡	1 NT
?	

Here is a rather different matter. In spite of the four aces the above hand is not worth its full nineteen points. The shortage of playing tricks should induce you to raise to two no trumps only. There will not be much of a play for game if partner cannot go on.

Many players tend to overvalue strong hands, particularly when they have forced what may be a very reluctant response from their partners.

♠ K Q J 10 9
♡ A K 6
◇ 10 9 4 3
♣ A

Game all. Dealer East

West	*North*	*East*	*South*
		1 ♣	Double
—	1 ♡	—	?

One spade is quite enough on the second round. If North has any values let him bid them himself. It is true that you have seven playing tricks, but you will need them all to make one spade if your partner has a balanced yarborough.

♠ A 9 5
♡ A Q 10 7 3
◇ A 2
♣ A Q 10

Game all. Dealer East

West	*North*	*East*	*South*
		1 ♡	Double
1 NT	—	—	Double
—	2 ◇	—	?

Faulty Valuation

With such a powerful hand it is tempting to bid once more, but North's takeout into two diamonds is a cry of weakness and South should pass. When the problem arose in a pairs tournament the pass represented the last chance of a plus score, for the full hand was:

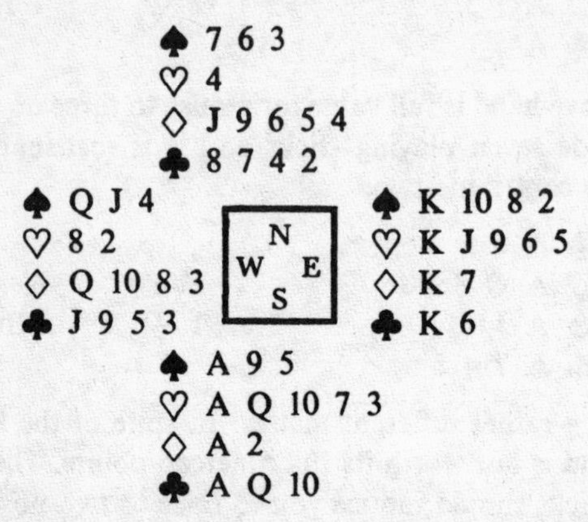

A vital element in card valuation is the assessment of the positional factor. The worth of a tenace holding such as K J 2 is determined by the position of the remaining honour cards, the ace, queen and ten. If these lie behind you the king and knave are as good as dead, but if they are favourably placed your holding will be good for two tricks.

There can be no guide to the position of the outstanding honour cards unless the opponents bid, of course. Even when the opponents do take an active part in the bidding it can still be very hard, indeed at times quite impossible, to work out whether your cards are well placed or not.

A hand from the 1969 final of the Scottish Masters Pairs contest illustrates this point.

Faulty Valuation

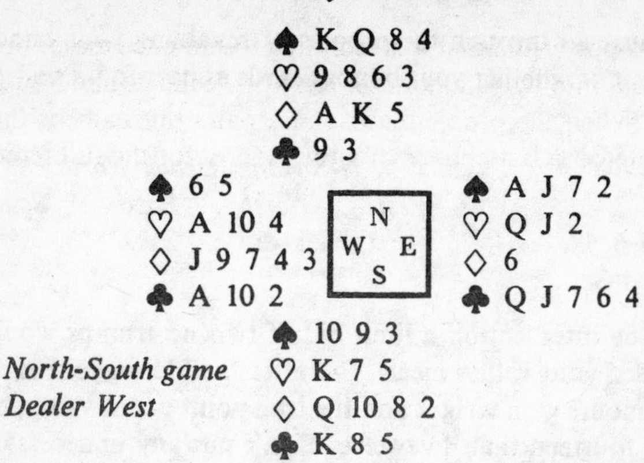

The points are evenly divided between the two sides but the cards are so placed that it is impossible for North and South to obtain a plus score. The largest minus was recorded after the following auction.

West	*North*	*East*	*South*
—	1 ◇	Double	Redouble
1 NT	—	—	2 ◇
Double	Redouble	—	2 ♡
Double	All pass		

With his bare twelve points North would have been wiser to have passed at this vulnerability. His choice of one diamond as an opening bid was particularly unfortunate, for it gave East the chance to come in with a shaded double.

South's redouble was also shaded and when he contested again on the second round his fate was sealed. Two hearts doubled cost 800 points, and two diamonds or two spades would have been no less expensive.

Sitting under the aces, South's kings are virtually useless to him on this hand. It is interesting to note that although East and West have no more than twenty points it requires a pretty smart defence to defeat them in a no trump game.

That is an extreme case, however, Normally when the opponents bid they will give some indication of where their high cards lie.

Then you must go through the process of revaluing your hand, taking account of whether your honour cards appear to be well or poorly placed.

♠ Q 4
♡ K J 2
◇ A J 6 5
♣ J 9 4 3

N-S game. Dealer North

West	*North*	*East*	*South*
	1 ♠	2 ♡	?

Without the intervention a limit bid of two no trumps would have expressed your values nicely. But after the bid on your right the heart honours gain weight and the true point count valuation is nearer to fourteen than to twelve. Don't put any unnecessary pressure on your partner, therefore. Jump to three no trumps yourself.

♠ K 8 7
♡ A 10 6 2
◇ 9 5
♣ 10 7 6 2

Love all. Dealer North

West	*North*	*East*	*South*
	1 ♡	—	2 ♡
2 ♠	3 ◇	—	?

This time if there had been no interference you would have been happy to accept your partner's game try and jump to four hearts. After the two spade bid on your left, however, it would be sensible to demote your king and sign off in three hearts.

For no trump purposes there are two distinct types of stoppers, and players who wish to value their cards accurately must learn to differentiate between them.

(*a*)		(*b*)	
♠	A K 7	♠	Q 10 8 3
♡	J 10 5	♡	J 10 5
◇	Q 10 8 3	◇	A K 7
♣	A J 3	♣	A J 3

If your right-hand opponent opens one spade the above hands just about warrant an overcall of one no trump. But what will you do if your partner raises to two no trumps?

I suggest that on (*a*) you should pass promptly, but that on (*b*) you should continue happily to game.

Apart from the transposition of the spade and diamond holdings the hands are identical, but (*b*) is much the stronger of the two when the opponents are known to have length in spades. A spade attack is likely to develop two tricks in the suit for you, and you have plenty of outside honour strength to help promote further tricks.

Other things being equal, it is always preferable to have third- and fourth-round stoppers in the enemy suit and quick tricks outside rather than quick tricks in the enemy suit itself.

The nature and location of the high cards in a hand is a vital factor to which sufficient attention is not always paid in the course of the bidding.

Hand	North	South
♠ K Q 7 6 3	*North*	*South*
♡ 9 7 2	1 ♡	1 ♠
◊ 8 4	2 ◊	?
♣ K J 5		

Here the honour cards in the black suits are of doubtful value and the hand is worth no more than a simple preference to two hearts.

Hand	North	South
♠ A 8 7 6 3	*North*	*South*
♡ Q 9 2	1 ♡	1 ♠
◊ Q 4	2 ◊	?
♣ 8 7 5		

This hand, with a point less, is much stronger. The ace of spades is bound to be a useful card, as are the two queens in partner's suits. All the points are working hard and that makes the hand worth a jump preference to three hearts.

A queen in partner's suit is always worth more than a queen outside. Consider the following cases.

(*a*)	(*b*)
♠ A 8 5 4	♠ Q 8 5 4
♡ 6 3	♡ 6 3
◊ 9 8 3	◊ 9 8 3
♣ Q 7 5 2	♣ A 7 5 2

Each of the above hands is worth a single raise if your partner opens one spade, but (*b*) is the better raise since you can be sure that both of your high cards are working. On (*a*) the value of the queen of clubs is dubious.

Duplication of values is one of the main hazards in hand valuation. Duplication is present to a certain extent on most hands, of course. The quota of 25 points considered normal for a game contract makes allowance for this.

		West	*East*
♠ K Q J 4 3	♠ A 8 7 6 2	1 ♠	3 ♠
♡ K J 7 2	♡ 6	4 ♠	—
◇ 8	◇ Q 9 5 2		
♣ A J 5	♣ K 7 3		

This is a fairly normal game hand, but just look at the number of unnecessary honour cards in the combined hands. Let us cut them out and see what we are left with.

♠ K 9 5 4 3	♠ A 8 7 6 2
♡ 9 8 7 2	♡ 6
◇ 8	◇ 10 9 5 2
♣ A 6 5	♣ K 7 3

Barring a 3–0 trump break the above hands will still produce game in spades, but neither West nor East can open the bidding. Games are often missed on hands with the complete lack of duplication that we describe as a perfect fit. Only if the opponents come to their aid will East and West have a chance of reaching game on the above hand. The bidding might start:

West	*North*	*East*	*South*
—	1 ♡	1 ♠	3 ♡
?			

West, knowing his partner to be very short in hearts, can now diagnose the perfect fit and jump to four spades.

What about this case?

	Game all. Dealer West			
♠ 9 8 6 5 2	*West*	*North*	*East*	*South*
♡ A 7 6 3	—	—	1 ♣	Double
◇ A Q 10 4	1 ♡	3 ♠	4 ♡	?
♣ —				

Faulty Valuation

Dedicated point-counters will be feeling very daring at having doubled in the first place, and it will give them a palpitation or two and a sense of living really dangerously if they manage to support their partners to four spades. They would be shocked to be informed that four spades is a pusillanimous underbid.

Forget about points and consider the losers for a moment. From your own hand you know that there are no club losers, and with hearts bid on your left and supported strongly on your right it requires little imagination to see your partner's singleton or void in the suit. For his bid of three spades partner should have a good six-card suit. There could be a trump loser or alternatively there might be a diamond loser. It must be highly unlikely that there will be a loser in both suits, and it follows that six spades is the only logical bid for South.

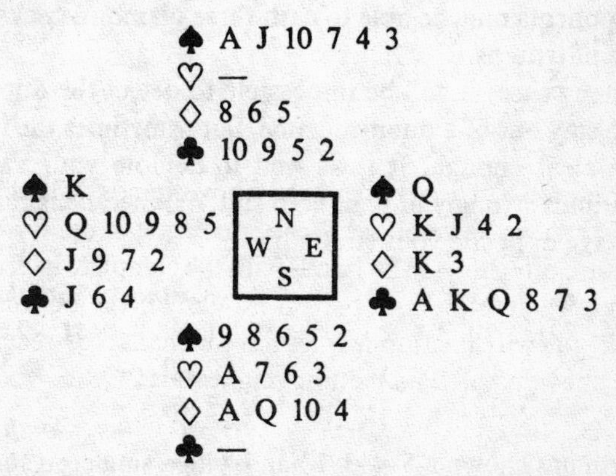

There you have it—a cold grand slam on a combined total of 15 high-card points. The grand slam can hardly be bid, of course, but the small slam certainly should be bid once the opponents co-operate by pin-pointing North's shortage in hearts.

The above may be an extreme case, but the lesson is clear that the point count—or for that matter any method of hand valuation —has severe limitations and should be used only as a rough guide. The point count assumes an abstract setting in assigning fixed values to each honour card. But card combinations do not occur in the abstract. We have to evaluate them within the setting of a particular hand and a given bidding sequence. Inevitably some honour cards will be completely redundant while others will be worth their weight in gold. The art of successful valuation lies in distinguishing the cards that are working hard from those that are not.

When excessive duplication of values is present players invariably get too high.

		West	*East*
♠ A K Q 6	♠ 9		
♡ K J 10 7 4	♡ Q 9 5 3	1 ♡	2 ♡
◇ J 9 4	◇ 10 7 5 2	4 ♡	—
♣ A	♣ K Q 6 3		

The above bidding can hardly be criticized. It is unfortunate that the opponents may be able to cash three diamond tricks as well as the ace of trumps.

In many cases it will be impossible to detect the duplication in time to stay out of a doomed game, but sometimes the indications will be clear enough. It is as well to demote your values when partner bids strongly in your void suit, or when he is marked with a shortage opposite your strength.

	North	*South*
♠ K Q J 6	1 ◇	1 ♡
♡ A 10 7 6 2	2 ♡	2 ♠
◇ 9 4	3 ♣	?
♣ 5 3		

North has shown a 5–4–3–1 hand with a singleton spade. South should recognize that there is serious duplication and sign off in three hearts.

4

Mishandling Trumps

THE introduction of a trump suit adds a further dimension to the play of the cards and provides a rich breeding ground for error. The manner in which a player utilizes his trumps, both in attack and in defence, is a reliable guide to his standard of play.

The declarer normally has the advantage of trump superiority. This gives him a certain measure of control, but the opponents' small trumps while they remain at large represent a serious threat to his high cards in the side suits. The declarer's natural inclination, therefore, is to draw the outstanding trumps as quickly as possible. It is unusual for anyone but a beginner to come to grief through failure to draw trumps.

Most of us err in the opposite direction by drawing trumps too hastily at times. On certain hands the trumps have a great deal of work to do, and it may be necessary to postpone the drawing of the opponents' trumps or indeed to abandon any attempt to do so. The obvious cases are those where there are losers to ruff in one hand or the other and the cross-ruff hands where the trumps need to be scored separately. There are other hands on which trumps cannot be drawn immediately for reasons of control. A trump may have to be left in dummy to protect against a forcing defence, for instance.

It may be necessary to delay the drawing of trumps simply because there is a more pressing job to be done. Perhaps dummy's trumps are required to help in establishing a side suit, or it may be just a matter of conserving your entries. If all the entries to one hand are in the trump suit it may be unwise to expend them too soon.

Mishandling Trumps

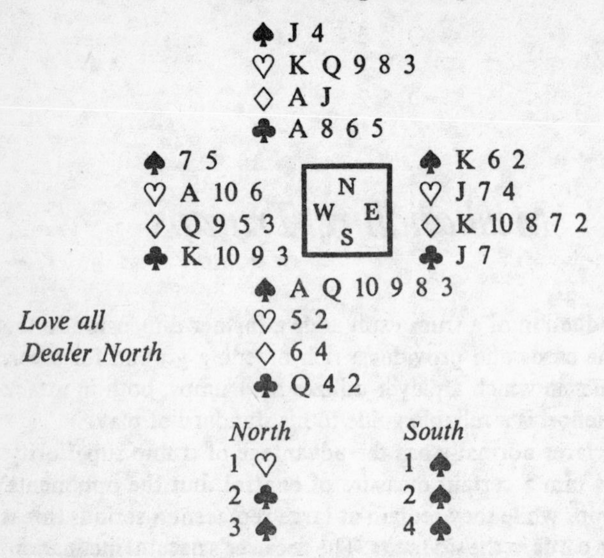

Against the optimistic four spade contract West led the three of diamonds. Winning with the ace, South ran the knave of spades successfully, finessed again and drew the last trump. A heart was then led and dummy's queen won.

With no quick way back to his hand, the declarer played the knave of diamonds from the table. East went up with the king and shot back the knave of clubs. This attack removed dummy's last entry and all the declarer could do was to return a club in the hope that the king was well placed. His luck had run out, however, and the contract was one down.

The lie of the cards in the major suits is so favourable that South should have had no difficulty in making eleven tricks. All he has to do is to try to gain two trump entries in his hand, which can be done by overtaking dummy's knave of spades with his queen. After a heart lead to dummy a second trump can be led, the ten finessed, and the last trump drawn. A further heart lead then establishes the suit for two club discards.

Perhaps the entry problem is a little harder to foresee in the next hand.

Mishandling Trumps

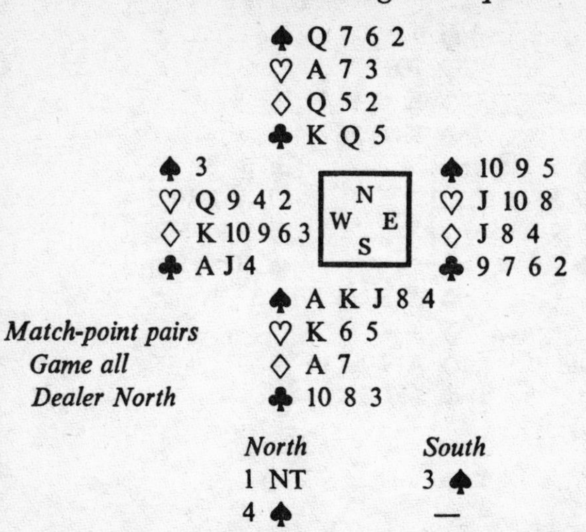

South won the opening heart lead in hand with the king and saw no reason for leaving any enemy trumps at large. After drawing three rounds of trumps with the ace, king and queen, he played the ace and another diamond and West took his king. The heart return was won by dummy's ace and South's heart loser discarded on the queen of diamonds. Next came a heart ruff, followed by the play of a small club to dummy's queen. This left the declarer stranded on the table, unable to return to hand for another club lead except by denuding both hands of trumps. West naturally threw the knave of clubs on this trump lead and made the last two tricks with the ace of clubs and the queen of hearts.

South's score of 620 was not good enough, for other pairs had registered 630 or 650. In order to make eleven tricks South must preserve entries to his own hand for the two club leads he must ultimately make. He should therefore draw only two rounds of trumps before playing the ace and another diamond.

Most players are optimistic in their outlook and can be caught unprepared by a bad trump break. Nine declarers out of ten would make the same mistake as South did on the following hand.

Mishandling Trumps

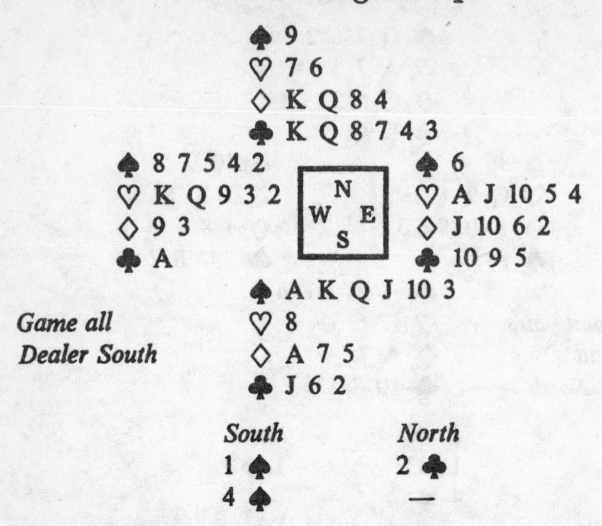

West attacked in hearts and South ruffed the second round. On a casual analysis it seemed impossible to lose more than one heart and one club, and at trick three South started on the trumps. When East discarded a heart on the second round South realized that he had miscalculated, but it was too late to change course. He drew all the trumps and then played on diamonds, hoping for an even break in the suit. But as the cards lay the contract had to go one down.

It was unlucky to find the trumps 5–1, but South ought to have guarded against the possibility. The way to retain control is to delay the drawing of trumps until the ace of clubs has been knocked out. Dummy's nine of spades will take care of a further heart lead and eleven tricks will be made without trouble. Playing on clubs first virtually guarantees ten tricks even if the enemy can negotiate a ruff.

Trump control can be precarious when you land in a 4–3 fit.

Mishandling Trumps

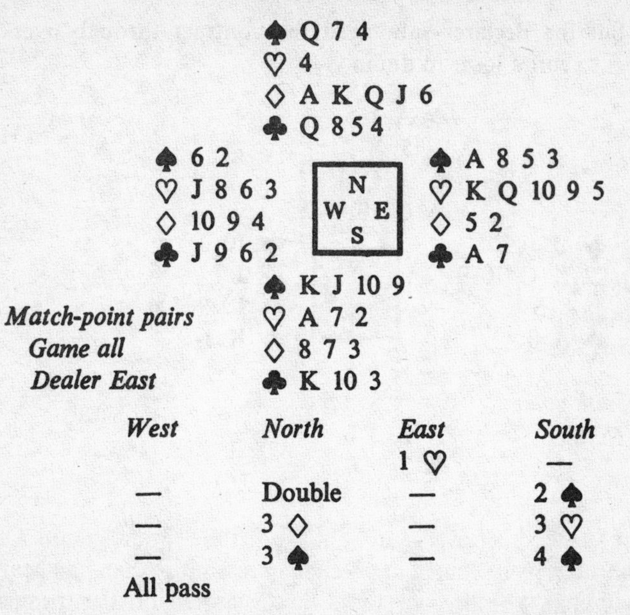

Five diamonds would have been easier, but South opted for the higher-scoring major suit game. He won the opening heart lead, ruffed a heart in dummy, led a club to his king and ruffed his third heart. East played the ace of spades on the queen and returned yet another heart, and this time South had to ruff in his own hand. When the trumps failed to break evenly he was held to nine tricks.

South would have made eleven tricks if the trumps had broken 3–3 but, since 620 would have been a good enough score, he should have tried to safeguard his contract against the more probable 4–2 break. The way to do that is to duck the first trick.

By refusing to part with the ace of hearts South retains control. If hearts are continued he ruffs in dummy and forces out the ace of trumps in comfort, while if East switches to the ace and another trump South simply draws the remaining trumps and establishes a club as his tenth trick.

There are several ways of making four spades on the hand shown below, but the declarer sabotaged the contract through over-eagerness to ruff a loser in dummy.

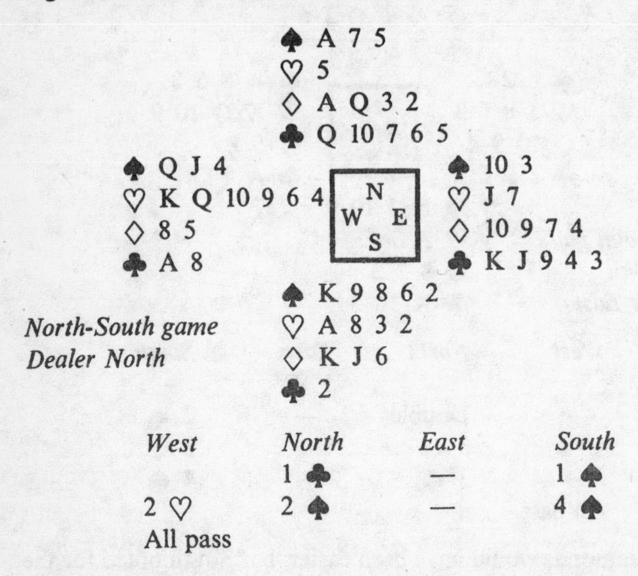

West	*North*	*East*	*South*
	1 ♣	—	1 ♠
2 ♡	2 ♠	—	4 ♠
All pass			

The opening lead was the king of hearts, and the declarer sealed the fate of the contract when he won and ruffed a heart immediately. After cashing the ace and king of trumps South turned his attention to the diamonds, but West ruffed the third round and cashed two hearts and the ace of clubs.

When a ruff has to be negotiated and a trump trick lost, an early duck will often retain control. If South allows the king of hearts to hold the first trick he will later be able to ruff a small heart and clear the trumps at leisure.

Alternatively South can win the first heart and duck a trump at trick two. He will subsequently get his heart ruff, draw trumps and claim ten tricks.

But the simplest way to play the hand is to win the first trick, cash the top trumps and play on diamonds, discarding the club on the fourth round if West declines to ruff. South can then ruff a club and score a heart ruff in dummy as the tenth trick.

Mishandling Trumps

The next hand, from a Gold Cup match, shows how dangerous it can be to judge by results.

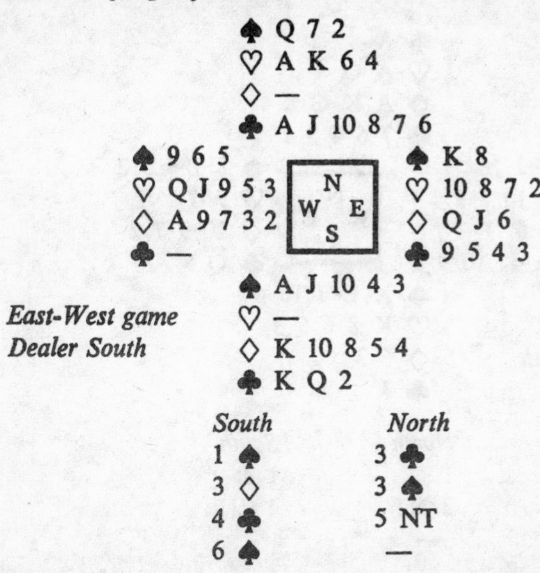

The final contract and the lead of the queen of hearts were the same in both rooms, but one declarer made an overtrick while the other went one down. Which team would you expect to win the match?

The hand is a classic trap for the expert. The declarer who went down allowed East's king of spades to hold the trick when it covered the queen. A club came back and it was all over.

The declarer was properly attempting to protect his contract against a 4–1 trump break. To capture the king with the ace and play two more rounds of trumps succeeds only 68 per cent of the time, while the duck ensures the contract nine times out of ten. This, unfortunately, was the tenth time.

Correct play may achieve a ludicrous result on any given hand, but it succeeds in the long run. I am happy to report that the team that lost points on this hand went on to win the match by a substantial margin.

Mishandling Trumps

Trump control can all too easily pass to the defenders if the declarer neglects the proper precautions.

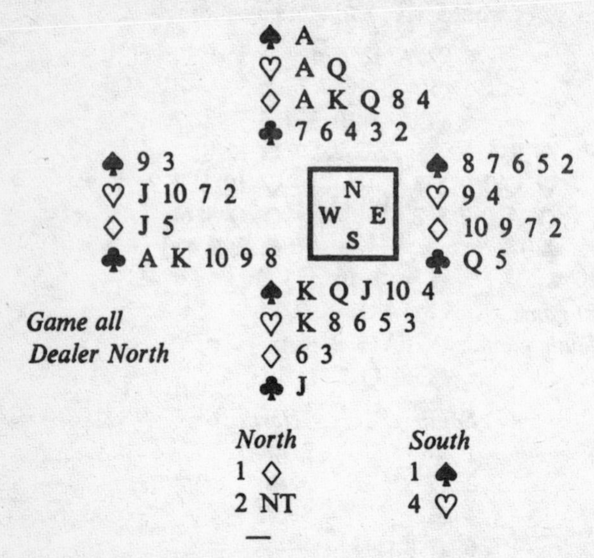

West led the ace of clubs and continued with the king which the declarer ruffed. After leading a spade to dummy's ace and playing off the ace and queen of trumps, South led out the top diamonds. West refused to assist by ruffing the third round but discarded a spade instead, and the declarer was in trouble. South ruffed a club, cashed the king of hearts and tried to slip the knave of spades through, but West ruffed and scored two more club tricks to defeat the contract.

The line of play adopted by the declarer would have succeeded if either of the red suits had broken evenly or if West had been kind enough to ruff the third diamond. South should have protected himself against a 4–2 trump break, however, by overtaking the queen of hearts with his king and playing on spades. This gambit sacrifices a trump trick but retains control, and the defenders can score no more than one club and two trumps.

A bad break in a side-suit often catches players off balance. In the following hand South did well to reach the grand slam in spite of high-level obstruction. If his play had been on a par with his bidding the story would have had a happy ending.

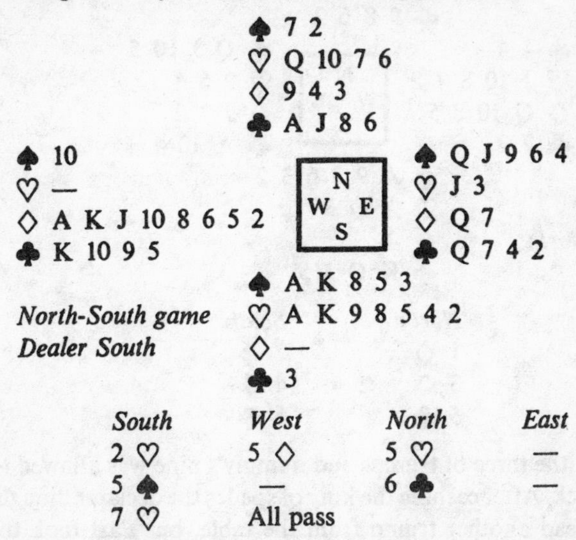

South	*West*	*North*	*East*
2 ♡	5 ◊	5 ♡	—
5 ♠	—	6 ♣	—
7 ♡	All pass		

South ruffed the opening diamond lead, confidently drew the outstanding trumps and cashed the ace and king of spades. When the suit broke 5–1 he realized with dismay that the grand slam could no longer be made.

The bidding might have warned South to expect bad breaks in the side suits, but even without this indication he should certainly have tested the spades before drawing the second round of trumps.

This play has nothing to lose, for the grand slam can never be made if East has fewer than two spades. If both defenders follow to two rounds of spades the outstanding trump can safely be drawn. And if, as in the present case, West shows out on the second round of spades, there are three trumps left in dummy to deal with the spade losers.

It is often necessary to establish a side suit before tackling trumps. In the next hand the declarer lost his slam through failure to appreciate this point.

Mishandling Trumps

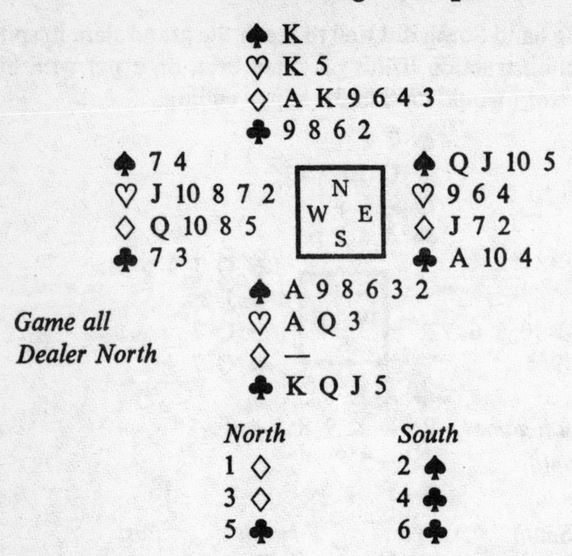

West led the three of trumps and dummy's nine was allowed to hold the trick. After cashing the king of spades the declarer thought it safe to lead another trump from the table, but East took the ace and returned his third trump and South found himself a trick short.

South should realize that if the spades are 4–2, as is probable, he cannot afford to lead a second trump until he has ruffed two spades in dummy.

The proper play at trick three is a heart to the queen followed by a spade ruff. The ace of diamonds is cashed for a heart discard, the king of hearts led to the ace, and another spade ruffed.

When that passes off successfully the remaining trump can be led from dummy, and as the cards lie the defenders are powerless to defeat the slam.

When ruffing a side suit in dummy it can be fatal to permit an early over-ruff. The declarer suffered from a blind spot on the following hand.

Mishandling Trumps

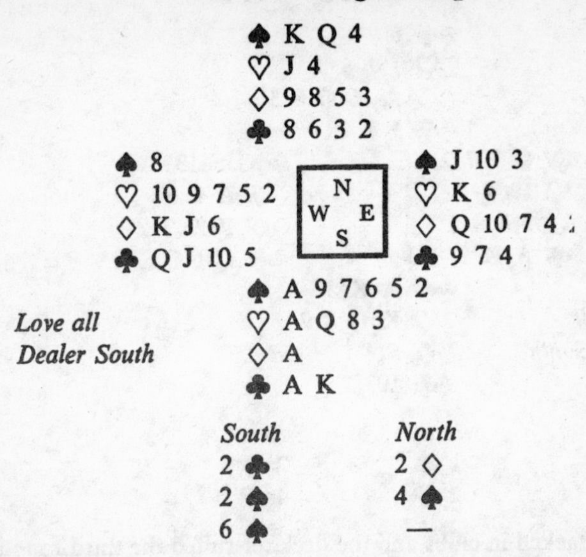

Winning the opening club lead, South led a spade to the king and returned the knave of hearts, which was covered by the king. After cashing the ace and queen South led a small heart and ruffed with dummy's four of spades. East over-ruffed and returned his last trump, and the declarer was left with a losing heart and a red face.

South lost sight of his target on this hand. His play would have been perfectly correct in a contract of seven spades, for he would then need to find the hearts 4–3 and the spades 2–2. In the small slam, however, there was no need to take any risk. As South realized the moment he had gone wrong, all he had to do was to ruff the third heart with the queen of spades, return to the ace of diamonds, and ruff the fourth heart with dummy's small trump. It could do no harm if East over-ruffed on the fourth round since that would be the only trick for the defence.

Possession of the ace of trumps gives the defenders a measure of control which they should be reluctant to lose. In missing his chance to defeat the game on the following hand, East was guilty of a very common mistake.

Mishandling Trumps

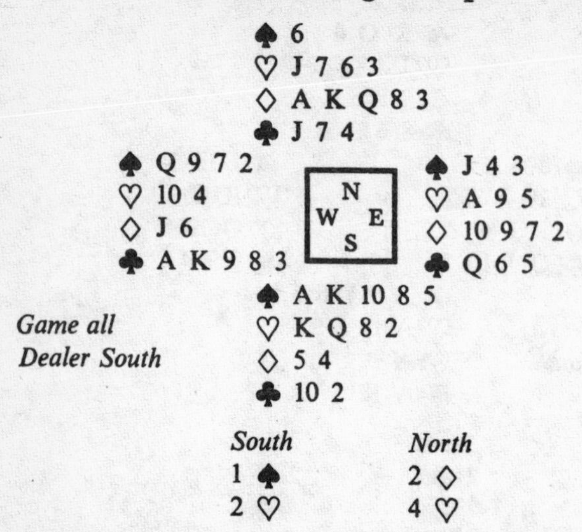

West attacked in clubs and the declarer ruffed the third round. The king of hearts was led to the ace, and the heart return won by South's queen. Before drawing the last trump the declarer correctly tested the diamond suit, and when West showed out on the third round South was able to ruff a fourth diamond with his remaining small trump. Ruffing the second round of spades on the table, South drew the outstanding trump and cashed the established diamond to make his contract.

Note the difference if East is bright enough to refuse to win the ace on the first round of trumps. The declarer cannot switch to diamonds immediately without allowing the defenders to make a second trump trick. And if South continues trumps East can win and play a third round to leave South a trick short.

It pays to be thrifty with trumps in defence. Players who are quick to seize any opportunity of scoring a trick with a small trump will usually have cause to regret their haste. The misuse of a small trump was fatal to the defence in the following hand, for the declarer obtained two tricks in exchange for the one he lost.

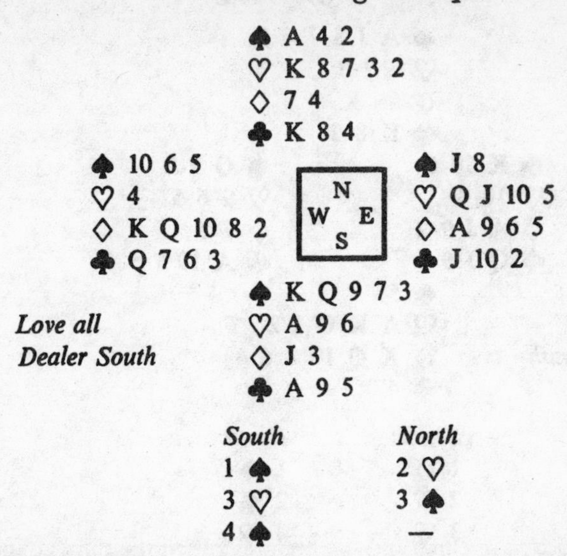

The defence started off with two rounds of diamonds and then switched to clubs. South won in hand with the ace and immediately played the ace and another heart. West pounced with a trump and led another club, but the declarer had no further problem. Winning with the king of clubs, he drew the remaining trumps with his king and queen and then established the fifth heart in dummy for a club discard.

It is usually a mistake for a defender to ruff when the declarer can play a loser on the trick. In effect West ruffed his partner's winner and disastrously shortened his own trump holding at the same time. If West discards on the second round of hearts the declarer can never come to more than nine tricks.

Players good enough to avoid that mistake might go wrong on the next hand, for many defenders are unable to resist an opportunity to over-ruff dummy.

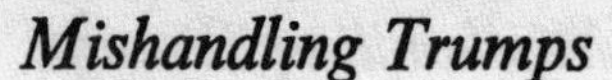

Mishandling Trumps

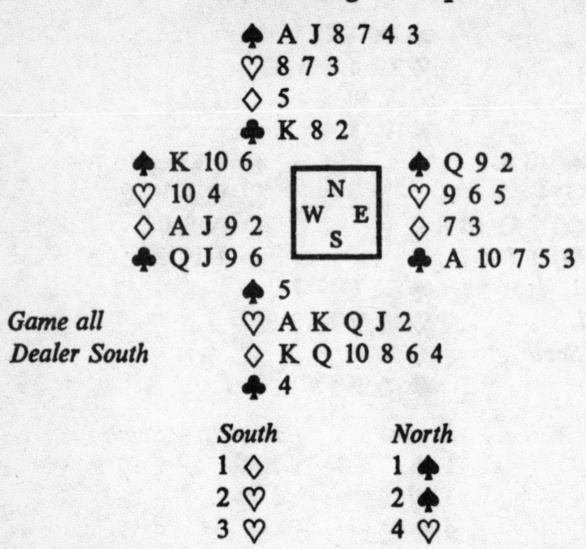

West leads the queen of clubs and South has to ruff the second round. The king of diamonds goes to West's ace, and the club return forces South to ruff again.

South cashes the queen of diamonds and ruffs a diamond with dummy's eight of hearts, and the critical point of the hand has been reached. If East makes the natural play of over-ruffing, that will be the end of the defence. South will ruff the club return with his queen, ruff another diamond with dummy's seven, draw the remaining trumps with his ace and king and claim the rest of the tricks.

East must refuse to over-ruff, discarding a spade or a club instead. Furthermore, when South plays a trump to his hand and ruffs the fourth round of diamonds with dummy's seven of trumps, East must again decline to over-ruff. Unable to return to his hand except by ruffing, South will then lose control and make no more than nine tricks.

A forcing defence is called for when the declarer has a two-suited hand, and the defenders must guard against weakening their trump holding at an early stage.

Mishandling Trumps

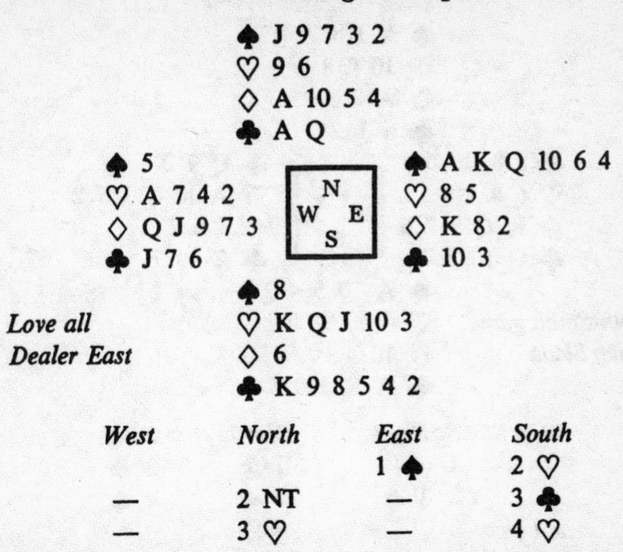

West	*North*	*East*	*South*
		1 ♠	2 ♡
—	2 NT	—	3 ♣
—	3 ♡	—	4 ♡

East won the first trick with the ten of spades and continued with the ace. When South ruffed with the three of hearts West seized the chance to over-ruff, thereby presenting South with the contract. West knocked out the ace of diamonds, but the declarer cashed the ace and queen of clubs and led the small trump from dummy. The ace of trumps was the only further trick for the defence.

It makes a difference of two tricks if West discards a diamond instead of over-ruffing. South will cash the ace and queen of clubs and then lead trumps, but West can defeat the contract in two different ways. The straightforward method is to hold off until the second round of trumps and then lead a diamond. South will be unable to return to hand without fatally shortening his trumps.

Alternatively West can win the first round of trumps and lead his club. South will have to ruff in dummy and the result will be the same.

Trumps are often mismanaged by both sides. In this hand the errors cancelled each other out.

Mishandling Trumps

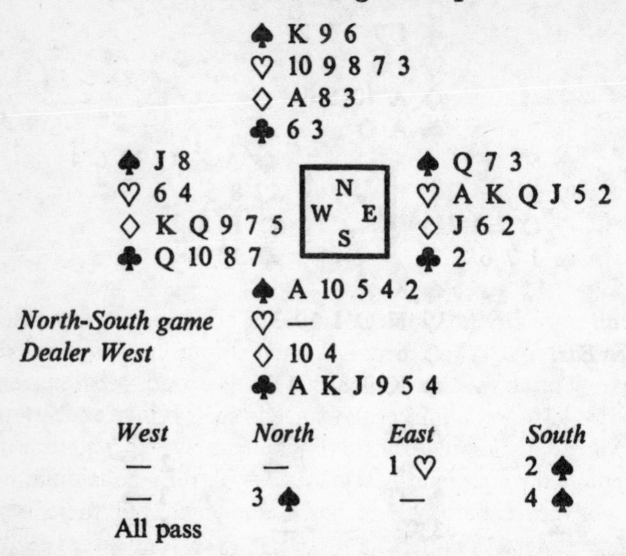

West	*North*	*East*	*South*
—	—	1 ♡	2 ♠
—	3 ♠	—	4 ♠
All pass			

South's jump overcall was of the Roman variety and showed a black two-suiter.

Ruffing the opening heart lead, South cashed the ace of clubs and the ace and king of spades and led the second club from dummy. The king won the trick when East discarded a heart, and a third club was ruffed in dummy and over-ruffed by East. South ruffed the heart return, conceded a club to West and claimed his contract, losing only a club, a trump and a diamond.

East made an elementary blunder, of course. He can defeat the contract by refusing to over-ruff dummy, thus preventing South from establishing the club suit.

But South also slipped up. He should draw only one round of trumps with the king before leading the second club from the table. The contract will then be unbeatable. If East declines to over-ruff on the third round of clubs, South simply returns to hand with the ace of trumps and leads another club.

5

Bidding on Misfits

FORTUNE normally favours the brave, in bridge as in any other sphere of activity. When there is a good trump fit it pays to bid aggressively up to the limit and even a little beyond. Most players absorb this lesson at a fairly early stage in their bridge education. Those who do not learn it have to resign themselves to a lifetime of losing points through faint-heartedness. A player who is timid by nature will never be anything but a door-mat, but there is a difference between timidity and discretion. Points can just as easily be lost by taking aggressive action at the wrong time.

Even amongst experienced players, making a bid too many on a misfit hand is one of the commonest causes of presents to the opponents. Those who are optimistic by nature find it easy enough to persuade themselves that their hands may be better than they think. It goes against the grain to devalue a hand when the bidding develops unfavourably. Players gaze fondly at their collection of picture cards and decide that the hand must surely be worth one more bid. And then the roof falls in.

The odd thing is that players seem to find it hard to learn from experience in this respect. The awful memories of four-figure penalties dissolve in an optimistic haze and the errors of last week are cheerfully repeated.

I have nothing new to offer in the way of advice. On misfit hands the only sound action is to stop bidding as soon as the misfit is diagnosed. You may not be in the best spot but this should not deter you, for by passing you will keep the loss to a minimum. It is the attempts to improve the contract that lead to disaster.

Here is a common situation.

♠ A Q 7 4 2
♡ 10
◇ K J 5 3
♣ J 7 3

Game all. Dealer South

South	*North*
1 ♡	1 ♠
2 ♡	?

As North, what would you do on the second round?

The general values are about right for a rebid of two no trumps, but the singleton heart should put you off. Partner had the chance to bid a minor suit or support spades but failed to do either. Clearly he has a weak hand with nothing much but a fair heart suit, and your only sensible action is to pass.

Is that too obvious? Apparently not, for when the problem arose in a pairs tournament the pass turned out to be worth 80 per cent of the match-points. Two hearts went one down, but most of the North players conceded two or three hundred after making a second bid. The full hand was as follows.

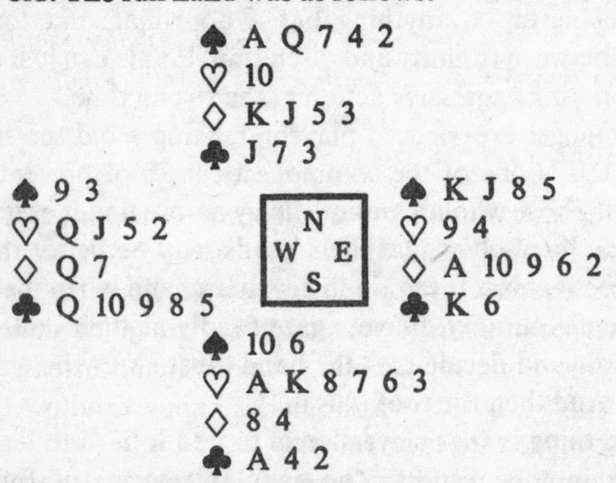

A two-suited misfit is even more to be feared. Players must school themselves to drop the bidding like a hot potato in situations like the following.

♠ 7
♡ A Q 8 6
◇ 8 5
♣ A Q 8 7 5 3

Love all. Dealer South

South	*North*
1 ♠	2 ♣
2 ◇	2 ♡
3 ◇	?

You begin to suspect the worst when partner bids diamonds on the second round but you can hardly pass at that stage. When South repeats the diamonds, however, the misfit is proved beyond doubt and a pass is likely to represent your only chance of achieving a plus score.

To be sure, partner might have the king and another club, although with that holding he might have bid two no trumps on the third round. If you can't bear the thought of missing any chance of game, go ahead and bid three no trumps. About one time in ten you'll get away with it. The other nine times I hope you're playing against me.

The trouble about diagnosing misfit hands in an uncontested auction is that it often takes a couple of rounds of bidding before you can be sure, and by then you may already be too high. When the opponents compete, however, your path is made smoother.

♠ 7
♡ A Q 6 5 3
◇ Q 9 4
♣ Q 10 7 3

Love all. Dealer South

South	*West*	*North*	*East*
1 ♠	2 ◇	?	

Without the intervention you would have to respond two hearts and pass the dreaded rebid of two spades on this hand. But the two diamond overcall solves your problem. Since the hand has every appearance of a misfit you should not dream of bidding two hearts. Take the money by doubling two diamonds instead. Whenever you suspect a misfit you should be happy to allow the opponents to struggle with the hand.

Here is a hand from a multiple team event where South exchanged a plus for a minus score by making a bid too many. Disaster was inevitable when his partner compounded the felony by bidding again himself.

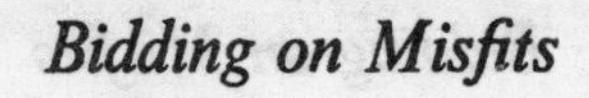

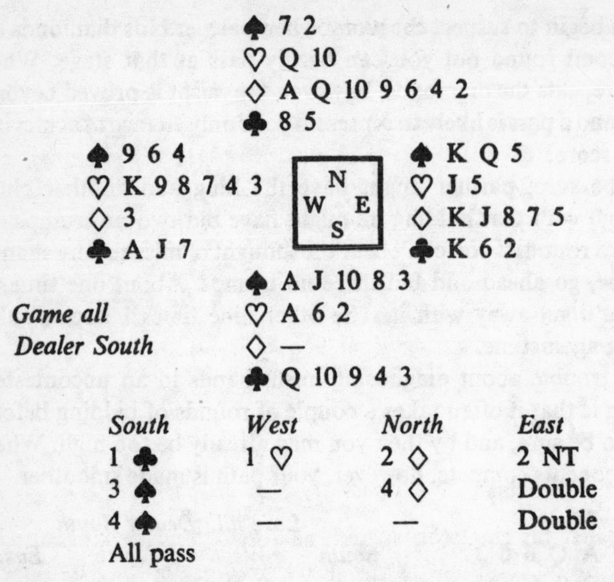

The five hundred penalty can only be attributed to a lemming-like urge to self-destruction. South had a weak hand and had no sound reason for making a second bid. With both opponents active, he should have realized that his partner could have little but a long string of diamonds.

All the evidence pointed to a misfit. South was void in his partner's suit, the opponents apparently had no good fit in hearts, and East was marked with values in clubs and spades. In the circumstances the bid of three spades was the height of folly. If South had made the obvious pass, the opponents would have gone down in two no trumps or three hearts.

North, for his part, should have passed three spades. The danger signs were there for him to read as well—shortage in his partner's suits and a no trump bid on his left.

The first evidence of a misfit may appear before you or your partner have uttered a word, and it is vital to be able to recognize it.

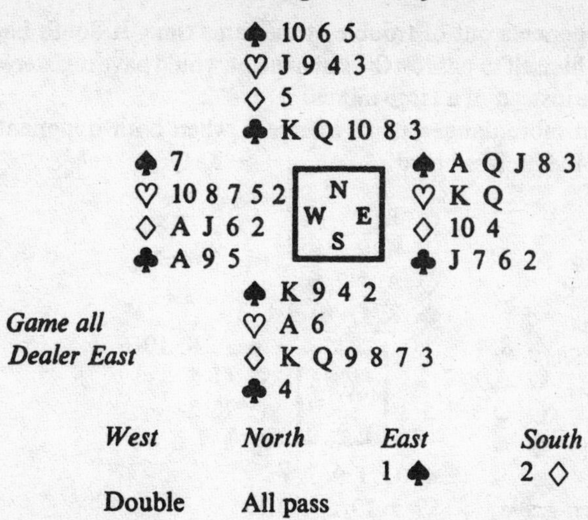

West led his singleton spade and ruffed South's king on the second round. South won the heart switch and tried to steal a club trick, but West put up the ace and led another heart to his partner's king.

After cashing the knave of spades East led a fourth spade which his partner trumped with the six of diamonds. A third round of hearts then enabled East to uppercut with the ten of diamonds, ensuring two further trump tricks and a penalty of 800 points for the defence.

South claimed that he was unlucky, but to concede such a penalty when there is nothing on for the opponents is the sure mark of a losing player. How should South have foreseen the catastrophe?

The answer lies in his four-card spade holding, which ought to have acted as a warning flag. Length in the enemy suit is the first indication of a misfit hand and should in itself be enough to deter an intervention. The point is often missed that if a hand is a misfit for one side it is also a misfit for the other. By making a voluntary intervention with length in the enemy suit you therefore risk a double loss. Not only do you offer your neck on the block but you bail the opponents out of trouble at the same time. If South had disciplined himself to pass on the last hand he would have registered a plus score instead of a large minus.

It is even more dangerous to intervene when both opponents have made themselves heard.

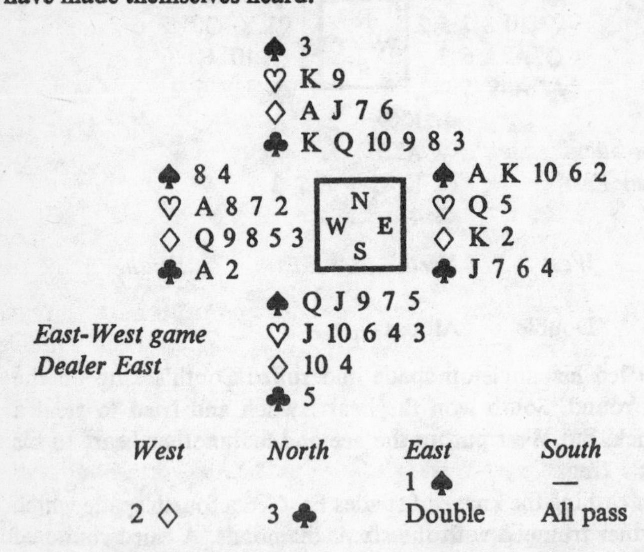

West	North	East	South
		1 ♠	—
2 ◇	3 ♣	Double	All pass

Once again all the signs of a misfit were there. North had four cards in diamonds himself, and since West had failed to support his partner's spades there was every reason to believe that South had length in the suit.

The non-vulnerable penalty was only 500 this time, but the true loss, as always, was somewhat more. East and West were certainly heading for a minus score until North came to their rescue.

The next hand from a team of four match is amusing in that one team managed to make fifteen tricks in hearts. It is also instructive.

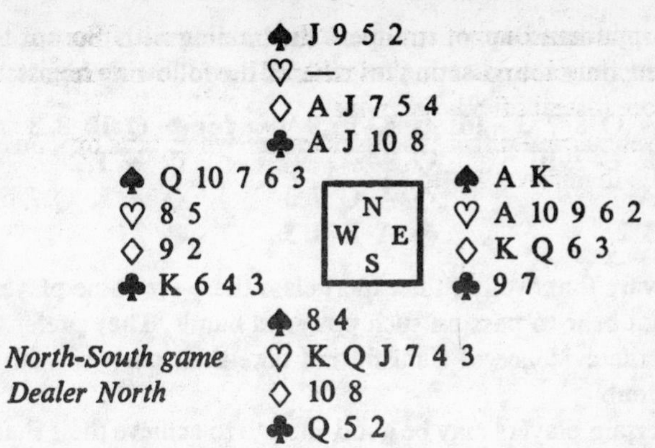

Room 1				Room 2			
West	*North*	*East*	*South*	*West*	*North*	*East*	*South*
	1 ◇	—	1 ♡		1 ◇	1 ♡	Double
—	1 ♠	—	2 ♡	All pass			
All pass							
◇ 9 led. Six tricks made				♡ K led. Five tricks made			
200 to East-West				300 to North-South			

Influenced by his length in diamonds, East in Room 1 decided that an overcall stood to lose more than it could gain. In Room 2, however, East was unable to resist a bid on his sixteen-point hand. When South doubled, North realized that at the vulnerability his partner was likely to have nothing much except hearts. In spite of his void, therefore, he decided to pass.

Par defence and dummy play was produced at both tables, and the swing of 11 i.m.p. is attributable solely to the sounder bidding methods of the winning team.

A pass is the correct action on most unbalanced hands of up to 17 high-card points in strength which contain length in the enemy suit. With 18 points or more, however, it is advisable to take immediate action of some sort. There is a limit to the protection you can expect from partner, and a game may well be missed if you pass.

Bidding on Misfits

If your right-hand opponent opens the bidding with one spade, a pass is the only sound action on each of the following hands.

(*a*)	(*b*)	(*c*)
♠ A Q 8 7 3	♠ K 10 9 4	♠ Q 10 8 3
♡ K Q J 10	♡ 8	♡ K J 2
◇ A 7	◇ A Q 7 3	◇ A K Q J 6
♣ 3 2	♣ A K J 5	♣ 2

I am aware that even in the expert class there are some players who cannot bear to pass on such powerful hands. They prefer to disregard the evidence of a misfit and take their chances with a bid or a double.

Well, certain players may be good enough to achieve their share of wins in spite of dubious bidding methods in such situations. Big-name players are in any case apt to enjoy a stoat and rabbit relationship with their less illustrious opponents. A large penalty may be within sight, but when the stoat fixes him with a beady eye the rabbit cannot believe it and fails to make the obvious double that he would cheerfully make in his home club. Instead he makes some inept no trump bid and the stoat is off the hook.

They may get by in spite of their methods, but I am convinced that these experts make the game much more difficult for themselves. An immediate overcall or double on hands such as the above is both dangerous and unnecessary. There is no risk of missing game by passing if partner is trained to give normal protection with about eight points. If one spade *is* passed out this is likely to produce a good result for the defence. And finally, if you are given another chance to bid you will be in a much better position to judge the potential of the hand and take appropriate action.

On balanced hands that are not strong enough for an overcall of one no trump, a pass is again the right answer. This is the only way of avoiding silly results such as the following.

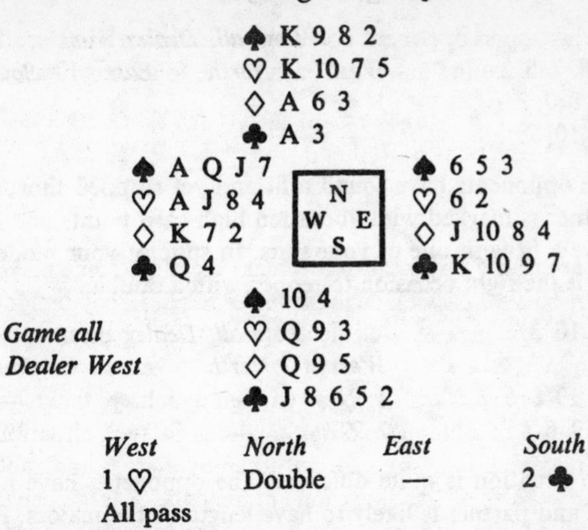

Two clubs went one down at a cost of 100 points. South could have saved the day by responding one no trump but, expecting shortage in hearts and club support in the North hand, he had no reason to make such a bid.

North had only to keep silent to pick up one or two hundred points defending against one heart. Many players would make the same mistake, failing to realize that it is quite unnecessary to double with the North hand on the first round. One heart will not be passed out if South has any respectable values.

Of course, if East raises to two hearts and this is passed round, North can think again. The initial evidence of a misfit has now been reversed. Since the opponents appear to have some sort of heart fit it is likely that the other side will have a fit as well and North can reopen with a double.

If East raises one heart to four North will be happy to defend, but if he had doubled on the first round his partner might thwart his intentions by bidding four spades on five to the queen.

In all reopening or protective situations the decision should be influenced by whether the hand seems to be a fit or a misfit.

♠ 8
♡ J 8 7 5 2
◇ A 8 7 3
♣ K 10 5

Love all. Dealer West

West	*North*	*East*	*South*
1 ♠	—	2 ♠	—
—	?		

Here the opponents have found a fit and yet stopped short of game. Partner is marked with about ten high-card points and he should have a fit with one of your suits. In spite of your modest values this is the right occasion to reopen with a double.

♠ K 10 3
♡ 6
◇ K 10 8 6 2
♣ A 9 6 4

Love all. Dealer West

West	*North*	*East*	*South*
1 ♡	—	1 ♠	—
2 ♡	—	—	?

Here the situation is quite different. The opponents have not found a fit and partner is likely to have length in the majors. He may not have enough to defeat two hearts, however, and a double or bid at this point could be disastrous. On a misfit hand the opponents would welcome the chance to double you.

♠ A 9 7 6 5
♡ A Q 6
◇ J
♣ A 9 6 3

Love all. Dealer West

West	*North*	*Wast*	*South*
1 ♠	—	—	?

In this case you have a good hand but nowhere to go. If you double, partner is likely to bid diamonds and what will you do then? The five-card spade holding is sufficient evidence of a misfit and you should allow West to struggle in one spade.

The problem arose in a pairs contest and the full hand was as shown opposite.

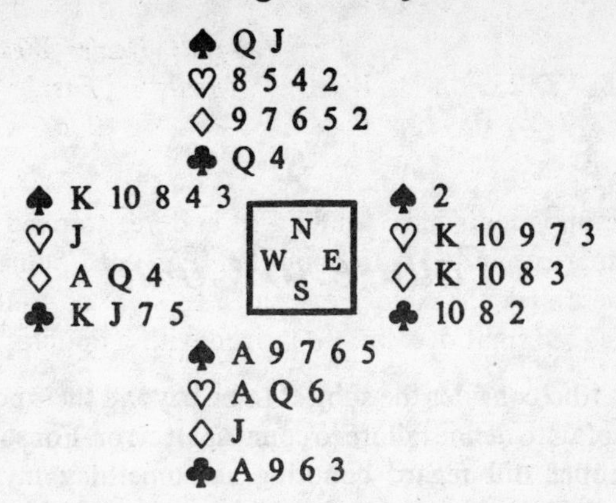

If South doubled or bid he was in trouble. The pass was the only way to obtain a plus score.

6

Failure to Count

PLAYERS who consider the subject to be beyond their powers may think it unfair to define failure to count as an error. For some reason many people still regard counting as something mystical and obscure which is the prerogative of the expert. Nothing could be further from the truth.

The counting that is required at bridge is so simple that any child can do it. A slight mental effort is called for, of course, and perhaps that is the real reason why a large number of players spend a lifetime at the bridge table without making any attempt to count. Most of us are lazy and hesitate to expend mental energy when we may get by quite nicely without doing so.

But there are a number of hands on which we cannot get by without counting. The small chore of counting out the distribution of the unseen hands is amply rewarded on those occasions when it turns a guess into a certainty.

The counting of points is also a neglected habit. It is such a simple thing to relate the high cards an opponent has produced to his bidding and infer that he must have, or cannot have, a particular card. But it never occurs to the average player to do so.

An even more basic exercise in arithmetic is the counting of tricks, both in the play of the dummy and in defence. This is something that is emphasized at an early stage in every bridge course. Count your tricks, the beginner is told, and look for a means of developing the extra tricks you need before playing a card from dummy. Nevertheless, declarers are often seen to embark on a hopeless line of play that cannot possibly produce enough tricks for the contract. Here is an example.

Failure to Count

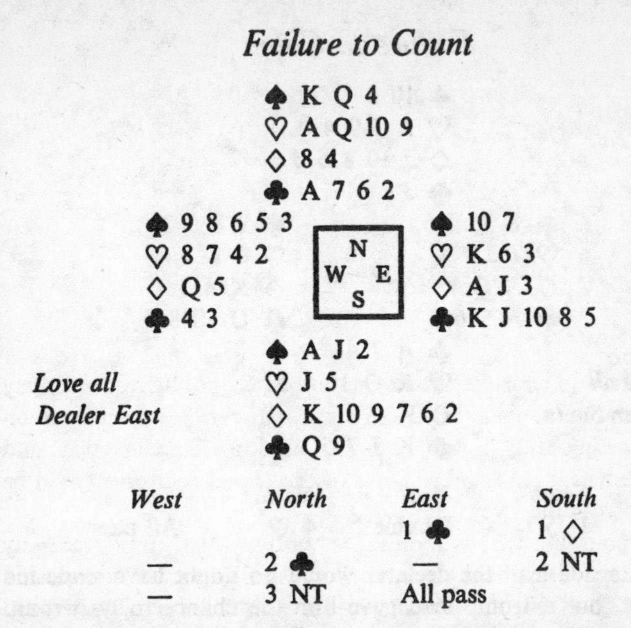

West	*North*	*East*	*South*
		1 ♣	1 ◇
—	2 ♣	—	2 NT
—	3 NT	All pass	

The four of clubs was led to the ten and queen, and South quickly chucked the game by running the knave of hearts. East won and cleared the clubs, and the contract went down.

The declarer was guilty of muddled thinking. With the heart king marked in the East hand by the opening bid, hearts could not possibly produce enough tricks for the contract.

The ninth trick must come from diamonds and the suit has to be tackled immediately. South should play a spade to dummy at trick two and lead a diamond from the table. If East plays low the king will score, and South can switch to hearts and establish enough tricks for game.

If East goes up with the ace of diamonds and clears the clubs, South will have to abandon the heart suit. Instead he can attempt to lose a second diamond to West, who will have no club to return if the suit breaks 5–2. South leads another diamond from dummy and plays the nine on East's three. West wins and returns a heart, but South puts on the ace and claims ten tricks.

The next hand is of a type that often catches players out.

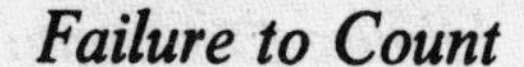

Failure to Count

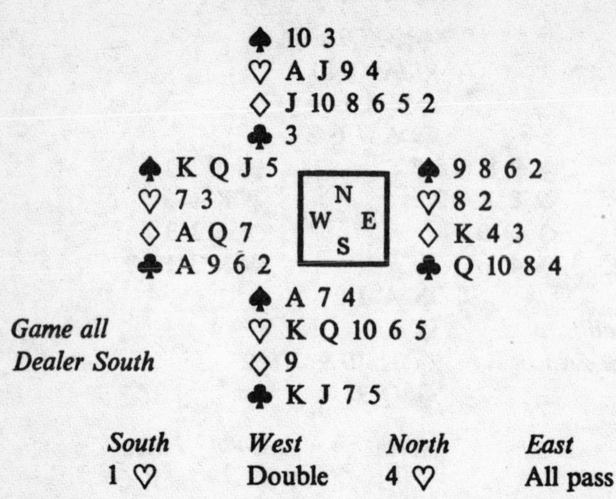

South	*West*	*North*	*East*
1 ♡	Double	4 ♡	All pass

On a spade lead the declarer would no doubt have made his contract, but a trump lead gave him the chance to go wrong. Winning with the nine in dummy, he led the club in an effort to find a parking place for the losing spade on the table. He succeeded in this objective when his knave of clubs drew the ace, but it did him no good. West returned another trump and there was no way for the declarer to make more than nine tricks—seven trumps, one spade and one club.

If South had counted his tricks more carefully he might have seen that the advantage of getting rid of dummy's losing spade is illusory. Ten tricks can never be made on this hand unless the diamond suit can be brought in. South must hope for a 3–3 break in the suit, and he must lead a diamond at trick two before a second trump entry can be taken out.

Many contracts that can be defeated are allowed to slip home when a defender has to make a critical discard at an early stage. Discarding correctly can sometimes be difficult, but a count of the declarer's tricks will usually save the defenders from going astray in cases like the following.

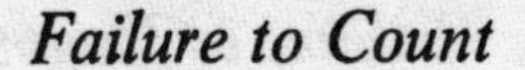

Failure to Count

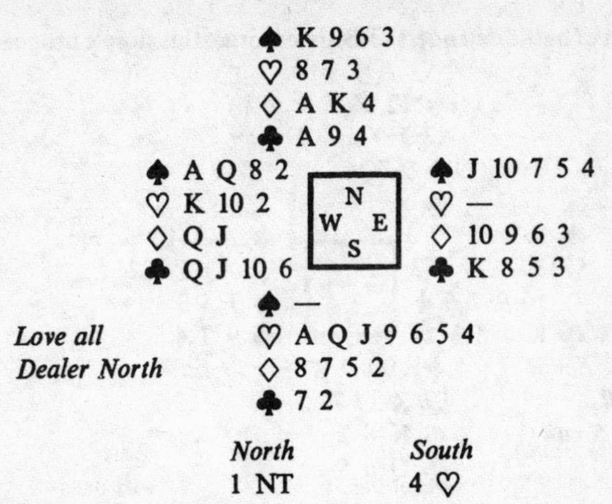

The opening lead was the queen of clubs which held the first trick. The declarer won the second club and led a trump, on which East discarded a club. West captured the queen of hearts with his king and led a third club for South to ruff.

On the next two trumps East had to find two discards without the benefit of a signal from his partner. On the first he discarded a spade, but on the second he thought he had a problem. Reluctant to part with a second spade, he let go a diamond instead. That was all the help the declarer needed to make his contract. After three rounds of diamonds the tenth trick was established.

Is this too elementary? I do not think so, for I have seen this sort of thing happen over and over again at the bridge table. East's problem existed only in his mind, of course. When his partner played the ten of hearts on the third round he could count the declarer for six trump tricks, and three additional winners were visible in dummy. It followed that if South had anything in spades —even as much as a singleton—he could not be prevented from making his contract. East should therefore have discarded his spades as the rubbish they were and hung on to his precious diamonds.

It takes four defensive tricks to defeat a major suit game, but in the heat of battle defenders sometimes forget this simple proposition.

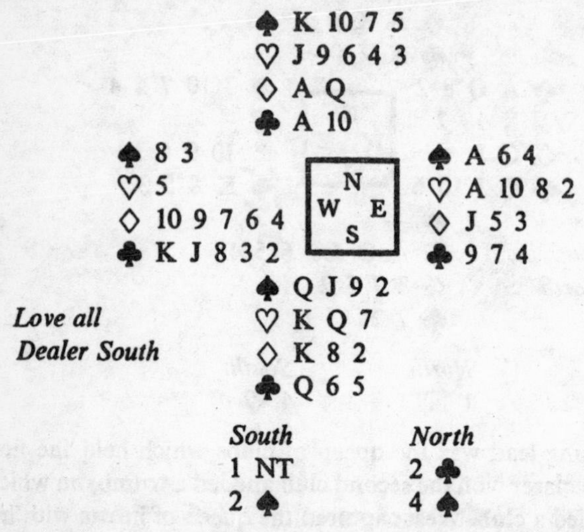

West led the five of hearts to his partner's ace and South dropped the queen. East recognized the lead as a singleton and returned the suit for West to ruff. After this there was no way for the defenders to defeat the contract. West tried a diamond lead, but the declarer won and played trumps and the ace of spades was the only further trick for the defence.

East was far too hasty here. If he had paused to count the defensive tricks he would have realized that two aces and a heart ruff would not be enough to defeat the contract. The only possibility of a fourth trick for the defence is in clubs. The club lead must come from East and it must be made immediately, before the hearts in dummy are available for discards.

The club lead at trick two gets the timing right for the defence. As soon as trumps are led East can play the ace, give his partner a heart ruff, and see West take the setting trick in clubs.

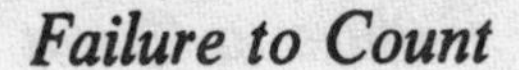

Failure to Count

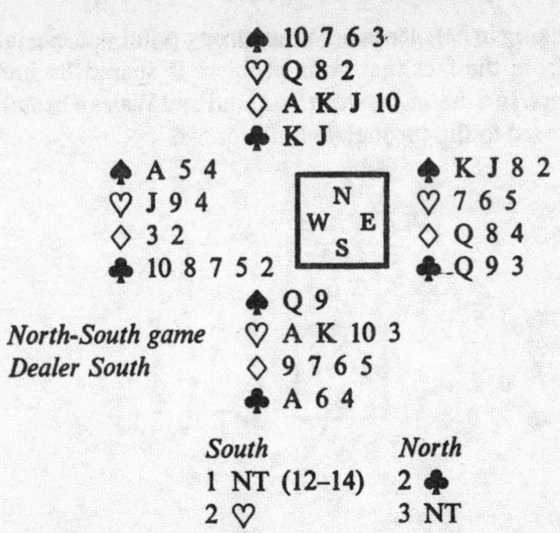

North-South game
Dealer South

South	*North*
1 NT (12–14)	2 ♣
2 ♡	3 NT

West's lead of the five of clubs was covered by the knave and queen and won by the ace. South played a diamond to the ace, returned to hand with the king of hearts, and took a losing diamond finesse. East returned a club to knock out dummy's king, but this did not trouble the declarer, who had nine tricks when the hearts broke evenly.

East's feeble defence was caused by his failure to count the declarer's tricks. South bid hearts and appeared to have the ace and king and therefore four tricks in the suit, and five further tricks are visible in the minor suits. When in with the queen of diamonds, East should realize that four fast spade tricks are needed to defeat the contract. There is quite a good chance of this, for a count of points indicates that South cannot have the ace of spades as well as the ace and king of hearts. In order to make four spade tricks East must lead the king. West wins the next trick with the ace and a further spade lead through dummy enables East to score his knave and eight.

South's play was inept in that he disclosed his heart holding prematurely. A better plan is to take an immediate diamond finesse at trick two.

Failure to Count

If clear thinking in defence is not your strong point you can take consolation from the fact that your problem is shared by international players. In a match between Scotland and Wales a beatable game was allowed to slip through in both rooms.

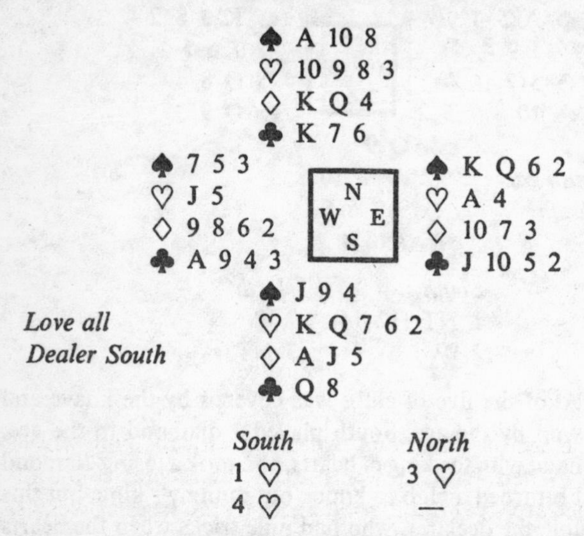

The opening diamond lead was won by the king and a heart was led to the queen. A club to the king was followed by another heart, and East returned the knave of clubs to the queen and ace.

The critical point of the hand had been reached. West should realize that two further tricks in the black suits are required. If the contract is to be defeated his partner will need to have either the king and queen of spades or the king of spades and a club winner. With the former holding East will now require a spade lead to protect him from an end-play.

Both West players returned a club, however, and that was the end of the defence. After ruffing and playing off the top diamonds, the declarers ran the knave of spades to the queen, and East was faced with the unhappy choice of returning a spade into the tenace or conceding a ruff and discard.

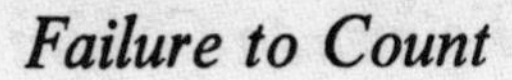

Failure to Count

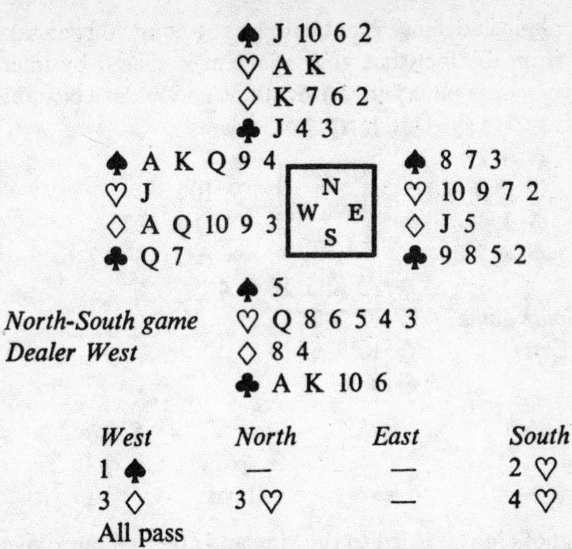

West	*North*	*East*	*South*
1 ♠	—	—	2 ♡
3 ◇	3 ♡	—	4 ♡
All pass			

West led the ace of spades and continued with the king which South ruffed. When West showed out on the second round of trumps, the declarer realized that he had a trump loser as well as spade and diamond losers. Needing to avoid the loss of a club trick, he led a small club from dummy and finessed the ten. But West produced the queen to put the contract one down.

If the declarer had taken the trouble to count West's distribution he would have seen that the club finesse was a hopeless play that could not possibly gain. West must surely have five diamonds for his three-level bid and he is also marked with five spades. Add the singleton trump and there is room for no more than two clubs in his hand. It follows that the club finesse, even if it wins, will do South no good, for he will still have to lose a club trick to East in the end.

In this hand the only hope of avoiding a club loser is that West has the queen singleton or doubleton. South should therefore have led a club to his ace, cleared the trumps, and then played to drop the queen of clubs.

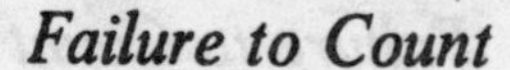

Failure to Count

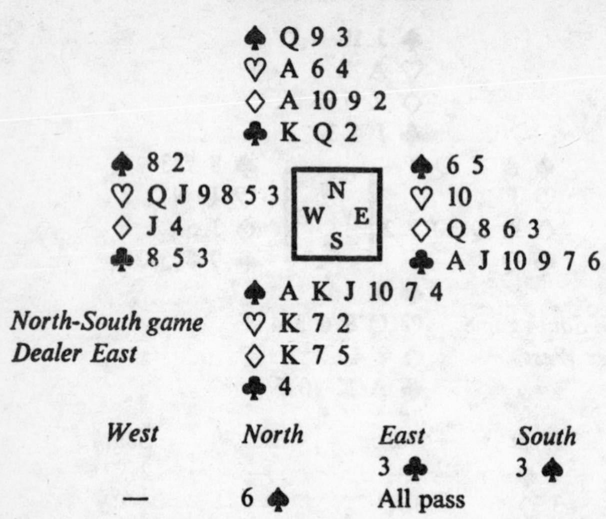

The eight of clubs was led to the king and ace, and the knave of clubs came back. South ruffed with the ace of spades, drew the outstanding trumps with the king and knave, and played the king of diamonds followed by a low diamond to the ace. After discarding his third diamond on the queen of clubs he led the ten of diamonds from the table and ruffed, hoping to bring down the queen. West showed out, however, and the contract had to go one down.

'The probabilities were with me,' said South gloomily. 'On the bidding East was more likely to have three diamonds than four.'

In a sense South was right, but there was no need to rely on probabilities in this hand. He could have found out for certain about East's distribution by the simple expedient of leading a heart to his king and a heart back to the ace. When East shows out on the second heart his hand can be counted as two spades, one heart, six clubs, and therefore four diamonds. The rest would be easy.

It is because players do not think of such things that they misplay simple hands like this one.

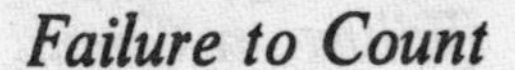

Failure to Count

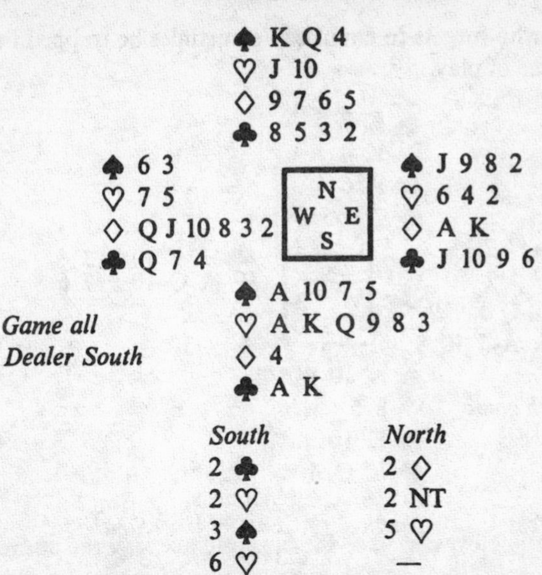

Good bidding reached the optimum contract, but South did not give himself much of a chance in the play. The queen of diamonds was led to the king and East switched to a trump. South drew three rounds and played off the king and queen of spades. On the way back he made the wrong guess, trying to drop the knave, and the slam went one down.

This is the sort of hand on which the declarer should attempt to discover how the side suits are distributed before facing the critical decision. South should win the first trump on the table, ruff a diamond, lead another trump to dummy and ruff another diamond. East is actually squeezed on this trick, but it does not matter if South fails to notice it. He can continue with a third round of trumps, discarding a club from dummy if he likes.

After cashing the ace and king of clubs, South enters dummy with a spade and ruffs the last club. The picture is now complete, West being marked with two trumps, six diamonds, three clubs, and therefore no more than two spades. The guess in the spade suit is thus transformed into a certainty.

Failure to Count

An expert who forgets to count can sometimes be trapped into an illogical line of play.

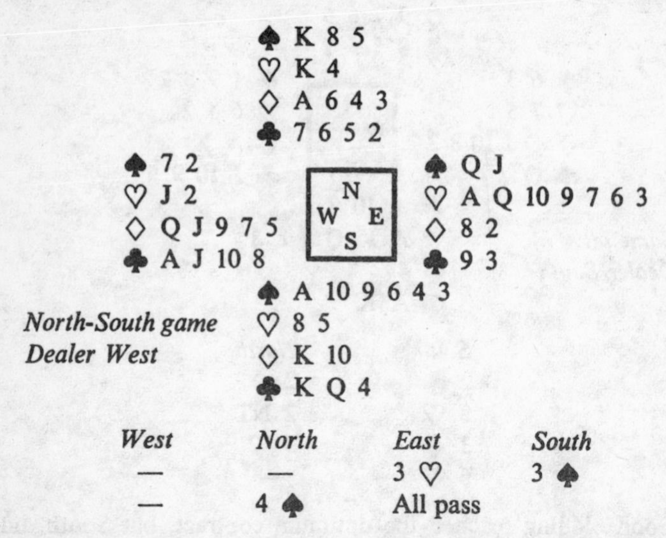

The opening lead was the knave of hearts, and after cashing two tricks in the suit East switched to the nine of clubs. South's king was taken by the ace and the knave of clubs was returned to the queen. South cashed the ace of spades and noted the drop of the knave. At the next trick he fell from grace by finessing the eight of spades to East's queen, and the contract was lost.

Although both the bidding and the Rule of Restricted Choice indicate that East's knave of spades is likely to be a singleton, the finesse on the second round is a hopeless play that cannot possibly succeed. Not only does South need to bring in the spade suit without loss, but he also needs a minor suit squeeze to fulfil his contract. If East has a singleton spade he will have three cards in one of the minors and the squeeze will fail.

South should therefore play for East to have a 7–2–2–2 distribution and put up the king on the second round of trumps.

Failure to Count

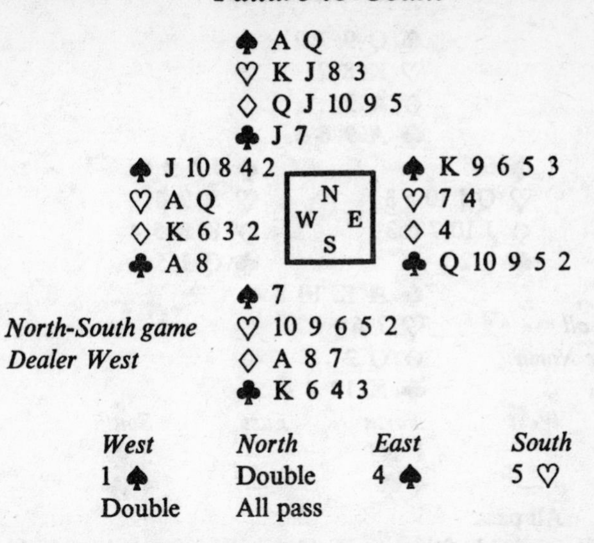

West	*North*	*East*	*South*
1 ♠	Double	4 ♠	5 ♡
Double	All pass		

The declarer won the opening spade lead with the ace, ruffed the queen of spades in hand, and led a trump. West played the ace and, for want of anything better, returned the queen of hearts. Dummy's king took the trick, and the queen of diamonds was run to West's king.

Thinking nervously about the discards the declarer would make on dummy's long diamonds, West decided that the time had arrived for the defenders to cash what club tricks they could. He led the ace of clubs, but that proved to be the last trick for the defence. The result was a penalty of 200 points which failed to compensate for the lost game.

West's generous defence was induced by his failure to count the declarer's hand. South is known to have started with one spade and five hearts, and therefore seven cards in the minor suits. It follows that there will be two clubs left in the declarer's hand after the diamonds have been cashed. There is thus no reason for West to panic. A passive diamond return is all that is required of him. The defenders will then come to two club tricks and earn a worthwhile penalty of 500 points.

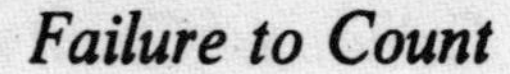

Failure to Count

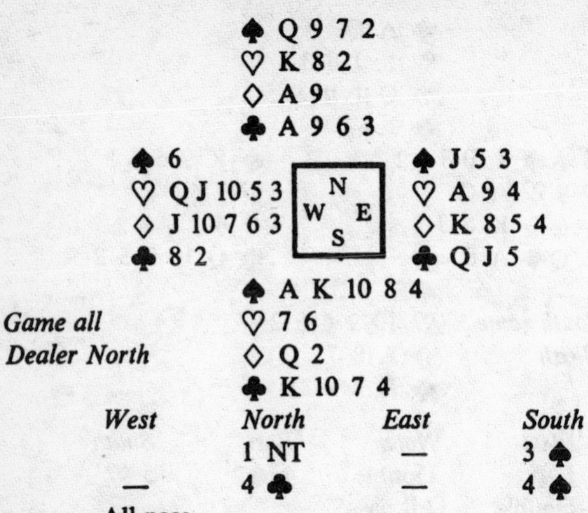

West	*North*	*East*	*South*
	1 NT	—	3 ♠
—	4 ♣	—	4 ♠
All pass			

The opening lead of the queen of hearts was covered by the king and ace, and a heart returned to the ten. West switched to the knave of diamonds, but the declarer put up dummy's ace, ruffed the heart, drew three rounds of trumps, and then put East on lead with the diamond.

Determined not to concede a ruff and discard, East tried the effect of leading the knave of clubs. South made the right guess, however, running the knave to dummy's ace and finessing on the way back to make his contract.

Once again it was failure to count that led East astray. South is known to have five spades and a doubleton heart. If he has only two diamonds he must have four clubs, in which case a ruff and discard will not help him. The diamond return is marked.

Another way of looking at the problem is to count the declarer's tricks. East knows that South has five trump tricks, one diamond, and at the most two clubs—a total of eight. A ruff and discard might give him the ninth trick, but it can never concede the tenth.

In the next hand the declarer played well up to a point. If he had only remembered the bidding he might have brought home a tricky contract.

Failure to Count

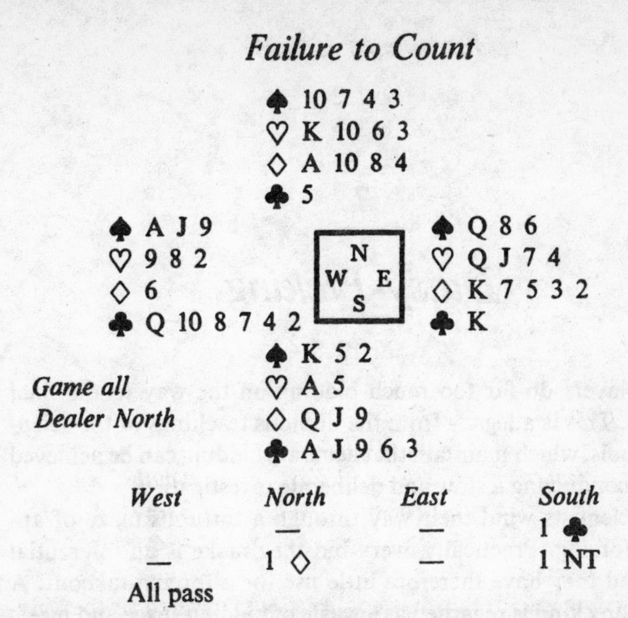

West	*North*	*East*	*South*
	—	—	1 ♣
—	1 ◇	—	1 NT
All pass			

The nine of hearts was led to the ace, and the queen of diamonds held the next trick. West threw the eight of clubs on the knave of diamonds and East won the trick with the king.

The king of clubs was allowed to hold the next trick, and the queen of hearts was also allowed to win. East finally got off lead with a third diamond.

South won in dummy and counted his tricks. With three diamonds, two hearts and a club, it seemed that the seventh trick would have to come from spades. Accordingly, without cashing the red suit winners in dummy, South led a small spade and put on the king. West won and returned his third heart, and the defence had to make seven tricks.

South had the right idea in leading a spade, but if it had occurred to him to count East's points he would not have tried to win the trick with the king. East, who passed originally, had already produced the queen and knave of hearts and the kings of clubs and diamonds. He could hardly have the ace of spades as well. If South ducks two spade leads he will always come to his seventh trick in one way or another.

7

Daisy-Picking

Most players do far too much bidding on the way to the final contract. This is a legacy from the dubious teachings of the scientific schools, which maintain that accurate bidding can be achieved only by conducting a slow and deliberate investigation.

The scientists wind their way through a tortuous maze of approach forcing. Practically every bid they make is an inferential force, and they have therefore little use for a forcing takeout. A jump of any kind is regarded as a waste of bidding space and meets with pained disapproval.

Such methods show up to best advantage in the cloistered setting of bidding competitions. With no uncouth opponents to disturb them, the scientists can be as fancy as they please and are unlikely to be penalized for taking seven rounds of bidding to reach a simple three no trump contract. But in real life things are different. The opponents are there, awkward creatures of flesh and blood, eavesdropping on every bid you make, butting in, sacrificing, and generally making a nuisance of themselves.

The notion of bidding as a duet between partners for the purpose of exchanging the maximum information about strength and distribution is widely held but quite unsound. There are *two* pairs at the bridge table and they do not sing in harmony. Each pair is out to get the better of the other, and the one most likely to succeed is the pair that is prepared to sacrifice a measure of accuracy for the sake of obstruction.

Extra rounds of bidding do not necessarily produce better contracts—only better defence. This is confirmed by a report in the 1969 Annals of the International Bridge Academy. A study of

Daisy-Picking

1,556 World Championship deals revealed that the most successful contracts were those reached in the fewest bids.

The real aim of bidding should be to exchange the absolute minimum of information that will enable you to arrive at a reasonable contract. Of course there are some hands that require detailed investigation and your system must include mechanism to deal with these. But it is vital to keep such investigations to a minimum and to avoid using your machinery for the pleasure of hearing it whirr. As soon as you have a good idea of what the final contract should be, bid it without picking daisies on the way.

The big secret of effective bidding is to limit your hand at the earliest opportunity. Limit bids in no trumps and quantitative raises have the virtue of feeding partner the information he needs while giving little away to the opponents. They also have a valuable obstructive effect, and practical players usually prefer an obstructive to a constructive bid when they are given the choice. Quantitative sequences such as 1 ♠–4 ♠, 1 ♡–3 ♡–6 ♡, or 2 NT–6 ♢ may have an untutored ring to them, but they can be devastatingly effective. The times you find yourself going down after such a sequence are more than compensated by the times when a favourable lead presents you with the contract.

Bidding is not, and never will be, an exact science. It is a rough estimation of probabilities, and there is no reason for supposing that a slow approach will lead to a better contract in the end. Perfection in bidding is an unworthy target and an unattainable one. The best of contracts may be defeated by a bad break or a double-dummy defence, and while the blaster can hope for the compensation of a favourable lead there is not much chance for the scientists. He has told the opponents so much about his hand that it is normally a simple matter for them to produce the best defence.

Consider three different methods of bidding this everyday hand.

Daisy-Picking

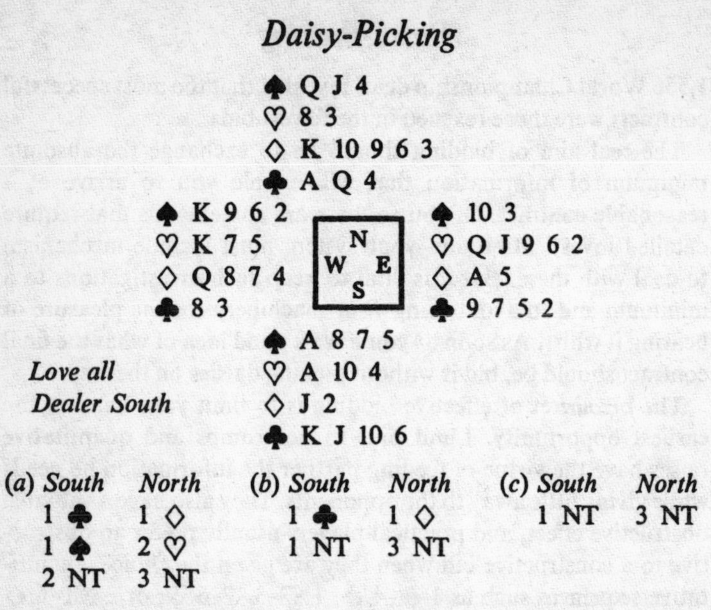

(*a*) *South*	*North*	(*b*) *South*	*North*	(*c*) *South*	*North*
1 ♣	1 ◇	1 ♣	1 ◇	1 NT	3 NT
1 ♠	2 ♡	1 NT	3 NT		
2 NT	3 NT				

(*a*) A nice scientific sequence, but the contract is doomed even though East failed to overcall on the first round and failed to double the fourth-suit bid of two hearts. Warned against the other suits, West has nothing to try but hearts.

(*b*) This is better, for West is now more likely to lead a spade. But note that East had the opportunity to overcall on the first round.

(*c*) South limits his hand with his opening bid and North is able to place the contract immediately, giving East no chance to indicate a defence. It would be unnatural for West to lead anything but a spade or a diamond.

Clearly the limit bid gives away the least information, and this is one of the main arguments in favour of the adoption of the weak no trump. With a frequency twice as high as the strong no trump, it gives many more opportunities for limiting your hand on the opening bid.

The hands that follow illustrate some of the embarrassing things that can happen to the daisy-pickers. The first example comes from a team of four match.

Daisy-Picking

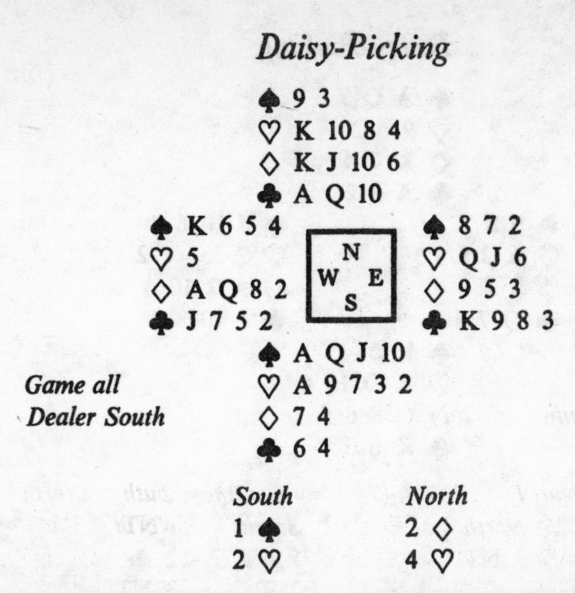

West led the two of clubs and the finesse of the queen lost to the king. When a spade came back the declarer was left with four inescapable losers.

It is perhaps unlucky to go down in four hearts on this hand, but it is certainly inept to be in it. The trouble was caused by North's first bid. Why fiddle around bidding diamonds when the perfect limit bid of three no trumps was available? I know that many players dislike this immediate jump to three no trumps, but when the right hand is held, as in the present case, there is no better bid. Even if North knew in advance that his partner had a five-card heart suit, he should not wish to play in hearts on this hand.

In the other room North made the obvious bid of three no trumps and was allowed to play there. East led a club and the declarer had no difficulty in making nine tricks for a swing of 12 i.m.p.

The Stayman convention is in almost universal use, but care should be taken to reserve it for the proper occasions.

Look at what happened in this hand from a match.

Daisy-Picking

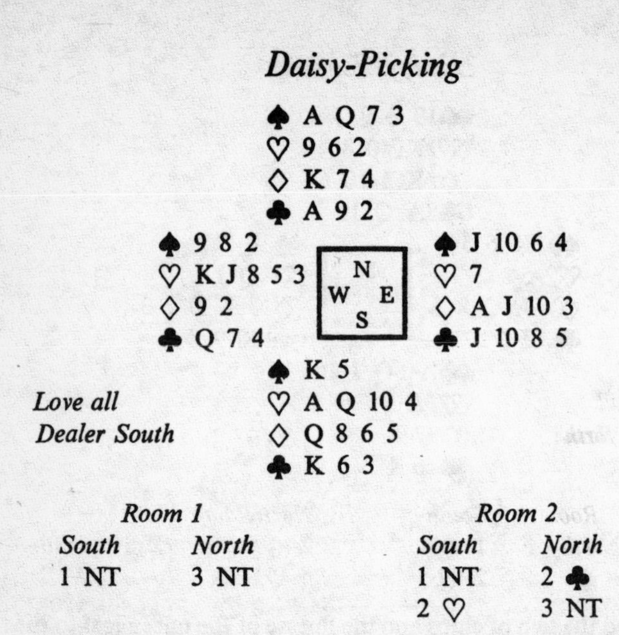

Room 1		*Room 2*	
South	*North*	*South*	*North*
1 NT	3 NT	1 NT	2 ♣
		2 ♡	3 NT

In Room 1 West led a heart and the ten won the trick. South played a diamond to the king and ace, ducked the club return, won the next club and ducked a diamond. The diamond suit failed to provide the ninth trick, but after cashing his top cards in clubs and spades South was able to end-play West in hearts to make his contract.

West in Room 2, warned against the heart lead, tried a club. The declarer ducked the first round, won the second club in dummy and ran the nine of hearts to the knave. A club came back, and South's next move was to knock out the ace of diamonds. East cashed his club for the fourth defensive trick and then led the knave of diamonds to the queen. After cashing the top spades the declarer was able to develop the same end-play in hearts, but that added up to only eight tricks.

Stayman should not be used on flat 4–3–3–3 shapes. There is little prospect of gain even if a suit fit is found, and the risk of giving too much information to the defenders is very real.

Two rounds of bidding proved to be better than five on this hand from a team of four match.

Daisy-Picking

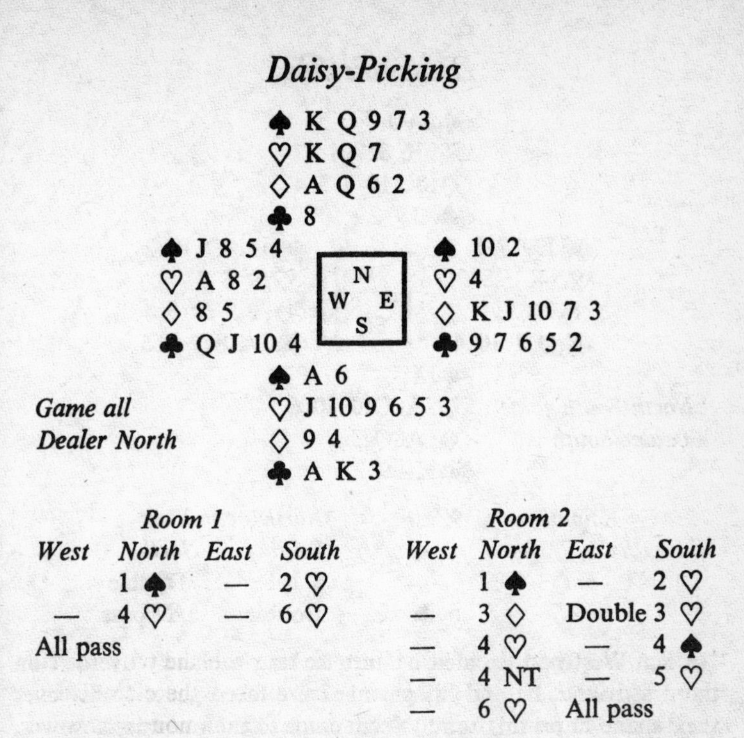

Room 1

West	*North*	*East*	*South*
	1 ♠	—	2 ♡
—	4 ♡	—	6 ♡
All pass			

Room 2

West	*North*	*East*	*South*
	1 ♠	—	2 ♡
—	3 ◇	Double	3 ♡
—	4 ♡	—	4 ♠
—	4 NT	—	5 ♡
—	6 ♡	All pass	

In Room 1 the bidding was straightforward and sensible. North showed his full values on the second round with a double raise, and South accepted the slight risk that there might be two top losers in the hand. On the natural lead of the queen of clubs twelve tricks were there for the taking.

In Room 2 North's fatuous bid of three diamonds gave East the opportunity to double for a lead. The slam was bid in spite of this, West dutifully led the eight of diamonds, and the declarer was in trouble. He put up the ace of diamonds and played on spades, but when East ruffed the third round there was no way of disposing of the losing diamond and the slam went one down for a swing of 17 i.m.p.

Over-indulgence in cue-bidding can be fatal in another way, as the next hand illustrates.

Daisy-Picking

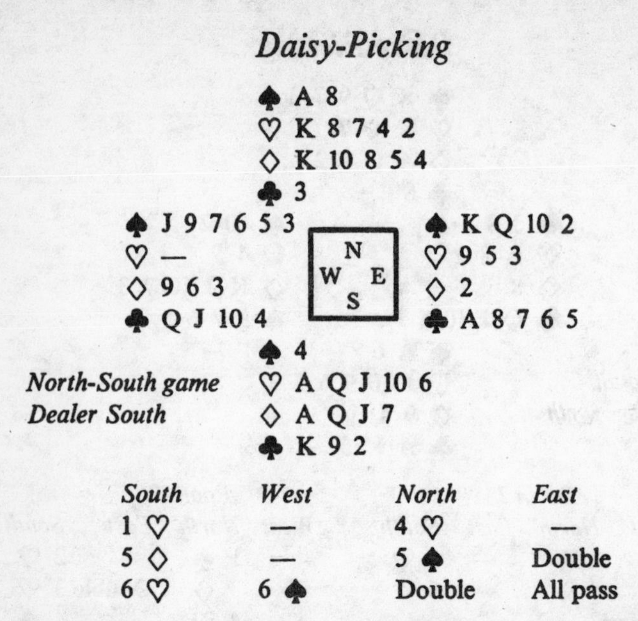

South	*West*	*North*	*East*
1 ♡	—	4 ♡	—
5 ◇	—	5 ♠	Double
6 ♡	6 ♠	Double	All pass

Once West had decided against making a cheeky overcall on the first round, he and his partner were fated never to discover their spade fit on this hand. North came to their rescue, however, with a daisy-picking bid of five spades. This gave East the opportunity to double, and West did not waste his second chance.

Nothing could be more futile than North's cue-bid of five spades in the above auction. There could hardly be a grand slam on the hand, since South had denied possession of the ace of clubs when he bid five diamonds. What, then, was North trying to achieve?

What he did achieve was a paltry score of 500 points instead of the 1,430 that would have accrued if he had made the sensible and obvious bid of six hearts.

Against the spade sacrifice North led the three of clubs and eventually obtained his club ruff, but there were no more than four tricks altogether for the defence.

Trial bids are not without their dangers.

Daisy-Picking

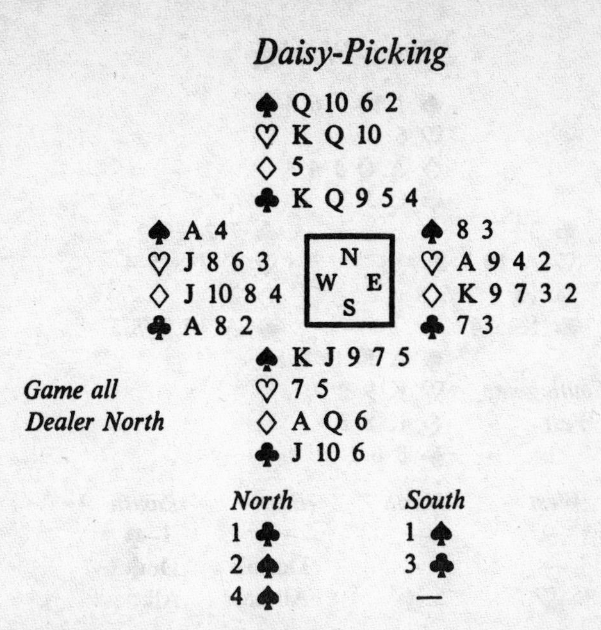

The correct final contract was reached, but the manner of getting there was again to prove fatal.

On the normal lead of the knave of diamonds the declarer would have had no trouble in making ten tricks. But the wanton display of club support alerted West to his partner's shortage and enabled him to find the killing defence of the ace and another club.

South won the second round of clubs in hand and tried to slip the knave of spades through, but West went up with the ace and led his third club. East ruffed and cashed the ace of hearts to defeat the contract.

If South felt impelled to make a trial bid, three diamonds might have been a wiser choice. But there is not much of a case for a trial bid at all. It is a mistake to try to land on the head of a pin in such cases. South's cards are so nearly worth a jump to game that the sensible course is to bid four spades and accept the responsibility for the slight overbid.

A big swing was lost on the next hand when North stopped to admire the view.

Daisy-Picking

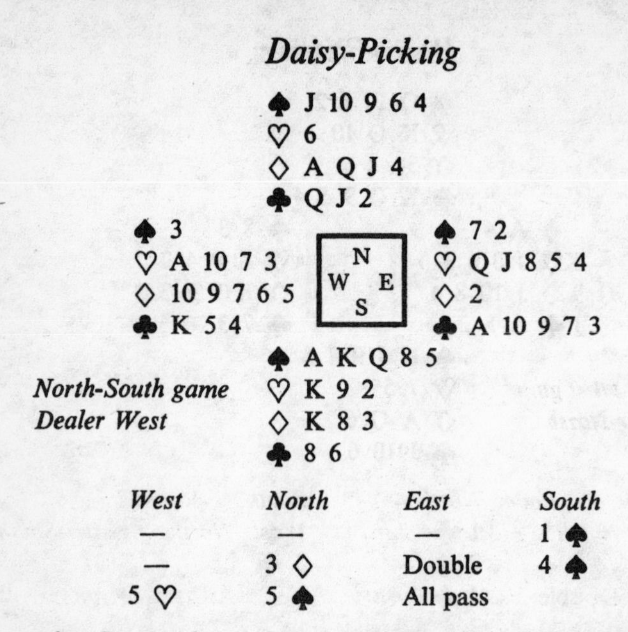

After South's fourth-in-hand opening of one spade North felt that he was too strong for an immediate raise to four. Instead he showed where his values lay with a jump to three diamonds, intending to bid four spades on the next round.

East seized the opportunity to make a distributional double, and although South jumped to four spades the damage was done. West was able to judge that his high cards were in the right places and took the cheap sacrifice in five hearts. The best North and South could then do was to double and collect 100 points. In fact North pushed on to five spades and lost 100 when the defenders cashed their three winners.

The direct raise to four spades is, of course, the only sound action on the North hand. This need not inhibit South from trying for slam if he has a strong hand.

In the other room North raised to four spades and the opponents had no chance to enter the auction. A diamond was led and South made eleven tricks for a swing of 13 i.m.p.

A daisy-picking bid was responsible for another large swing on the following hand.

Daisy-Picking

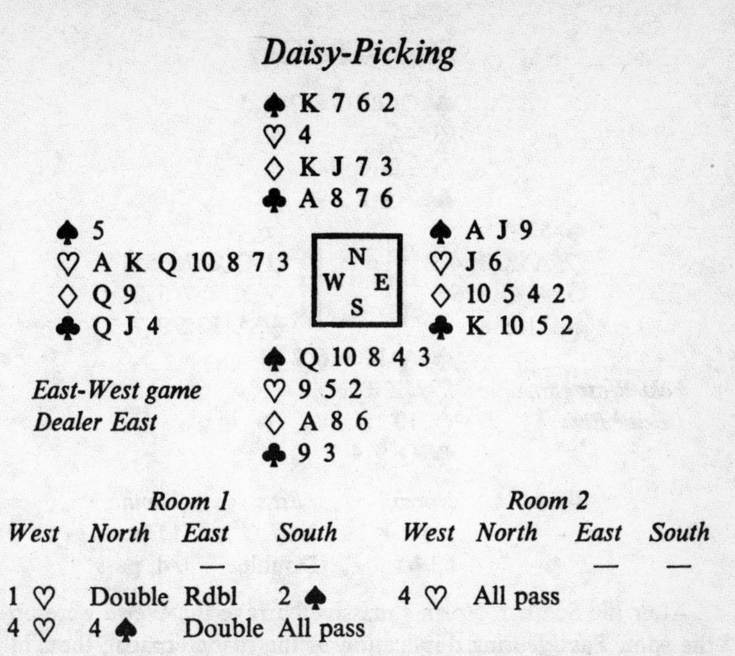

Room 1				*Room 2*			
West	*North*	*East*	*South*	*West*	*North*	*East*	*South*
		—	—			—	—
1 ♡	Double	Rdbl	2 ♠	4 ♡	All pass		
4 ♡	4 ♠	Double	All pass				

Although his partner had passed, West in Room 1 for some reason considered his hand too strong to open four hearts. His one heart bid allowed the opponents to enter the auction at a low level. West jumped to four hearts on the next round, but the damage had been done and he was left with a choice between defending against four spades and bidding on to an unmakable five hearts.

It takes an initial trump lead and smart defence to defeat four spades. In practice West began with a top heart, and South was able to make his doubled contract by finessing against the knave of spades and ruffing his third heart high in dummy.

In the other room West made the obvious bid of four hearts, which gave his opponents no chance to get into the bidding. Ten tricks were made for a score of 620 and a total swing of 15 i.m.p.

Here is a hand from a Camrose match between Scotland and Wales where a pointless cue-bid reduced the Welsh chances.

Daisy-Picking

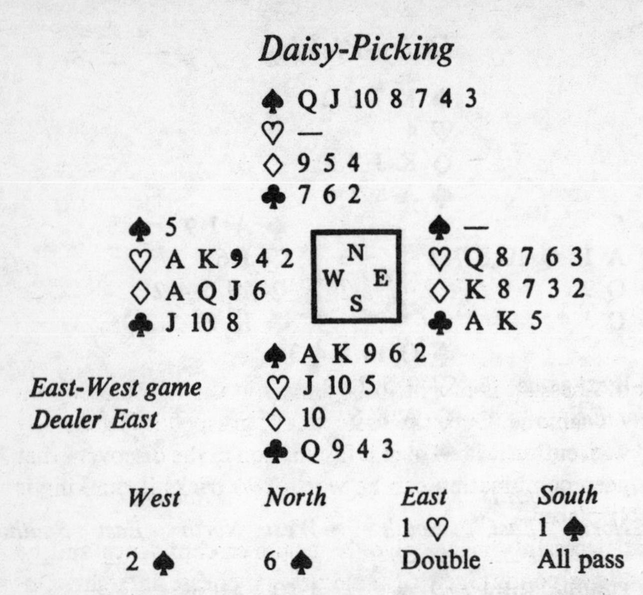

After the Scottish North's massive barrage the Welsh were on the spot. East, fearing duplication of the spade control, thought it best to indicate minimum values by doubling, and West was in no position to reverse this decision. Six spades went only two down, needless to say.

The situation would have been altogether different if West had forced with three diamonds instead of using the over-worked cue-bid in the enemy suit. Then East would be in a position to indicate his void by passing the six spade bid and West, knowing little could be missing in the other suits, might have found the courage to bid seven hearts.

South would no doubt have sacrificed to the limit in seven spades, but at least East and West would have reached their par on the hand.

In the other room Scotland was allowed to play in six hearts for a big swing.

8

Over-Finessing

THE art of finessing is taught to beginners in their first lesson on card-play technique. Once the basic idea is grasped it is generally adopted with enthusiasm. There is fascination in the discovery that an ace-queen combination can be worth two tricks if the king is favourably placed.

A few successful finesses give the beginner confidence and he soon becomes conditioned to taking every finesse in sight. Opportunities are not hard to find, since every other hand contains at least one finessing position. Unfortunately many players never carry their card-playing technique much beyond this point. They learn the elements of trump extraction and suit establishment, and perhaps acquire a little knowledge of hold-up play. For the rest they lean heavily on the familiar finesse, making their contracts when the finesses are right and going down when they are wrong.

The trouble with the finesse is that it often tempts players to take unnecessary risks. Good players dislike taking finesses. A fifty–fifty chance is not sufficiently attractive to the expert who will usually look for a way of obtaining better odds, keeping the finesse in reserve as a last resort.

The finesse is a specific tool which should be kept for the proper occasion. For average players, indiscriminate finessing is one of the commonest errors and one of the most expensive. The clearest cases of abuse occur when players go out of their way to take a finesse that is completely unnecessary to the success of the contract. Sometimes greed for an overtrick lies at the root of the trouble, but more often it is simply a case of failure to apprehend the risk involved. Here is an example of a type that occurs every day.

Over-Finessing

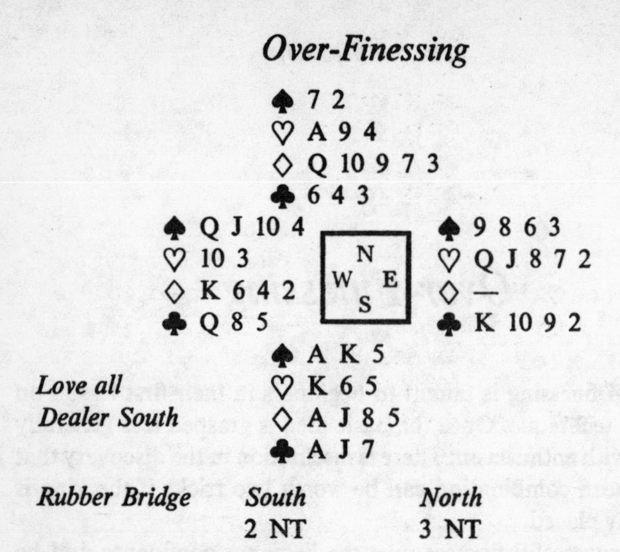

West's opening lead of the queen of spades is won by the king, and at this point a large number of the world's bridge players will enter dummy with the ace of hearts in order to take the diamond finesse. West will hold up the king of diamonds and the contract will be defeated, not so much because of the losing finesse but because dummy's only entry was used in order to take it.

No player who can count up to nine should have any trouble with this hand. Five quick tricks in the outside suits together with four diamond tricks are enough to ensure the success of the contract. South should therefore reject any idea of finessing in diamonds and simply lead out the ace and another.

At match-point pairs it would be correct to cross to the ace of hearts and take the diamond finesse, for the chance of an overtrick is nine times greater than the risk of defeat. But at other forms of the game there can never be any excuse for jeopardizing the safety of the contract.

Over-Finessing

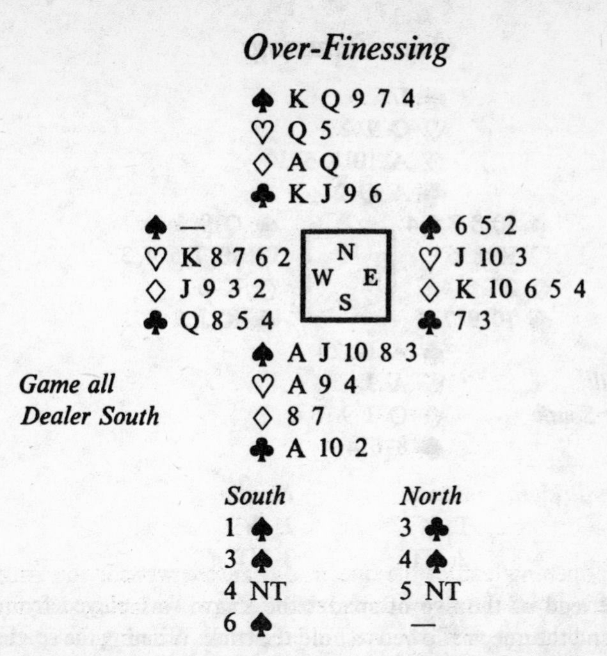

West led the two of diamonds and South hopefully tried the finesse of the queen. East produced the king and returned a heart, and there was no way for the declarer to avoid a further loser.

Although there is no certainty of making this contract, South was guilty of sloppy thinking when he finessed the queen of diamonds. This play gains nothing even when it succeeds, for South must still guess correctly in clubs in order to make his contract. And if the correct guess is made in clubs, the losing diamond can always be discarded on the fourth round of clubs.

The proper play is to put up the ace of diamonds at trick one, draw the outstanding trumps, and then hope to take a favourable view on the club position. Actually, the declarer should probably guess correctly in this case. When West shows out on the first round of trumps it is logical to place him with length in clubs and take the finesse the right way. The losing diamond can then be discarded on the fourth round of clubs and the contract made for the loss of only a heart trick.

The next hand is more complex.

Over-Finessing

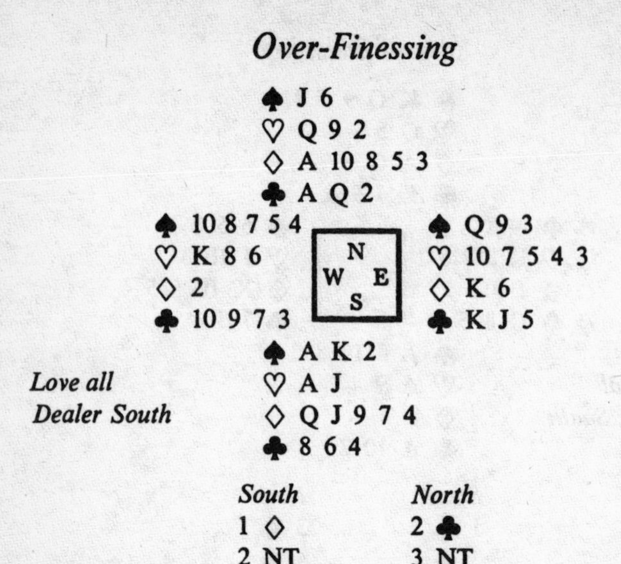

South	*North*
1 ◇	2 ♣
2 NT	3 NT

On the lead of the five of spades the knave was played from dummy and the queen allowed to hold the trick. Winning the spade return, South ran the queen of diamonds to the king. East knocked out the last spade stopper and South, with only eight tricks, had to try the club finesse and then the heart finesse. When both proved to be wrong the contract was defeated.

It was certainly unlucky to find all three finesses wrong, but the declarer ought to have foreseen the danger and taken steps to safeguard his contract. On this hand it is necessary to reject two of the finesses and postpone the third.

At trick three South should attack the only possible entry card in the long spade hand by leading the knave of hearts from hand. West will probably win and, seeing no future in a spade continuation, switch to the ten of clubs. South must refuse this finesse and put up the ace. After returning to hand with the ace of hearts he will at last be in a position to finesse in diamonds with complete safety.

A finesse should often be rejected when its failure will give an opponent the chance to make a damaging switch.

Over-Finessing

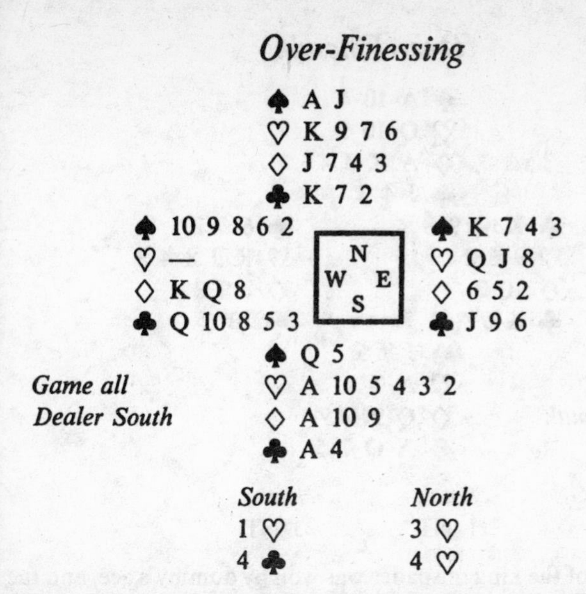

West led the ten of spades and South's initial impression was that he and his partner had underbid the hand. The spade finesse lost, however, East returned the six of diamonds to the nine and queen, and West switched back to spades.

When West discarded on the first round of trumps the risk of defeat was apparent, but South had nothing better to do than try another diamond finesse. When that failed the contract was one down.

In spite of the bad breaks the contract ought to be made. The safe course for the declarer is to play the ace of spades at trick one and test the trumps. When it transpires that there is a trump loser, all South need do is cash the ace and king of clubs, ruff a club in hand and lead his queen of spades. East can lead a diamond but, after winning with the queen, West will be end-played, forced to yield the tenth trick either by returning a diamond into the tenace or conceding a ruff and discard.

The next hand has a similar theme. A combined total of 28 high-card points may not always be enough to ensure game at no trumps, but in this case the declarer received a favourable lead and should have made his contract.

Over-Finessing

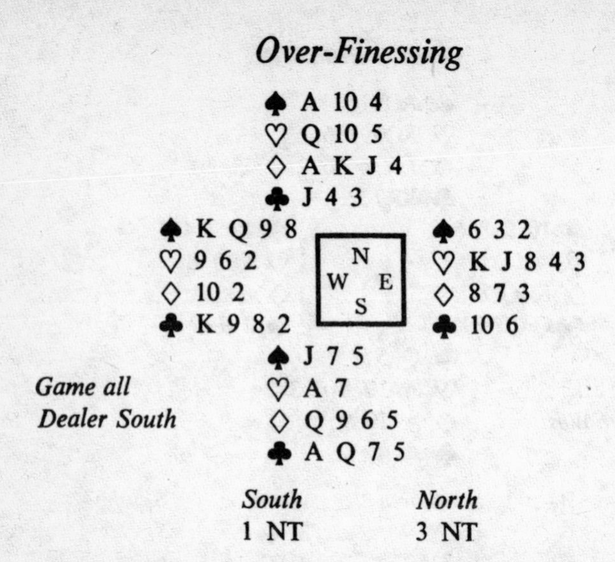

The lead of the king of spades was won by dummy's ace, and the declarer reckoned that five tricks in the red suits along with two in each black suit would bring in the game. Accordingly he led a club at trick two and finessed the queen. But when West won and found the deadly switch to the nine of hearts South was in trouble. He covered with dummy's ten and allowed the knave to hold the trick, but East was not to be fooled. The return of a small heart knocked out the ace, and when the clubs failed to break evenly the contract had to go one down.

The natural-looking club finesse was a clear mistake because it allowed the dangerous hand to gain the lead too early. South should instead have come to hand with a diamond and led a small club towards the knave. If East is able to win the trick he can do no harm, while if West goes up with the king South will score three club tricks. If West ducks, South can switch back to spades to establish his ninth trick.

There is a certain type of hand on which the expert usually makes a trick less than the average player.

Over-Finessing

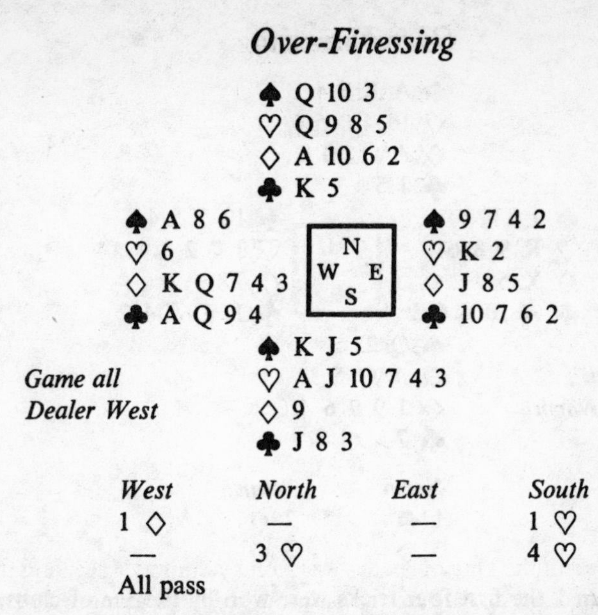

On the normal lead of the king of diamonds, most players will take the heart finesse at trick two and wrap up eleven tricks, losing only to the two black aces.

The expert's approach is more cautious. He recognizes that if the heart finesse is right there is no need for him to take it. If East has the king of hearts the contract is never in any danger for East cannot, in view of his failure to respond to his partner's opening bid, have the ace of clubs as well. The expert therefore plays a heart to his ace and returns the suit, allowing East to score his king.

When the cards are distributed as above the expert makes only ten tricks, but if West happens to have the bare king of hearts and East the ace of clubs the expert will still make his contract while the average player goes down.

Virtue had to be its own reward on the next hand as well. In a team match the result was a flat board, both sides making game in diamonds, but a study of the first four leads in each room is instructive.

Over-Finessing

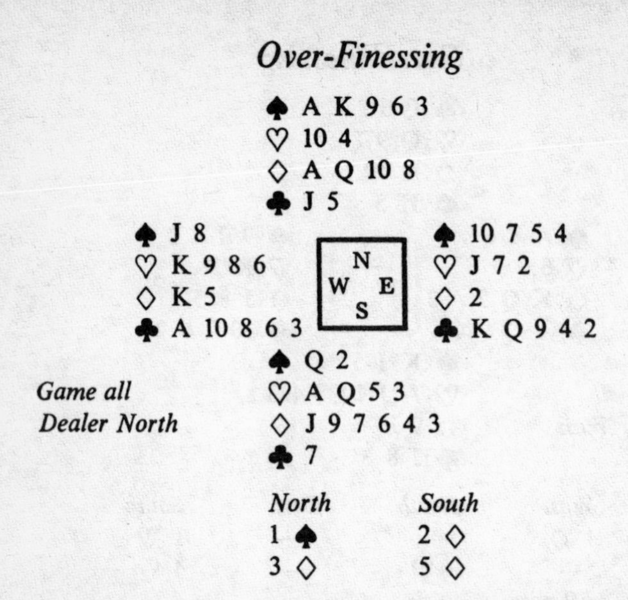

North	*South*
1 ♠	2 ◇
3 ◇	5 ◇

In Room 1 the first four tricks were won by the ace of clubs, the three of diamonds (ruffing a club), the queen of diamonds and the ace of diamonds. By taking a successful diamond finesse the declarer confined his losers to one club and one heart.

In Room 2 the first four tricks were won by the ace of clubs, the three of diamonds, the ace of diamonds and the queen of spades. This declarer rejected the diamond finesse, cashed the top spades and ruffed a fourth spade in his hand. When West refused to over-ruff he was thrown in by a diamond lead to make a fatal return.

If East had held the bare king of diamonds the first declarer would have gone down while the second would still have made his contract. The play of the ace of diamonds on the first round also gives an extra chance when East has king and another diamond, for the declarer cannot be forced to make a decision in the heart suit before he knows how the spades are breaking.

The next hand quickly sorted out the sheep from the goats when it turned up in a pairs tournament.

Over-Finessing

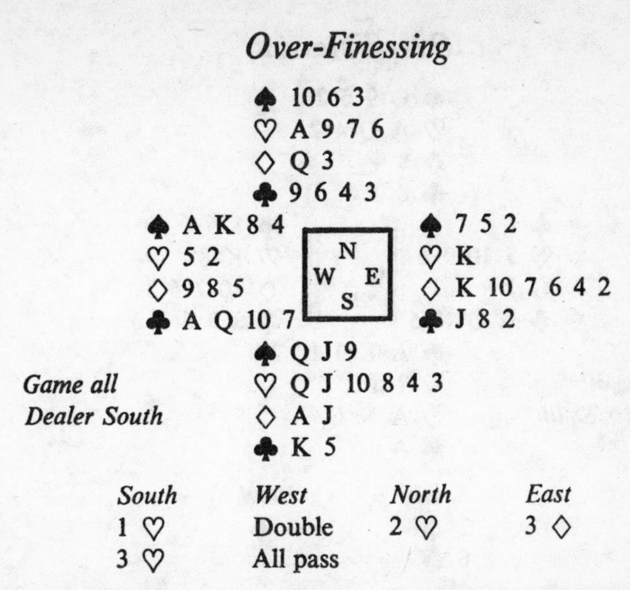

South	*West*	*North*	*East*
1 ♡	Double	2 ♡	3 ◇
3 ♡	All pass		

The West players normally started with a top spade and, on seeing East's discouraging two, switched to the nine of diamonds. This was covered by the queen and king and won by South's ace.

Most of the declarers then tabled the queen of hearts and ran it. When East produced the king and returned a club the defence had five tricks.

One or two enlightened declarers led the queen of spades at trick three in order to force out West's remaining winner in the suit. After winning the diamond return these declarers led a heart to the ace, and the fall of East's king solved all their problems. They would have made the contract even if West had held the king and another heart, however. After the ace of hearts a spade to the knave would clear the decks and a further heart lead would throw West in to open up the clubs or concede a ruff and discard.

West could have given the declarer a real problem by switching to a heart at trick two.

Sometimes there is no alternative to a finesse, but it may be possible to improve on the fifty-fifty chance by delaying the finesse for a round or two.

Over-Finessing

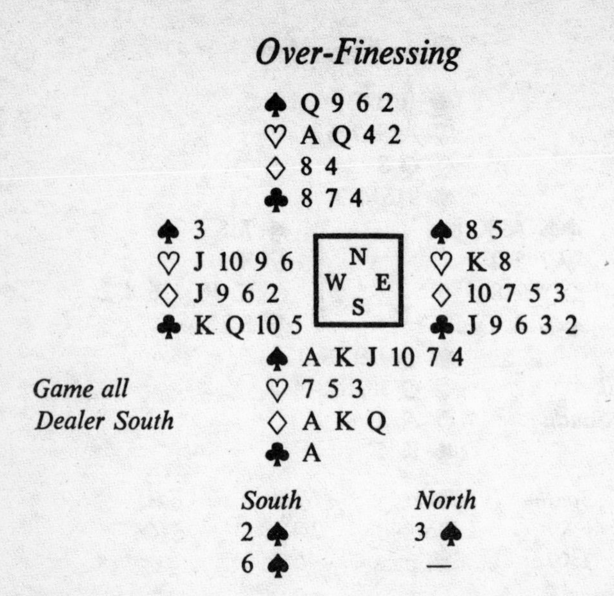

The opening lead was the king of clubs, and after drawing trumps South saw nothing better to do than to lead a heart and finesse the queen. East won and returned a club, and eventually South had to lose another heart trick.

When a trick must always be lost in a suit it is poor play to finesse on the first round. If the king is favourably placed the queen will still score on the second or third round.

After the ace and queen of trumps South should ruff a club and cash the diamonds, discarding the last club from dummy. A heart is then led, and if West plays the six South can duck in dummy to end-play East. If West plays a higher card South should put up dummy's ace, return to hand with a trump, and lead another heart to the queen. On winning with the king, East has nothing but minor suit cards to return and South discards his losing heart while ruffing in dummy.

This line of play makes sure of the contract not only when West has the king of hearts but also when East has the king singleton or doubleton.

A deferred finesse is again the answer on the next hand.

Over-Finessing

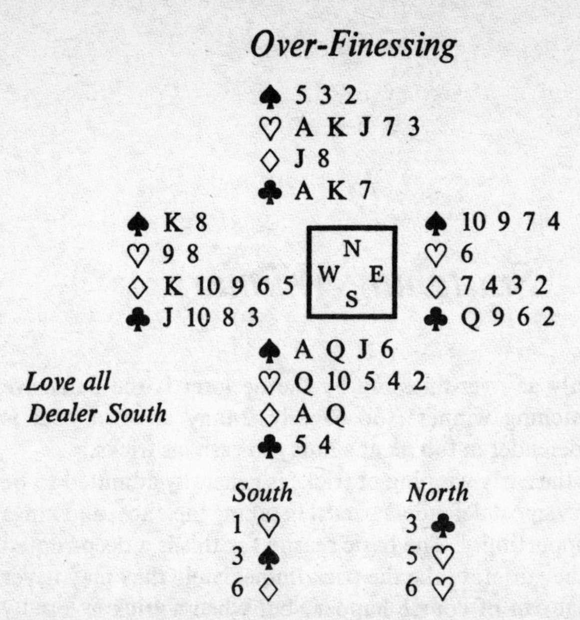

West leads the knave of clubs to dummy's king. At first glance the slam appears to be doomed, since both the spade and the diamond finesses are wrong. Correct technique can see the declarer safely home, however.

South should lead a heart to his queen, return a club to the ace, and ruff the third round of clubs high. Then cash the ace of spades before leading a second trump to dummy. A spade lead follows and the queen loses to the king, but West has to return a club or a diamond, either of which presents South with the slam.

On the above line of play South will not have to risk the diamond finesse unless West turns up with four or more spades including the king.

9

Snatching Winners

JUST as costly as over-finessing by the declarer is the defensive error of snatching winners too eagerly. Many an own goal is scored by a defender in too great a hurry to cash his tricks.

Although the early winning of tricks is generally admitted to be a losing policy, most defenders persist in taking their aces and kings at the first opportunity. The basic reason for this is a deep-rooted fear that if they do not take the trick immediately they may never make it. That can of course happen, but when a trick is lost by ducking it often comes back with interest in the subsequent play. It is helpful, however, if defenders can learn to differentiate between those of the declarer's losers which may disappear and those which can never do so.

Ducking plays are often deceptive in nature. Defenders who release their stoppers at an early stage make life simple for an experienced declarer by allowing him to make the most of his technical chances. It is another matter if the defenders refuse to commit their high cards for a round or two. Unsure of the position of the outstanding honour cards, the declarer will find it hard to determine the best line of play and may go down in an ironclad contract.

Quite apart from the deceptive angle, there may be sound technical reasons for a defender to postpone the winning of a trick—reasons connected with communications or control.

Here is a simple hand that might have been included in the chapter on timing.

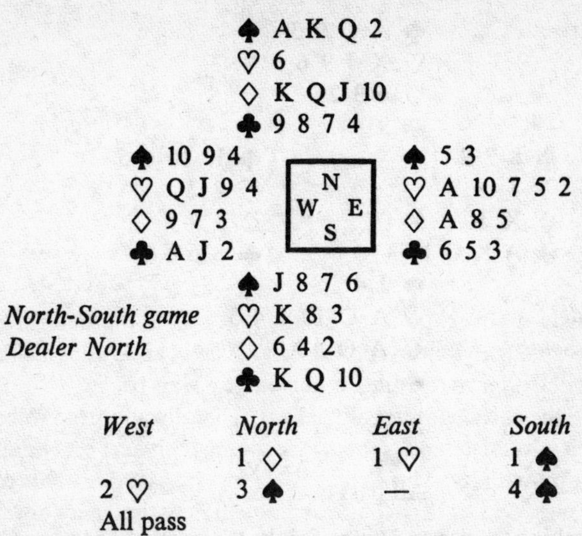

West led the queen of hearts to his partner's ace, and East returned the six of clubs on which the declarer played the king. West took the trick with his ace and wondered what to do next.

In fact it made no difference what he did next for the chance to defeat the contract had come and gone. West's mistake is a fairly obvious one. It should have been clear to him that if the contract was to be defeated his partner would need to have the ace of diamonds and the defenders would need to make two club tricks before South could get the diamonds going.

To get the timing right West must duck the first club trick. It need not worry him that the two of clubs might seem like a discouraging card to his partner. When East regains the lead with the ace of diamonds there is really nothing for him to try but another club.

It is seldom a winning move to 'beat air' with an honour card, but many players would make the same mistake as the defender on the following hand.

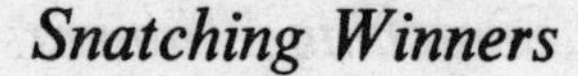

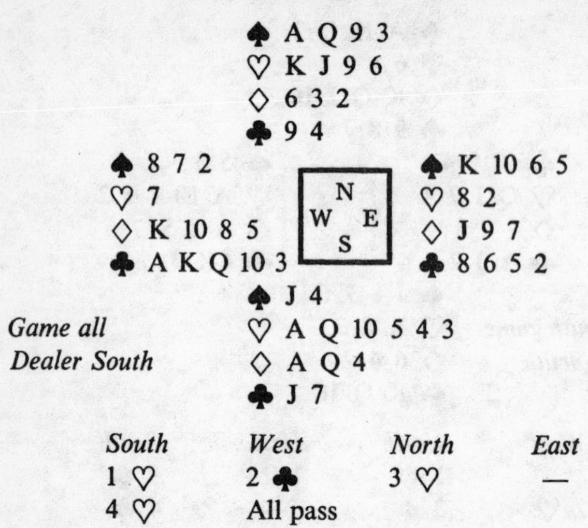

After cashing the ace and king of clubs West switched to trumps. The declarer won in dummy and, before drawing the outstanding trump, led the three of spades from the table. East went up with the king and returned a diamond, but it was no longer possible to defeat the contract. South played the ace of diamonds, drew the last trump, cashed the knave of spades, and entered dummy in trumps to discard his losing diamonds on the ace and queen of spades.

East feared that he would never make his king of spades if he did not take it at once. It is true that by ducking he would have sacrificed his spade trick, but the defence would have gained two diamond tricks in return.

Note that the declarer gave himself the best chance by denying East a count of trumps and leading the small spade from dummy. An orthodox spade finesse was unlikely to be superior unless West had four spades to the king and ten, but with that holding West might well have doubled the opening bid of one heart.

The next hand is similar in outline but the danger is if anything even more obvious.

Snatching Winners

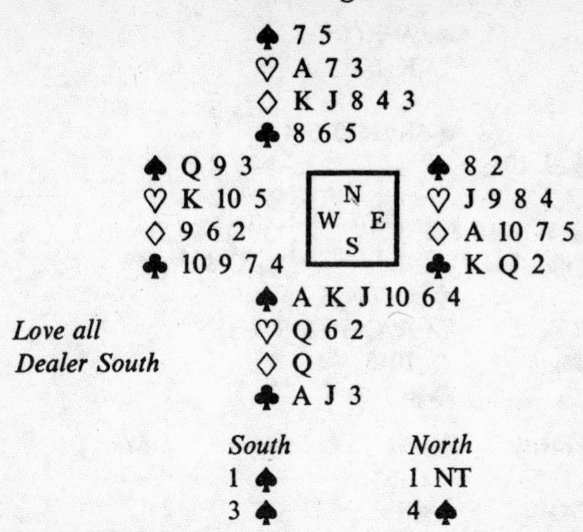

The ten of clubs was led to the queen and ace, and the declarer played the queen of diamonds at trick two. On seeing his partner's two of diamonds East realized that the queen must be a singleton, so he took his ace 'before the rats got at it' and returned the four of hearts.

This defence was not good enough. The queen of hearts was covered by the king and the ace, South's losing hearts were discarded on the king and knave of diamonds, and a club was led from the table. East won the king and shot back the ten of diamonds, but the declarer was untroubled. He simply ruffed small, and West scored a trump for the last defensive trick.

The knowledge that South's queen of diamonds was a singleton should have guided East to the right defence. It must clearly be better to allow the declarer to score one diamond trick immediately rather than two at a later stage.

To snatch the ace of diamonds could be right only if West had two trump tricks, which is hardly possible on the bidding.

Game can always be made on the next hand, but the declarer might have played himself down if a defender had not come to his rescue.

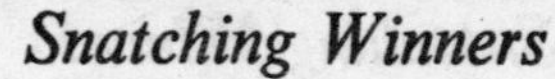

Snatching Winners

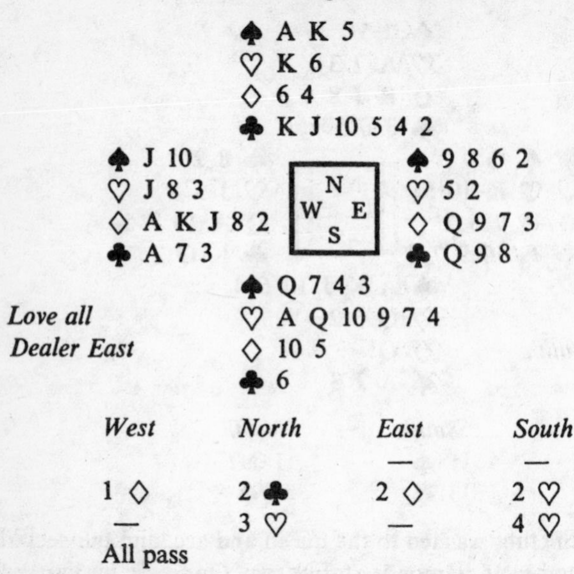

West	*North*	*East*	*South*
		—	—
1 ◇	2 ♣	2 ◇	2 ♡
—	3 ♡	—	4 ♡
All pass			

After cashing the ace and king of diamonds West switched to the knave of spades, and East played the two on dummy's ace. South drew trumps and led his club, on which West hastily played the ace. That was the end of the defence, for the king of clubs provided a parking place for South's losing spade.

That was feeble defence by West. He could count South for six trumps and three top spades and should see that one club trick would give South the game. He ought therefore to give South a guess by playing smoothly low on the club lead. There's no law against trying.

South did not make the most of his chances, of course. He should have won the first spade lead with the queen and led his club immediately. Even with a wrong guess in clubs he will still make the contract if West has a doubleton honour or if the clubs break 3–3, for dummy has enough entries to establish the suit.

A defender who is trying to establish his long suit at no trumps must preserve his entries at all costs.

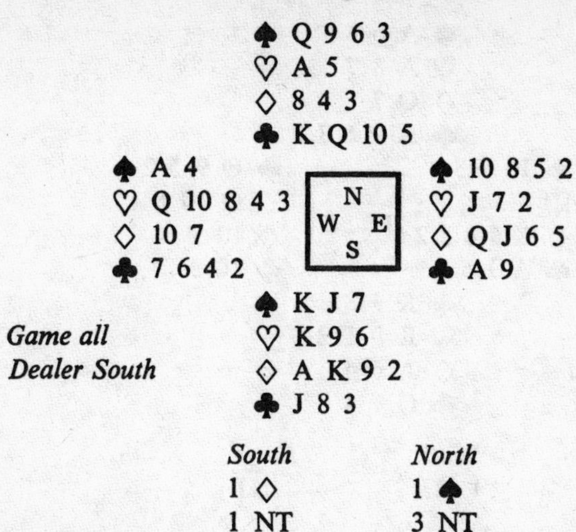

West led the three of hearts and the knave was allowed to hold the trick. The heart return went to dummy's ace and the three of spades was led to the king. Not wishing to 'beat air' with his ace on the next round, West won at once and continued the heart attack. When East won his ace of clubs, however, he had no heart to return, and South eventually made ten tricks by squeezing East in spades and diamonds.

It should be clear to West that there will be no chance of defeating the contract if he parts with the ace of spades before the hearts are established. He should therefore play low without batting an eyelid on the first round of spades. The chance of defeating the contract is well worth the risk of giving the declarer an extra trick in spades.

South might do the right thing by continuing spades, but he might also decide that East had the ace of spades and switch to clubs with fatal results. East will win the first club and clear the hearts, and the declarer will be unable to make more than eight tricks.

The next hand shows a different way in which a hold-up may gain.

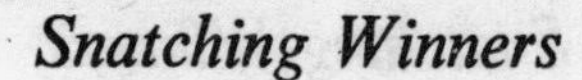

Snatching Winners

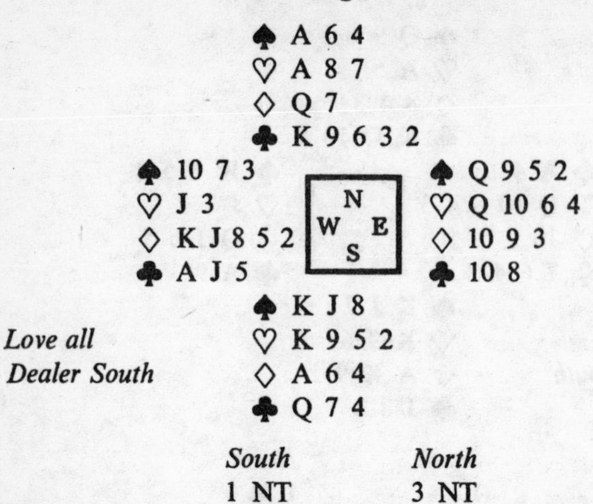

South	*North*
1 NT	3 NT

West led the five of diamonds and dummy's queen scored. The two of clubs was led to the queen, and West took his ace, hoping to score a further trick with the knave. South ducked the king of diamonds, won the third round, and led the seven of clubs, running it to the ten when West played low. Having no diamond to return, East tried a heart and again the declarer made ten tricks.

The play might have taken a very different course if West had allowed the queen of clubs to win and played the knave on the second round. The declarer would be likely to place West with knave, ten, five in clubs and play low from dummy in the expectation that the ace would fall. West would then be in a position to clear the diamonds while still holding the ace of clubs and the contract would go one down.

This may strike you as a difficult defence, but it need not be beyond your powers. Follow the simple principle of hanging on to your entry card at all costs and the deceptive aspect will take care of itself.

Defenders are often in too much of a hurry to cash what they think will be the setting trick. This can lead to disappointment, as the following hand shows.

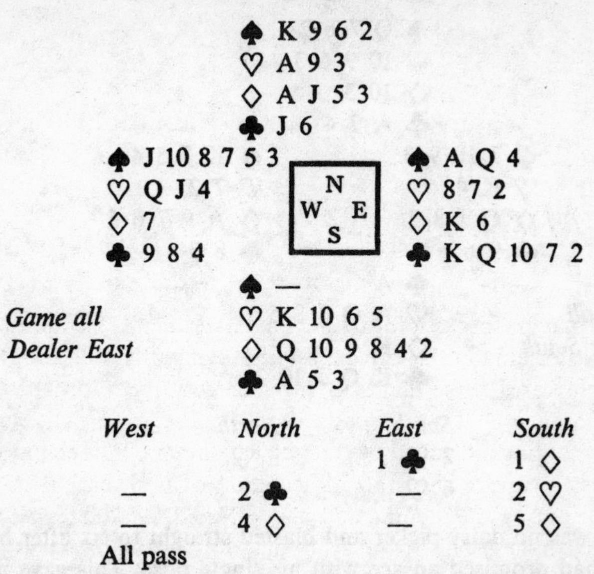

♠	K 9 6 2
♡	A 9 3
◇	A J 5 3
♣	J 6

West: ♠ J 10 8 7 5 3 ♡ Q J 4 ◇ 7 ♣ 9 8 4

East: ♠ A Q 4 ♡ 8 7 2 ◇ K 6 ♣ K Q 10 7 2

South: ♠ — ♡ K 10 6 5 ◇ Q 10 9 8 4 2 ♣ A 5 3

Game all
Dealer East

West	*North*	*East*	*South*
		1 ♣	1 ◇
—	2 ♣	—	2 ♡
—	4 ◇	—	5 ◇
All pass			

West led the nine of clubs to the knave, queen and ace, and the declarer took a losing trump finesse. After cashing the king of clubs, East tried to take the setting trick with the ace of spades.

South ruffed, led a trump to the ace, discarded a heart on the king of spades, ruffed another spade in hand and ruffed his last club in dummy. The play of the remaining trumps then squeezed West in the major suits and the game was made.

East was altogether too eager to score his ace of spades. The declarer might have had a spade loser, but if so he would have no possible means of disposing of it. A passive defence was therefore indicated. After cashing his club winner East should simply have returned his trump and waited for the contract to go down.

The next example has a similar theme.

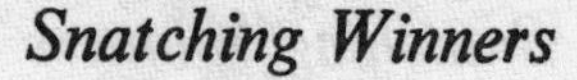

Snatching Winners

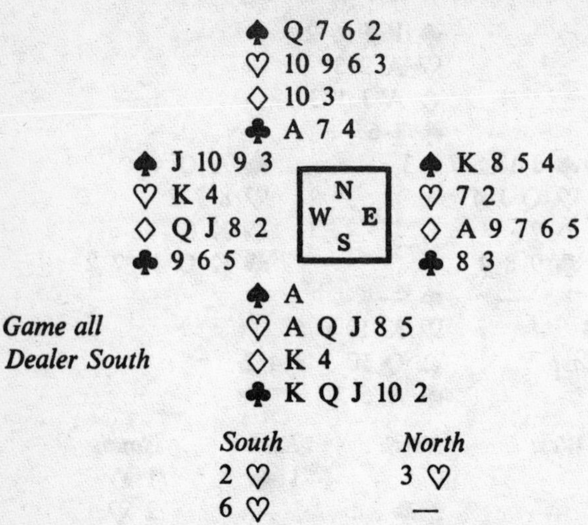

South was no daisy-picker and blasted straight to six after his partner had promised an ace with his single raise. This gave no help to the defence, but West seemed to have made an auspicious start when the lead of the knave of spades was covered by the queen and king and won by South's ace.

The declarer entered dummy with the ace of clubs and ran the ten of hearts to West's king. Flushed with success, West tabled the ten of spades, but the declarer ruffed, drew the remaining trumps, discarded dummy's diamonds on the clubs and then cross-ruffed for twelve tricks.

Well, all one can say is that West's over-eagerness to score the setting trick led him astray. The point is that the spades can wait. If South has a spade loser it can never run away, for he can hardly have six clubs. There *is* a danger of dummy's diamonds disappearing if South has five clubs, however, and West should therefore have tried the queen of diamonds after winning his trump trick.

On the next hand the declarer was allowed to get away with an impudent game contract.

Snatching Winners

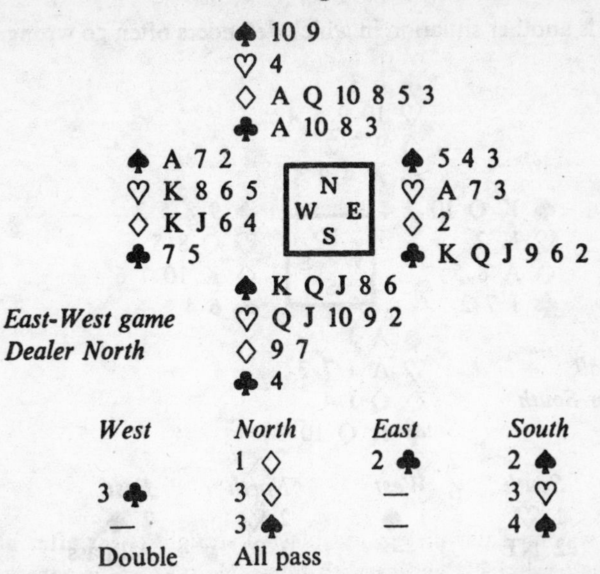

West	*North*	*East*	*South*
	1 ◇	2 ♣	2 ♠
3 ♣	3 ◇	—	3 ♡
—	3 ♠	—	4 ♠
Double	All pass		

The opening club lead was won by the ace and the four of hearts led from the table. East shot up with the ace and returned a trump to cut down heart ruffs. West captured the king with his ace and returned another trump, but this defence did not worry South in the slightest. He drew the outstanding trumps, conceded another heart, and came to ten tricks by way of the diamond finesse.

No defence can succeed once East has snatched at his heart trick. When the declarer is marked with length in a suit and has few trumps to ruff with in dummy, there is no need to panic when a singleton is led from the table. East should have played low and given his partner a chance to win with his king. A club return will then leave South short of entries to establish the hearts, and best defence will hold him to nine tricks. A one-trick defeat is all that the defenders can hope for in spite of their 21 high-card points.

Snatching Winners

Here is another situation in which defenders often go wrong.

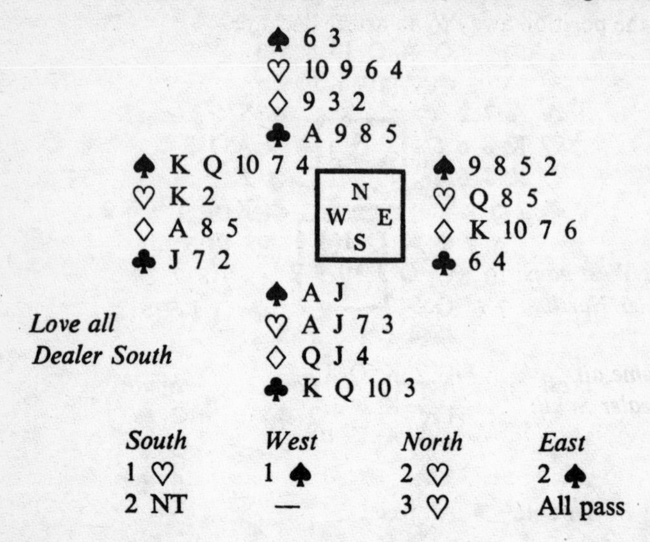

South	*West*	*North*	*East*
1 ♡	1 ♠	2 ♡	2 ♠
2 NT	—	3 ♡	All pass

The opening lead of the king of spades was won by the ace. Having only one sure entry to dummy, the declarer tried the effect of leading the three of hearts from hand. West went up with the king, cashed his spade winner, and led a club. Dummy's nine won the trick and the declarer ran the ten of hearts successfully, thus confining his losers to one spade, one heart and two diamonds and making his contract on the nose.

The declarer played well but the defence might have put up a more spirited resistance. There was no need for West to be in such a hurry to score his trump trick. By playing the king he gave South no chance to go wrong on the next round. If West had played low and allowed his partner to win the queen, the declarer would have had a problem. He might still have done the right thing by playing for split honours, but he might equally well have misread the position and finessed on the second round, allowing the defenders to make a second trump trick.

Most defenders know better than to snatch an ace on lead against a slam. It is tempting to make an exception when you have hopes of scoring a trump trick as well, but the lead of your ace may give the position away to an astute declarer.

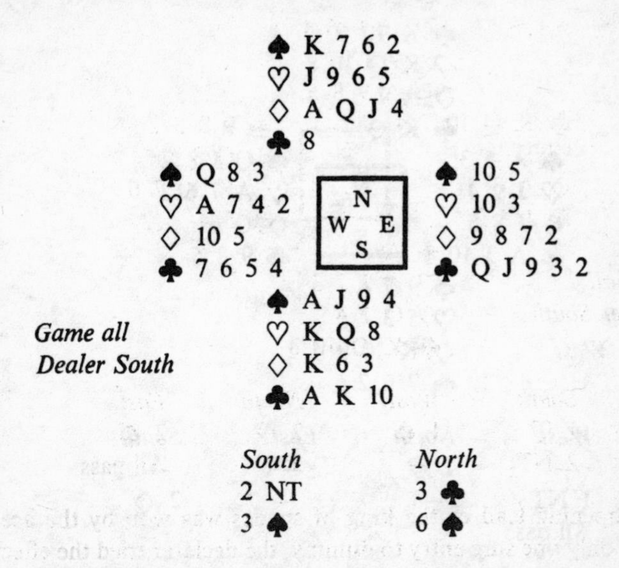

Having high hopes of making his queen of spades, West led the ace of hearts and continued the suit. South won the second round and paused to consider. He knew West to be an experienced player not given to leading aces indiscriminately, and suspected that it could only be possession of the queen of trumps that had inspired the lead.

South therefore led the knave of spades for a backward finesse. West played low smoothly enough but, with the courage of his convictions, South ran the knave to make the contract.

On this bidding there could be little chance of the declarer being able to discard his heart losers, and West should have avoided the lead of the ace. On a passive diamond or club lead the declarer, not being gifted with second sight, would have taken the normal trump finesse and lost his slam.

There have been too many bad defences in this chapter and it should be a relief to have a look at a good one. By concealing their assets on this hand both defenders played their part in bringing about the declarer's downfall.

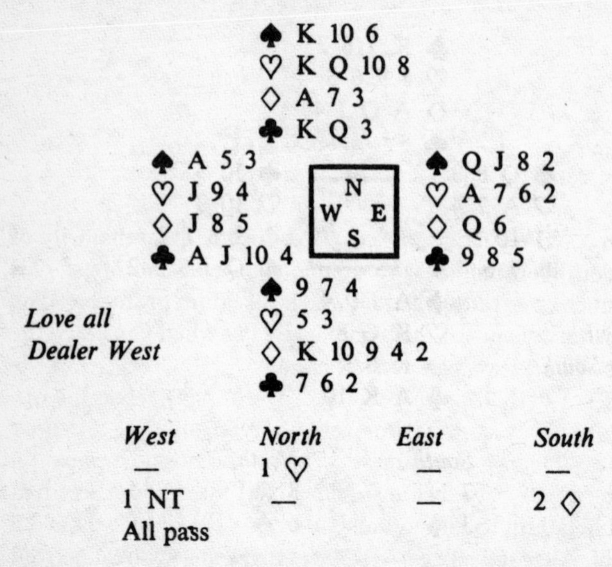

West	*North*	*East*	*South*
—	1 ♡	—	—
1 NT	—	—	2 ◇
All pass			

With no very attractive lead, West made the happy choice of the three of spades. The declarer played low from dummy, and East blinked but gave no other sign of surprise when his knave held the trick. He returned the nine of clubs and dummy's queen was allowed to win.

After cashing the ace and king of diamonds the declarer led a heart to dummy's queen, and East smoothly played the two. South then conceded the third round of diamonds to West's knave.

West produced the five of spades with the proper degree of unconcern and the declarer can hardly be blamed for going astray. It appeared to South that West had the aces of hearts and clubs plus a couple of knaves. Since West passed originally he could not have three aces. South therefore played the ten of spades from dummy and the defenders took six well-earned tricks.

10

Over-Doubling

A GRIEVOUS and recurring source of loss for the great majority of players lies in their readiness to double high-level contracts. This is a very much over-rated pastime which is seldom profitable. The big penalties accrue not at the higher levels but when you catch the opponents at a low level on a misfit hand.

There is normally little to be gained by doubling when the opponents voluntarily contract for game. If you inflict a one-trick defeat the double brings in a mere 50 or 100 points. The potential loss is much greater, for the double may alert the declarer to a bad break and help him to find a double-dummy line of play to make his contract. Alternatively a double may drive the opponents from a hopeless contract into a good one.

In competitive situations the danger is even more acute. It is so easy to forget that distribution can compensate for a shortage of high cards. Very often the effect of wild distribution is to create a 60-point pack, enabling both sides to make game or even a slam in their best suit. This is what produces the big swings in matches, where the same team scores a doubled game in each room. Experienced team players aim to minimize the losses caused by competitive misjudgements by bidding on rather than doubling in borderline cases.

Because over-doubling is seldom recognized as a clear-cut bidding error, it tends to become a habit. After an unsuccessful double a player will shrug his shoulders and say, 'Well, that was unlucky. I certainly had my double,' and go on to do the same thing next day.

In preparing this chapter I have not had to look far for copy.

Over-Doubling

My only problem lay in deciding which examples to use and which to reject from the mass of material in my files.

Hands full of Eastern promise like the one below often end in disappointment for the holders.

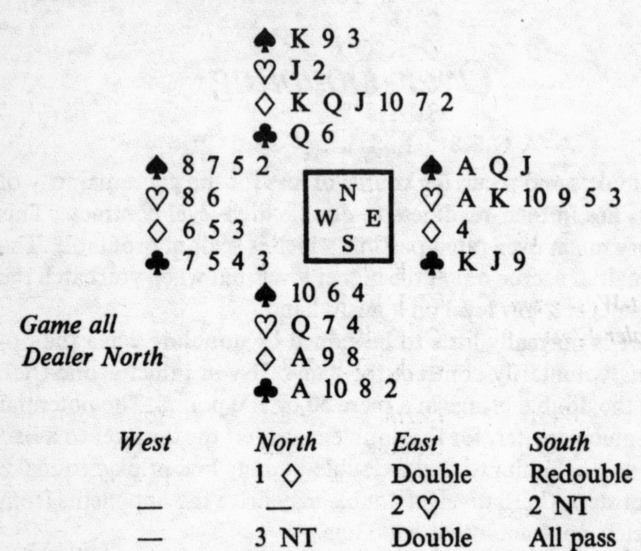

West	*North*	*East*	*South*
	1 ◇	Double	Redouble
—	—	2 ♡	2 NT
—	3 NT	Double	All pass

West led a heart and South's queen won the third round, a spade being discarded from dummy. Six rounds of diamonds followed and East's beautiful hand was put through the mincer. In order to keep the club king guarded East had to throw the queen and knave of spades and two winning hearts. The lead of a small spade from the table then established the ninth trick for the declarer.

An initial spade or club lead would have made no difference to the result; South can always make nine tricks.

East should have realized that his hand was too rich in honour cards to make the double a sound proposition. The danger of being squeezed on the run of the diamonds was not hard to foresee. Note the difference if the East hand is weakened by transferring the king of clubs to West. Three no trumps is now defeated without difficulty.

Over-Doubling

Those who double high-level suit contracts with an inadequate trump holding are usually given cause to regret it. The point-count is an unreliable guide to trick-taking potential when distribution is freakish.

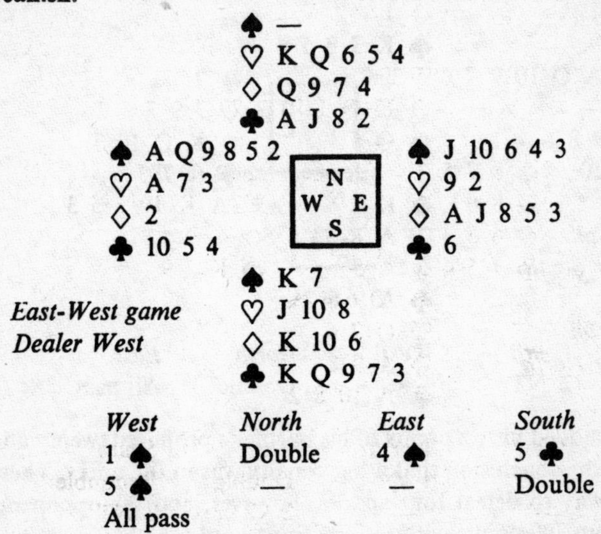

West	*North*	*East*	*South*
1 ♠	Double	4 ♠	5 ♣
5 ♠	—	—	Double
All pass			

South made the right decision on the first round by bidding five clubs, but when the bidding came round to him again he could not restrain himself from doubling on the strength of his twelve points.

An assortment of kings and queens can be virtually useless in defence against a high-level distributional contract. Such proved to be the case here. For all their twenty-four points the defenders could make no more than one heart and one club trick. The declarer took the right view in trumps and brought home the doubled contract for a score of 850 points.

In the other room South took out insurance against a disastrous swing by bidding six clubs. This was doubled and went two down for a loss of 300 points.

Over-Doubling

A poor decision led to a double game swing on the next hand.

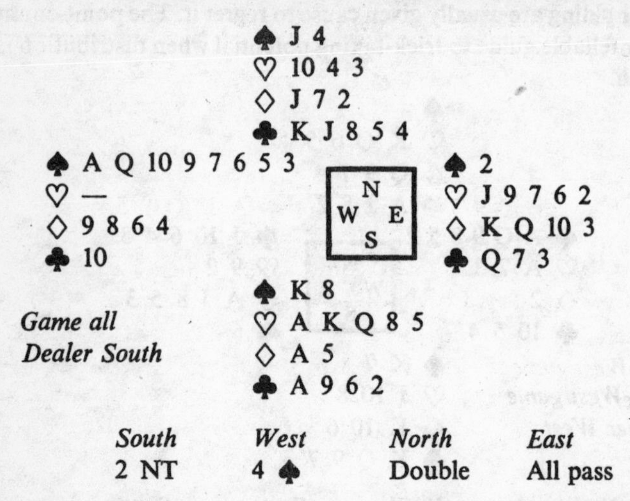

South	*West*	*North*	*East*
2 NT	4 ♠	Double	All pass

North added his six points to his partner's promised twenty and came to the conclusion that a big penalty was in the offing. There was no way to defeat four spades, however, and the opponents chalked up 790 points without breathing hard.

West was certainly lucky to find his partner with just the right cards, but North had no reason to expect his hand to be worth anything in defence.

At the other table the bidding began in the same way, but North showed better judgement by bidding four no trumps over West's four spades. West found the best lead of the nine of diamonds, but the declarer won the trick, cashed the ace of hearts, and made the key play of leading the nine of clubs to dummy's king. The knave of clubs was returned and allowed to run when East played low. The lead of the ten of hearts then forced a cover from East, and after running the rest of the clubs South was able to finesse the eight of hearts for his tenth trick.

That was a further 630 points and a total swing of 16 i.m.p.

Aces are much more valuable in defence than are kings and queens, but even when holding aces it can be dangerous to double a high-level suit contract. The next hand comes from the 1970 Life Masters Pairs Contest.

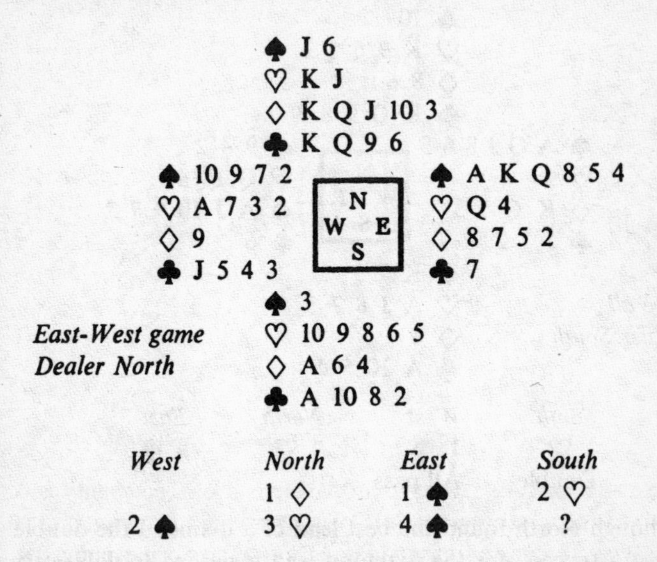

West	*North*	*East*	*South*
	1 ◊	1 ♠	2 ♡
2 ♠	3 ♡	4 ♠	?

There are times when the opponents have to be trusted. South should not double in spite of his two aces. In my opinion he has a clear-cut bid of five diamonds at this point. This bid ensures a minimum loss, and the contract might even be made if East fails to lead his singleton club.

If North rebids three clubs instead of the slightly unorthodox three hearts on the second round, South has even more reason to bid on rather than double. Five clubs might also be made if the defence slips slightly, but any sacrifice—even five hearts—will give North and South a reasonable score.

It must be recorded, however, that at most of the tables the contract was four spades doubled, making ten tricks for a score of 790 to East-West. The ranks of the Life Masters are full of optimists, it appears.

In a competitive auction the double of a high-level contract ahead of partner should show trump tricks and warn against bidding on. Failure to observe this principle led to a poor result on the following hand.

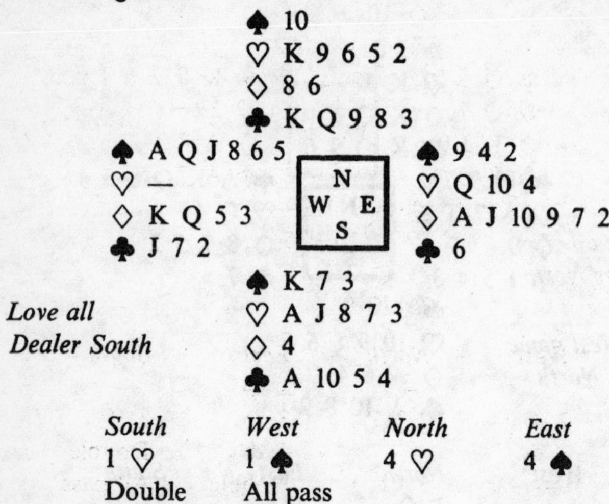

South	*West*	*North*	*East*
1 ♡	1 ♠	4 ♡	4 ♠
Double	All pass		

Although North found the best lead of a diamond the double was not a success, for the diamond lead is needed to defeat *six* spades. West had no difficulty in making eleven tricks for a score of 690.

The double was wrong on two counts. Firstly, South did not have the trump tricks he promised, and secondly, with his good controls he had no reason to discourage his partner from bidding on.

If South had passed four spades North would have contested again with five clubs, and this evidence of a fit for both sides might have enabled South to find the good sacrifice in six hearts if the opponents had bid to five spades. Six hearts costs a mere 100 points.

Naturally enough it is the players prone to making dubious doubles themselves who are most likely to double-cross their partners in situations like the following.

Over-Doubling

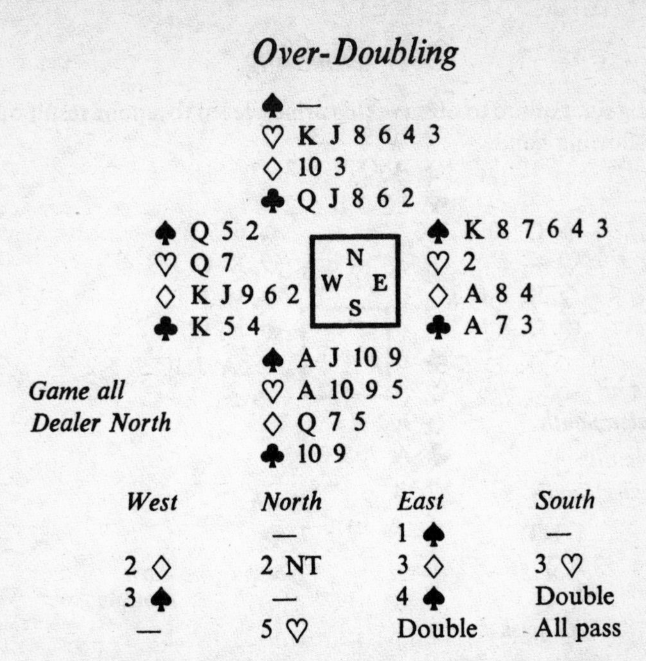

West	*North*	*East*	*South*
	—	1 ♠	—
2 ◇	2 NT	3 ◇	3 ♡
3 ♠	—	4 ♠	Double
—	5 ♡	Double	All pass

The defenders cashed two tricks in each of the minor suits for a penalty of 500. That represented a total swing of 700 points, since four spades would have been one down on the natural lead of the ace of hearts.

This type of competitive misjudgement is very common. North's takeout into five hearts is, of course, a classic example of the double-cross. North argued that his hand was so weak defensively that he could not expect to defeat four spades, but this showed a sorry lack of confidence in his partner. By passing originally and then contesting with an unusual no trump bid, North had given a very good picture of his hand. Knowing there could be little in the way of defensive strength across the table, South must surely have the beating of four spades in his own hand.

Many juicy penalties will be missed if South is inhibited from doubling on this sort of hand for fear that his partner may take out.

With a massive trump holding defenders feel on safe ground, but even then a double may be unwise.

Over-Doubling

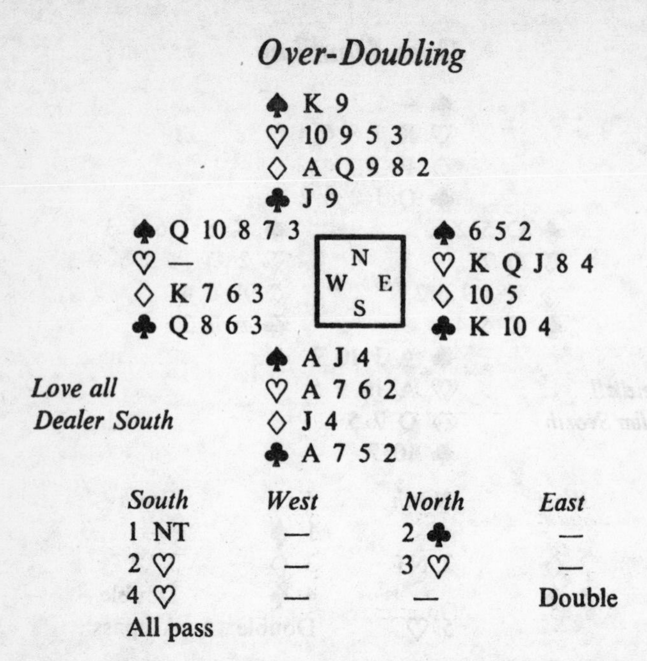

South	*West*	*North*	*East*
1 NT	—	2 ♣	—
2 ♡	—	3 ♡	—
4 ♡	—	—	Double
All pass			

West led the seven of spades and dummy's nine won the trick. South cashed the king of spades, led a club to his ace, and discarded dummy's losing club on the ace of spades.

After a successful diamond finesse the ace was cashed and a third round led. East ruffed with the eight of hearts and was allowed to hold the trick. The club return was trumped in dummy and a fourth diamond led, ruffed by the king and over-ruffed by the ace. South then ruffed his last club on the table, conceded two trump tricks and claimed his contract.

East was unlucky in that any lead but a spade would have defeated the game, but his double was ill-advised. It stood to gain a mere 50 points if the contract had gone one down, while the actual loss was 640. Without the double to alert him to the possibility of a 5–0 trump break, South would probably have mistimed the play and gone down.

A certain type of defensive trump holding is not as good as it looks.

Over-Doubling

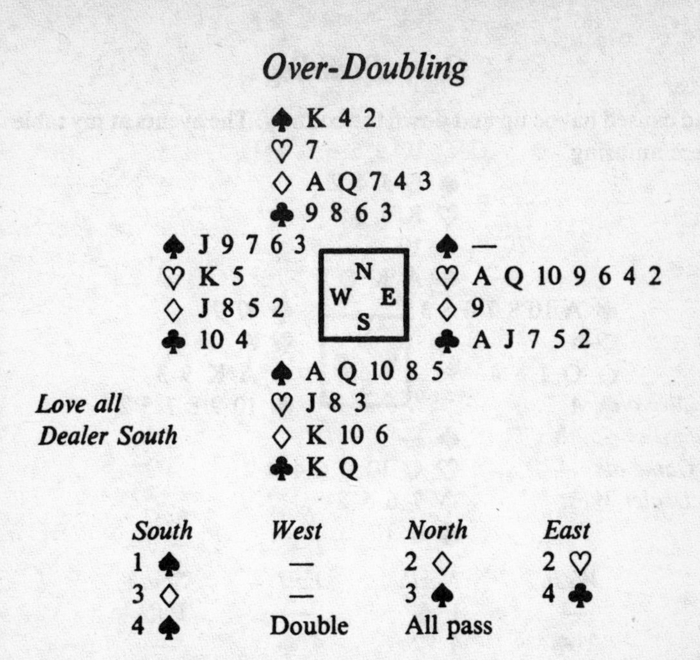

South	*West*	*North*	*East*
1 ♠	—	2 ◇	2 ♡
3 ◇	—	3 ♠	4 ♣
4 ♠	Double	All pass	

West led the king of hearts and continued the suit. The declarer ruffed on the table and led a club to the ace. East plugged away with a third round of hearts, enabling his partner to discard his second club while dummy ruffed.

The lead of the king of spades exposed the trump position and South turned his attention to the diamonds, ruffing the fourth round in his hand. Having nothing but trumps left, West was thrown in by a club lead and had to concede the last three tricks to South.

It is true that four spades can be defeated if the defenders start with two rounds of clubs, but a double that succeeds only on one particular line of defence is a bad double. Perfect defence is often hard to produce at the table, and West would have been better advised to raise his partner to five hearts. At the worst this contract would be one down, and it might be made if South fails to find the killing trump lead.

A hand originally played in the Crockfords Cup was selected by Alan Hiron for the Charity Challenge Cup event in March 1970 and caused havoc up and down the country. The events at my table were amusing.

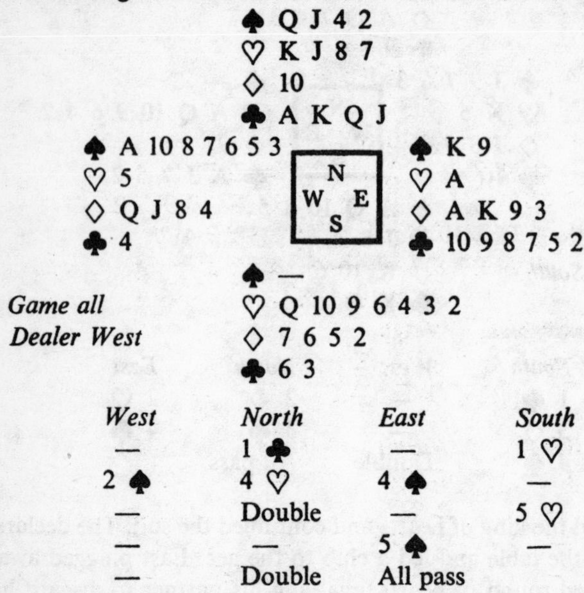

West	*North*	*East*	*South*
—	1 ♣	—	1 ♡
2 ♠	4 ♡	4 ♠	—
—	Double	—	5 ♡
—	—	5 ♠	—
—	Double	All pass	

My partner chose to pass originally and contested with two spades on the second round. South properly refused to stand the double of four spades and took out into five hearts. I could see little profit in defending and therefore tried again with five spades. When this came round to North he doubled once more and, it being a light-hearted game, added as an aside: 'If he takes it out again I'll shoot him.'

South took the warning to heart and passed, but West had no difficulty in wrapping up eleven tricks for a score of 850.

North showed poor judgement on the hand, for the bidding marked his partner with a void in spades. It should be clear to North that if South has either red ace six hearts must be on ice. As it happens South does not have an ace, but six hearts is of course a very cheap sacrifice.

Over-Doubling

The next hand comes from a pairs tournament and illustrates another way in which a rash double can lose points.

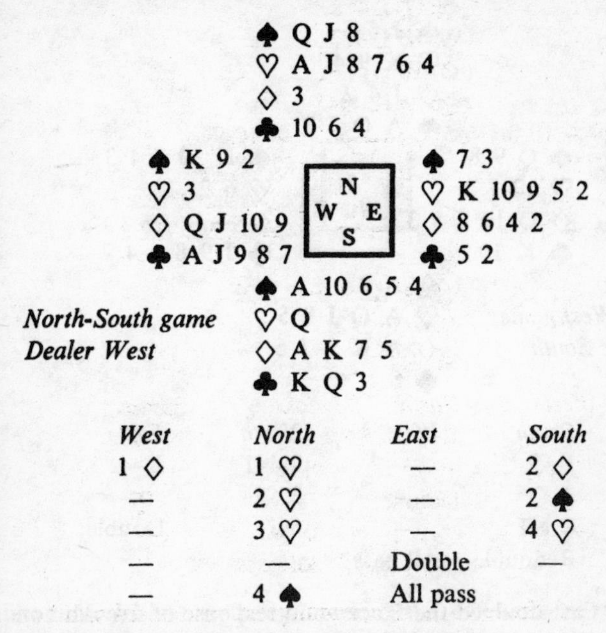

West	*North*	*East*	*South*
1 ◇	1 ♡	—	2 ◇
—	2 ♡	—	2 ♠
—	3 ♡	—	4 ♡
—	—	Double	—
—	4 ♠	All pass	

To share the top East-West score of 200, all East had to do was to pass four hearts. His double was a greedy bid which gave North the chance to correct his earlier error and switch to a more sensible contract.

The declarer won the opening heart lead with dummy's ace, cashed the ace and king of diamonds, and ruffed a small diamond with the eight of spades. A club was led to the king and ace and West switched to a small trump, won by dummy's knave. South returned to his hand with the queen of clubs, ruffed his last diamond with the queen of spades, and got off lead with the ten of clubs.

West continued with a fourth round of clubs, but East's seven of spades was not big enough for an effective uppercut and the declarer made ten tricks.

The doubling of cue-bids to indicate a lead is not without its dangers. In the following hand the manœuvre recoiled upon the doubler in an unexpected way.

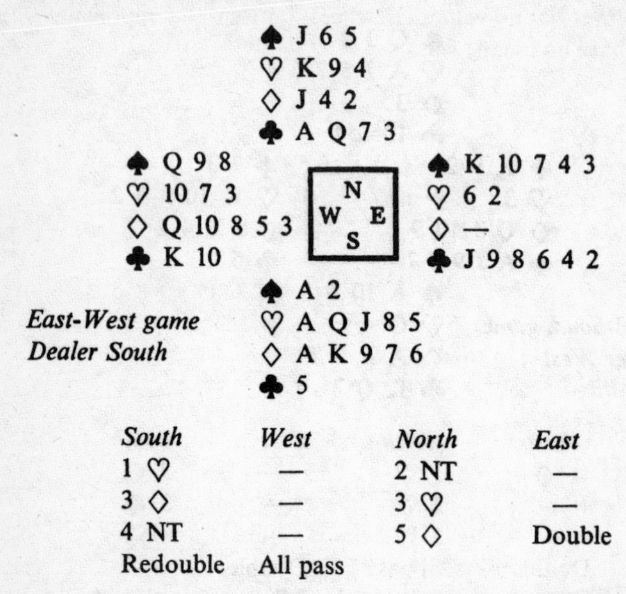

South	*West*	*North*	*East*
1 ♡	—	2 NT	—
3 ◇	—	3 ♡	—
4 NT	—	5 ◇	Double
Redouble	All pass		

When East doubled the Blackwood response of five diamonds South seized the opportunity to show a good suit by redoubling. North passed on the strength of the knave of diamonds, and the defenders found that there was no way of defeating the contract.

West hit the most troublesome lead of a spade, but South won and took an immediate club finesse to dispose of his spade loser. A spade ruff was followed by the ace, queen and king of hearts and another spade ruff. The ace and king of diamonds brought the declarer's total up to ten tricks, and the lead of a heart promoted the knave of diamonds as the eleventh trick.

Incidentally, East was mistaken in thinking a diamond lead to be desirable against a six heart contract. Far from defeating the slam, a diamond is the only lead that allows it to be made.

The doubling of part-score contracts is a sounder mathematical proposition than the doubling of game contracts. On misfit hands the opponents can often be caught for a big penalty at a low level. A time to avoid low-level doubles, however, is when you have good trumps but no values elsewhere, for then the opponents will usually have an escape suit.

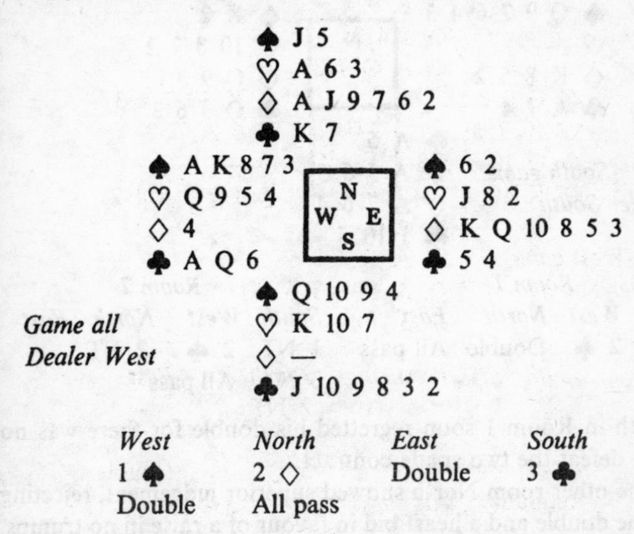

No one can blame West for doubling three clubs although the contract proved to be unbeatable. It was East's rash double of two diamonds, promising values he did not possess, that was responsible for the bad result.

East's only proper course on the above hand is to pass two diamonds. No doubt South would also pass and West, not being clairvoyant, would reopen with a double. This would be passed round to South who would again rescue into three clubs. But West would now have no reason to double, and South would score a normal 110 in the par contract instead of 670 for making three clubs doubled.

Another occasion on which players are often too ready to double part-score contracts is when their partners have opened with a weak no trump bid. The following hand from a Gold Cup semi-final match produced a large turnover of points.

Over-Doubling

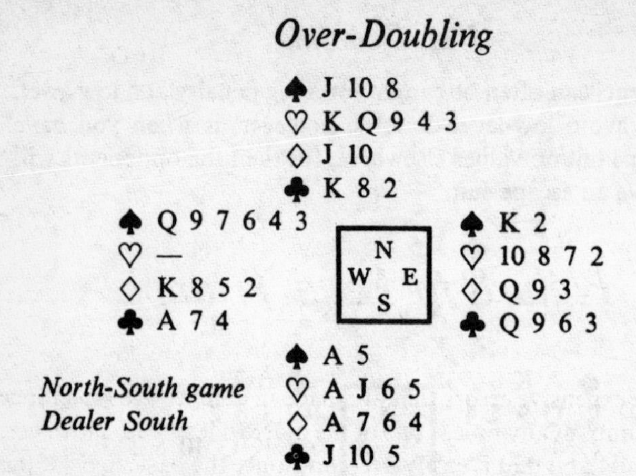

Room 1				*Room 2*			
South	*West*	*North*	*East*	*South*	*West*	*North*	*East*
1 NT	2 ♠	Double	All pass	1 NT	2 ♠	2 NT	—
				3 NT	All pass		

North in Room 1 soon regretted his double for there was no way to defeat the two spade contract.

In the other room North showed superior judgement, rejecting both the double and a heart bid in favour of a raise in no trumps. South was happy to proceed to game.

An initial diamond lead might have defeated the contract, but West led the six of spades to the knave, king and ace. At the second trick South led the knave of clubs and put on dummy's king when West played low. With a club trick in the bag, South was able to return to hand in hearts and establish his ninth trick by leading towards the ten of spades.

The swing was 1,070 points or 14 i.m.p.

11

Failure to Lead Trumps

OF all the expensive errors that are made in defence the reluctance to lead trumps at any time is one of the most widespread. However, this is a bad habit that is easily overcome once the basic logic of the trump lead has been grasped.

The subject of opening leads in general is a thorny one, and many players will hold that the failure to find a critical trump lead should be classed as a 'wrong view' rather than an error. I disagree. The bidding will almost invariably give sufficient indication, and I believe that the failure to find a trump lead on the proper occasion is normally a clear-cut and demonstrable mistake.

Reluctance to lead trumps often stems from lack of confidence. The trump lead is a long-range form of attack which does not produce immediate benefits. It also has the appearance of surrendering an early tempo, which players have been taught to regard as a bad thing. Most defenders are happiest when launching an active attack on the declarer's honour cards in an attempt to develop tricks in the side suits. There are many hands on which this is the correct policy but there are others where it is not, and it is vital to learn how to listen to the bidding and distinguish between the two situations.

In one short chapter it will not be possible to cover the whole range of bidding sequences that demand a trump lead. All we can do is to have a look at some of the more common ones. The most obvious occasion for leading a trump is when dummy has given preference and you have a substantial holding in the declarer's side suit. Here is a typical example.

Failure to Lead Trumps

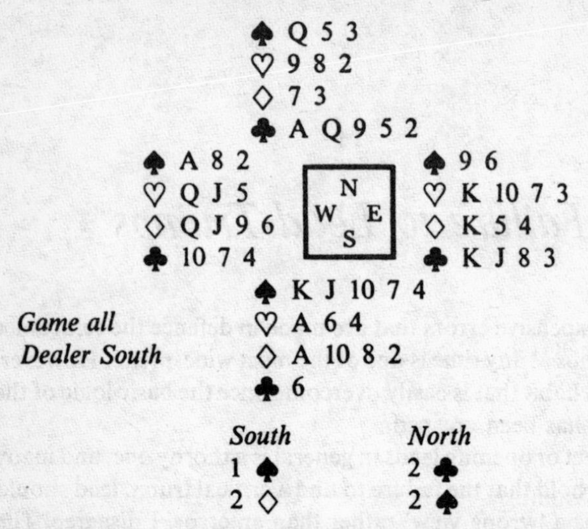

West led the queen of hearts to the ace and South immediately ducked a diamond. West won with the nine and switched to the ace and another trump, but it was too late. South could not be prevented from scoring his eighth trick by ruffing a losing diamond in dummy.

On the above bidding, the danger of dummy scoring a small trump by ruffing should have been clear to West. The initial lead of a small trump was called for. On regaining the lead in diamonds, West could then have prevented any ruffs by playing two further rounds of trumps. In actual fact, on a trump lead the declarer would probably have abandoned any hope of ruffing diamonds and would have tried for his eighth trick by taking the club finesse, but as the cards lie that play is also doomed to failure.

Note that North's daisy-picking bid of two clubs gave West a good chance to find the killing defence. If North had raised to two spades immediately there would have been less to guide West in his choice of lead, and he could hardly be faulted for trying a heart or a diamond.

On the next hand a light opening bid resulted in the declarer playing at a dangerously high level.

Failure to Lead Trumps

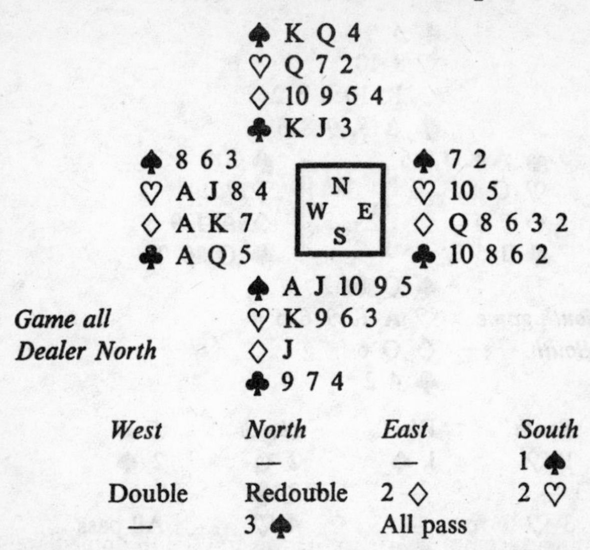

West	*North*	*East*	*South*
	—	—	1 ♠
Double	Redouble	2 ◇	2 ♡
—	3 ♠	All pass	

With a strong all-round hand and a good holding in hearts, West had little excuse for failing to lead a trump against this bidding. Players who find it hard to resist 'having a look at dummy', however, will sympathize with his choice of the ace of diamonds.

Having had a look at dummy West switched to a trump, but once again it was too late. South won in hand and led a club, putting in dummy's knave when West played low. A diamond ruff was followed by another club lead.

West played the ace and led another trump, but South had the hand under control. Winning with the queen, he ruffed another diamond, crossed to the king of clubs and ruffed the fourth diamond with his last trump. That made seven tricks and he still had a heart trick and the king of spades to come.

An initial trump lead would have killed the dummy reversal and held the declarer to eight tricks.

It can be difficult to break the taboos instilled by faulty teaching.

Failure to Lead Trumps

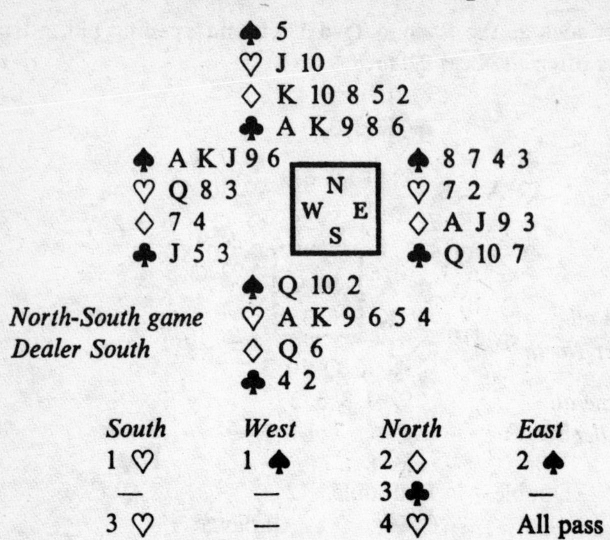

South	*West*	*North*	*East*
1 ♡	1 ♠	2 ◇	2 ♠
—	—	3 ♣	—
3 ♡	—	4 ♡	All pass

West knew better than to cash a high spade, but he had been taught that a trump lead away from the queen should be avoided. Accordingly he led the seven of diamonds in the hope that his partner would be able to win and lead a trump.

East covered dummy's eight of diamonds with the nine (it does no good to play the ace) and South won with the queen. The queen of spades was won by West, who led another diamond to his partner's knave. East returned a trump which was allowed to run to the queen, and West played a second round.

Although prevented from ruffing spades in dummy, the declarer had an easy alternative play for his contract. After drawing the outstanding trump, he led a club to the ace and ruffed out East's ace of diamonds. The established diamonds in dummy then provided discards for the losing spades.

It takes an initial trump lead to defeat this contract. Defenders should not be timid about leading from an honour when the bidding calls for a trump lead. Any trick given away by the lead usually comes back with interest.

When opponents find a fit by means of some distributional

gadget such as the Roman Two Diamond opening bid, a trump lead is often the best defence.

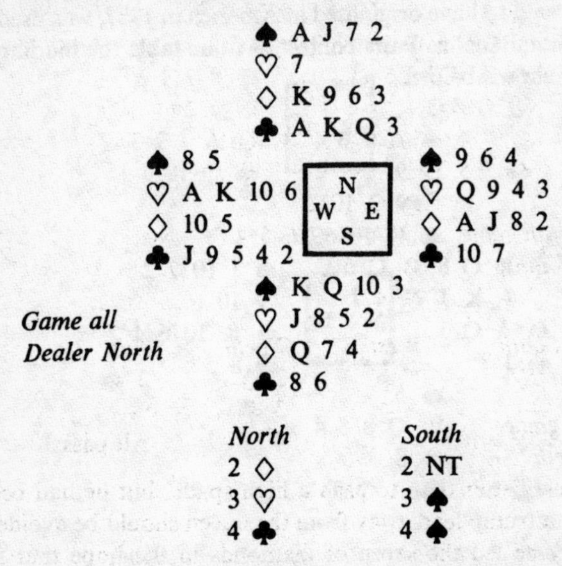

This is the old-fashioned version of the Roman Two Diamonds, with two no trumps as the positive response and the rebid in the short suit.

West led the ace of hearts and wondered what to do next, but he had already thrown away his chance of defeating the contract. South had no difficulty in ruffing two hearts on the table to bring his bag up to ten tricks.

Note the difference if West leads a trump initially. South is unable to negotiate two ruffs in either hand without running into entry trouble and it is a simple matter for the defenders to hold him to nine tricks.

Other conventions that lead to distributional contracts are Roman Jump Overcalls, Tartan Two Bids, Astro, Landy, Michaels Cue-Bids, etc. Against contracts reached by any such means a trump lead is always worth considering.

The greater the high-card strength a defender holds the more he should incline towards a trump lead. If the opponents are short of points they will surely have distributional compensation.

This hand, said to have originated in America in 1937, was used in a B.B.L. Simultaneous Pairs contest. At one table the bidding proceeded as shown below.

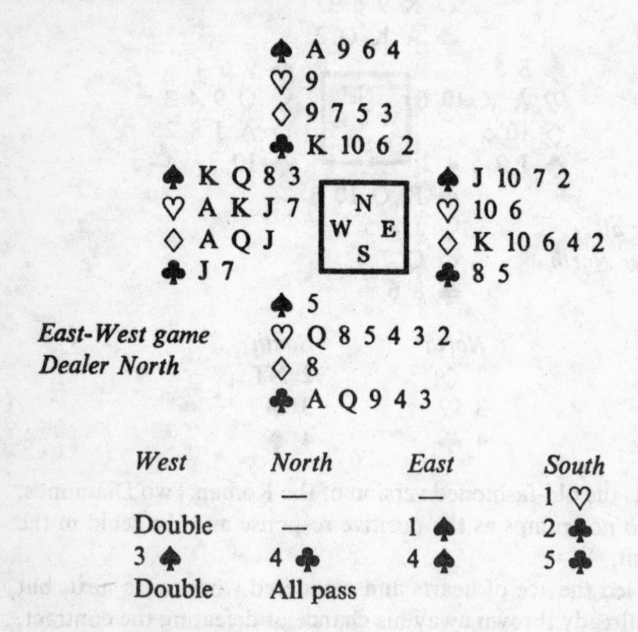

West	*North*	*East*	*South*
	—	—	1 ♡
Double	—	1 ♠	2 ♣
3 ♠	4 ♣	4 ♠	5 ♣
Double	All pass		

Strictly speaking this is a phantom sacrifice since four spades cannot be made on a heart lead. Best defence is not always found in practice, however, and it was reasonable for South to bid on.

Rendered over-confident by his picture gallery, West began by cashing a top heart and that was the end of the defence. The declarer needed no further help to make his doubled contract for a very fine score.

An initial spade lead fares no better, and although a diamond lead and continuation defeats the contract this is purely fortuitous. The bidding cries out for the trump lead that gives the declarer no chance.

Failure to Lead Trumps

Over-bold bidding landed the declarer in trouble on the next hand, but an inept opening lead let him off the hook.

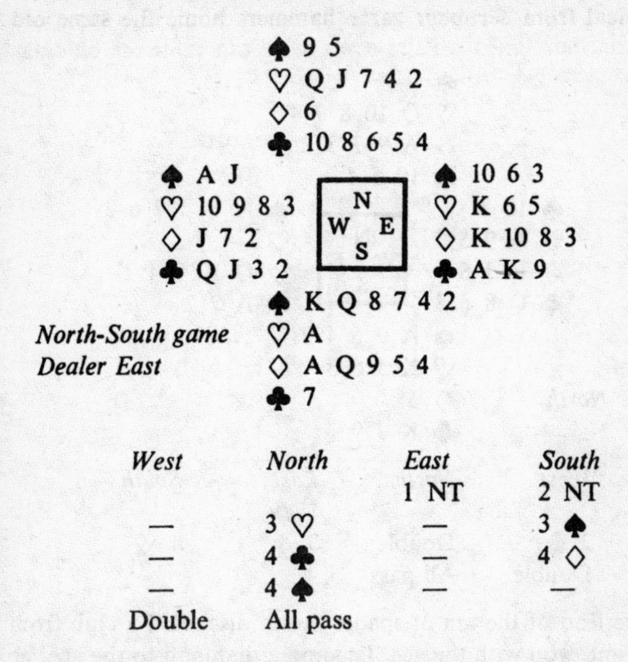

West	*North*	*East*	*South*
		1 NT	2 NT
—	3 ♡	—	3 ♠
—	4 ♣	—	4 ◇
—	4 ♠	—	—
Double	All pass		

West led the ten of hearts to the ace and the declarer was quick to seize his chance. He cashed the ace of diamonds, ruffed a diamond and led the queen of hearts from the table. When East covered with the king South ruffed, entered dummy with another diamond ruff, discarded his club on the knave of hearts, ruffed a club, and led the king of spades.

Taking his ace, West returned a club for South to ruff. With eight tricks in the bag, South had queen and another trump and queen and another diamond left in his hand. He led a diamond to the king, and no return by East could prevent him from making two further tricks and his contract.

A trump lead was marked when North gave preference to spades. The lead of the ace of spades followed by the knave would have cost the defence a trump trick but it would have gained no fewer than three tricks in return, ensuring a penalty of 500.

This deal from a rubber game hammers home the same old lesson.

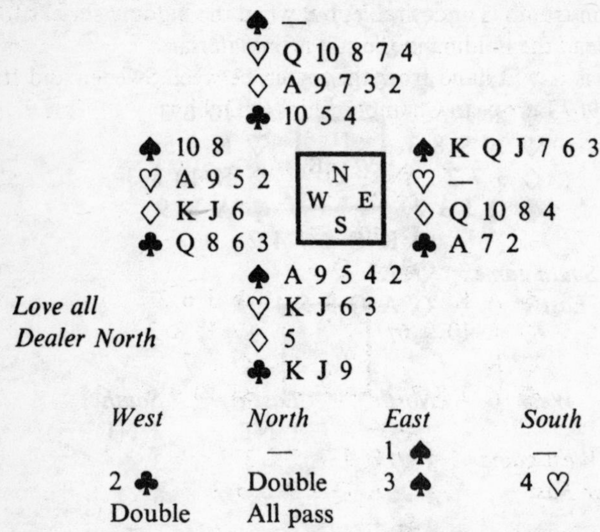

West	*North*	*East*	*South*
	—	1 ♠	—
2 ♣	Double	3 ♠	4 ♡
Double	All pass		

On the lead of the ten of spades South discarded a club from dummy and won with the ace. Leading a diamond to the ace, he continued with a diamond ruff, a spade ruff, another diamond ruff and another spade ruff. A fourth diamond was then ruffed with the king of hearts. West over-ruffed with the ace and led a trump, and the declarer played the queen from the table, felling his own knave. When the established nine of diamonds was led from dummy West could do no better than ruff and return his last trump. The declarer then had to guess the club position, but in view of the bidding this was not too difficult and he duly scored the tenth trick with his king.

After the initial spade lead the defence was helpless. Knowing his side to have more than half the points in the pack, West's aim should have been to draw the declarer's small trumps before they could be used for ruffing.

Failure to Lead Trumps

On the obvious lead of the ace and another heart the declarer is unable to establish dummy's diamond suit and the contract fails.

It is a pity that there is such a strong prejudice against leading singleton trumps. Obviously there are times when the lead of a singleton trump is undesirable, but when the bidding shrieks for a trump lead the holding in the suit is immaterial.

Here is a wild hand from the match between Sweden and Italy in the 1967 European Championships at Dublin.

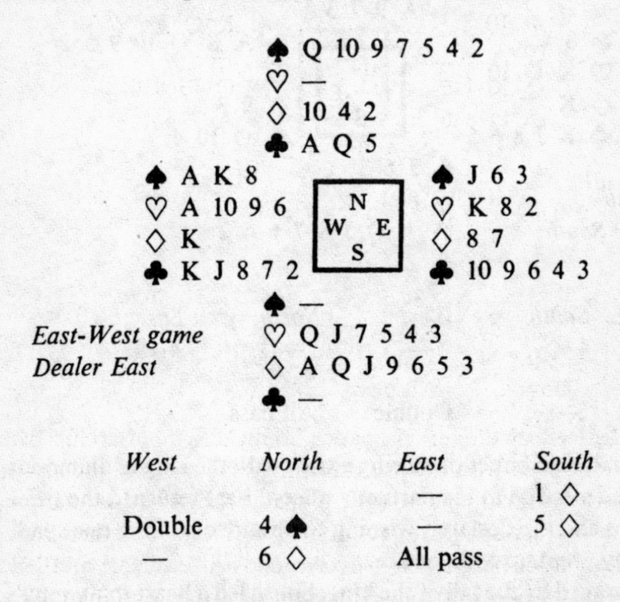

West	*North*	*East*	*South*
		—	1 ◇
Double	4 ♠	—	5 ◇
—	6 ◇	All pass	

This inelegant sequence occurred when Sweden held the North-South cards. Although not a very good slam, it happens to be unbeatable on any lead but a trump. After ruffing three hearts in dummy South is in the fortunate position of being unable to take the diamond finesse and thus cannot go wrong.

Few players would produce the right lead from the West hand, but the Italian defender, Bellentani, made no mistake. Out came the king of diamonds and the contract had to go down.

In the other room North-South for Italy played in the more

sensible contract of five diamonds. A swing of 21 i.m.p. thus hung on Bellentani's choice of lead.

A defender took a less realistic view of his singleton king of trumps on the next hand.

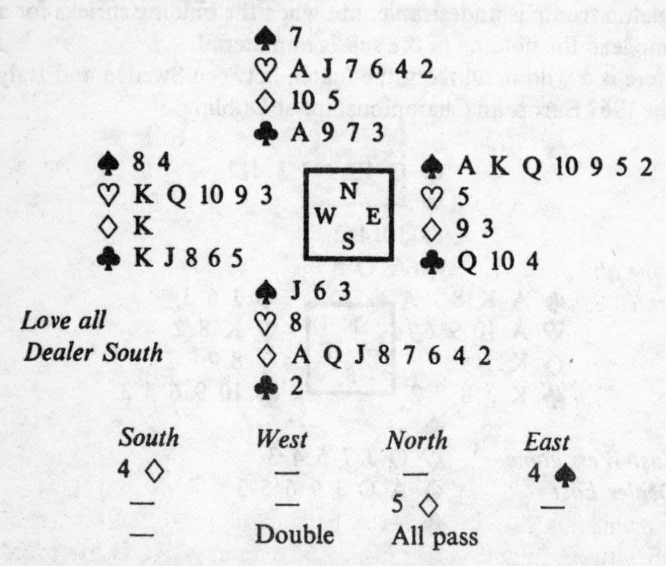

South	*West*	*North*	*East*
4 ◇	—	—	4 ♠
—	—	5 ◇	—
—	Double	All pass	

West had high hopes of scoring a trick with the king of diamonds and he led a spade to his partner's queen. East returned the three of trumps and the declarer, wishing to be sure of ruffing one spade in dummy, went up with the ace.

Encouraged by the fall of the king, South led a heart to dummy's ace and returned the suit. When East showed out South was able to lay down his hand and claim twelve tricks on a double squeeze.

West's idea that the declarer might finesse in trumps and allow him to score the king was wishful thinking of the worst kind. With all the side suits securely buttoned up, West should have leapt at the opportunity to lead his king of diamonds in order to cut down dummy's ruffing power.

The trump lead would have made a difference of two tricks and 750 points.

Failure to Lead Trumps

It is important to be able to recognize the occasions when a trump lead will not be the right answer against a high-level doubled contract.

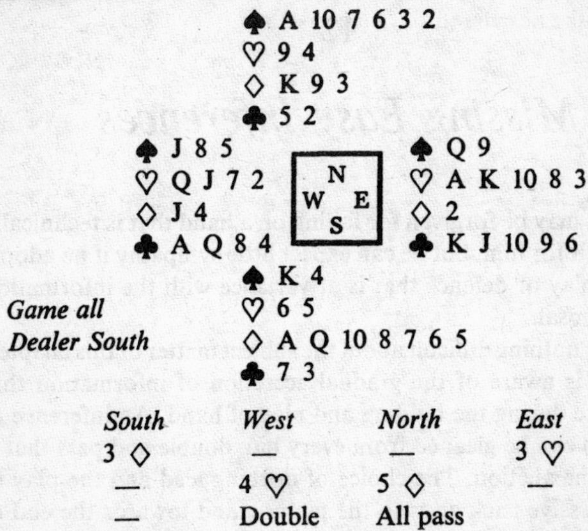

Knowing his side to have the balance of power, West led a trump with the intention of cutting down dummy's ruffs. He soon regretted it, for on the trump lead the declarer was able to establish dummy's spade suit and get rid of three of his losers, thus making the doubled contract with an overtrick.

The clue to the proper defence lies in East's failure to double the pre-emptive opening bid of three diamonds. This marks East with shortage in spades and West should expect to see a long spade suit in dummy.

The danger of the declarer obtaining discards on the spades is clear, and West should attack in hearts or clubs in order to cash what tricks he can before losing the lead.

12

Missing Easy Inferences

A PLAYER may be forgiven for failing on a hand that is technically too difficult for him, but he can expect little sympathy if he adopts a line of play or defence that is at variance with the information at his disposal.

There is nothing difficult about the subject matter of this chapter. Everyone is aware of the gradual accretion of information that takes place during the bidding and play of hand. An inference of some kind can be gleaned from every bid, double and pass that is made in the auction. The choice of opening lead and the play to each successive trick adds to the picture, and towards the end of the hand there is normally no mystery left and the play becomes a double-dummy problem. A 'wrong view' at this stage will usually turn out to be a clear-cut error by a player who has missed some simple clue.

We tend to observe only what we are trained to observe, which explains why so many players suffer from a curious myopia in their card play. These players do not see what is under their noses because they do not know what to look for. I am not talking about subtle inferences, some of which are so obscure that they will pass unnoticed by all except first-class players. The inferences commonly missed are so obvious that they only have to be pointed out for a player to wonder how he could have been so blind.

Whether consciously or not, we all make use of certain inferences from the auction. When an opponent opens the bidding we infer that he has at least twelve points. If he bids no trumps we put him with a balanced hand, while if he mentions a suit we presume that he has four or more cards in it. The opening lead provides another rich vein of information that is mined by all. If a player leads an honour card we normally infer that he has a sequence, while the lead of the two is presumed to be either from an honour card or a singleton.

What is more likely to be missed is the negative inference from the failure to lead a certain suit.

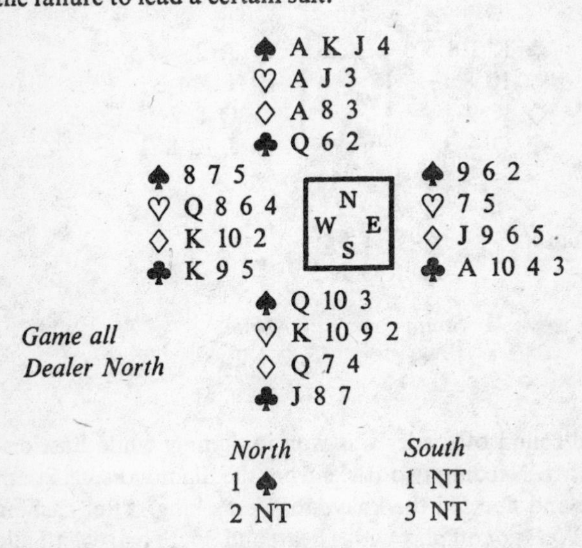

The opening lead of the eight of spades is won in hand with the ten. To be sure of making his contract South must bring in the heart suit without loss, and there is nothing to guide him except the opening lead.

A neutral lead such as this carries the inference that the leader will have honour cards in the other suits. With equivalent holdings in spades and hearts, for example, West might equally well have chosen a heart lead. The fact that he did not affords a presumption that he is likely to have the queen of hearts.

It may not be much to go on but it is better than a guess. South should therefore lead the ten of hearts and run it if West plays low.

Since each hand is limited to thirteen cards, a player marked with length in one suit is likely to be short in another. Many seem to be unaware of this simple proposition.

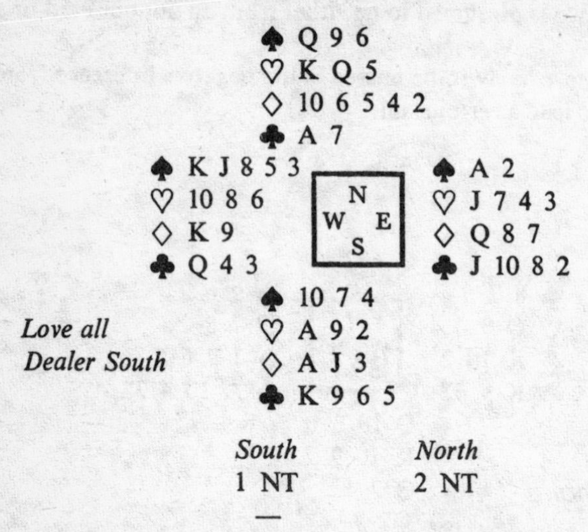

The third round of spades was won in dummy while East discarded a heart. Needing two tricks from the diamond suit, South led the two and finessed the knave to West's king. After cashing his spades, West got off play with a heart and South had eventually to lose another trick.

Considering the diamond suit in isolation, South made the proper percentage play, but in the context of the hand as a whole his play was wrong. West, with five spades to East's two, was more likely to have the doubleton diamond. Both in theory and in practice the better play is the ten of diamonds from the table on the first round. If this is allowed to run to West, South repeats the finesse at a later stage. If East covers the ten of diamonds, South ducks and plays the ace on the next round.

This play loses marginally when West has a singleton diamond, failing when the singleton is a small card and succeeding when it is an honour. But it makes sure of the contract when West has any doubleton except king and queen.

Missing Easy Inferences

A player acquainted with the simple logic of distribution would not have gone down in this slam contract.

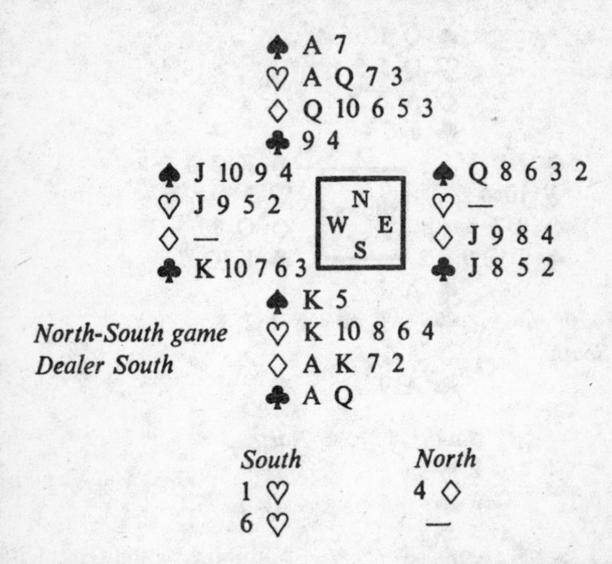

When West led the knave of spades and dummy went down South's first impression was that he should have been in seven. After winning with the king of spades and making the natural play of a heart to the ace, however, he found it impossible to make six.

Of course it was unlucky to find both red suits breaking so badly, but the declarer should have considered the possibility before playing to the first trick. It is clear that the contract can be in danger only if there is a diamond loser. And if West is void in diamonds he can hardly be void in hearts as well, for that would give him thirteen cards in the black suits which would surely have prompted some bidding.

South should therefore have won the first trick in dummy and led the three of hearts to his king in order to cater for four hearts in the West hand.

It is important to acquire the habit of noticing the cards the opponents fail to play as well as those that they play. A negative inference can very often turn a guess into a virtual certainty.

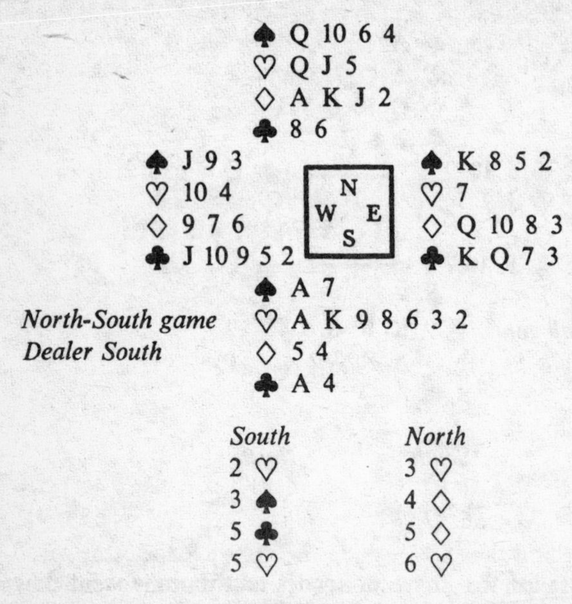

Receiving the damaging lead of the knave of clubs, the declarer played the hand well up to a point. He won the first trick, cashed the ace of hearts, and turned his attention to the diamonds, ruffing the third round with the king of hearts. When the queen failed to appear, South led a second trump to dummy, ruffed the last diamond and got off lead with his club.

West won with the ten and led the three of spades. South gave this a great deal of thought but eventually made the wrong decision by playing dummy's queen. A spade trick then had to be lost and the slam was defeated.

South thought the play a fifty-fifty guess, but he was mistaken. While there was no guarantee that the play of the ten of spades would win, the queen could do nothing but lose. The clue lies in East's action on the second round of clubs. Clearly either opponent could have won this club trick, and if East had not held the king of spades he would certainly have overtaken his partner's ten of clubs and led a spade through.

In the next hand the declarer allowed the probabilities of distribution to blind him to other considerations.

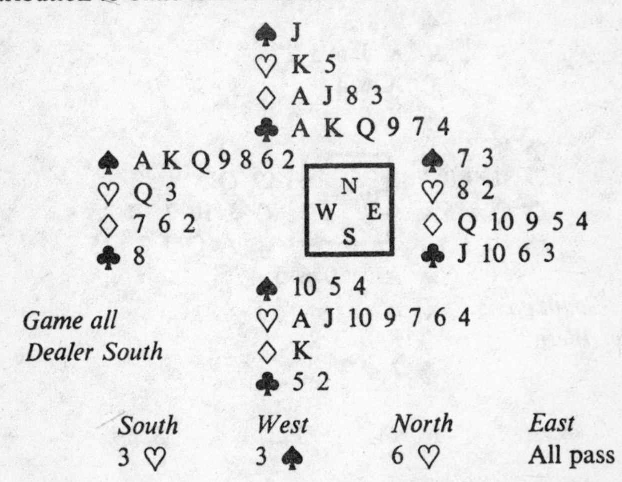

South	*West*	*North*	*East*
3 ♡	3 ♠	6 ♡	All pass

After cashing the ace of spades West switched to the seven of diamonds. South won in hand, led a heart to the king and finessed on the way back to go three down.

Since West was marked with considerable length in spades it might not seem unreasonable to play him for a singleton heart, but the declarer missed a simple negative inference which would have guided him to the winning play. If West had started with a singleton heart he would surely have continued with a second round of spades in order to remove the small trump from dummy and protect a possible guarded queen in his partner's hand. This would also be the obvious line of defence, of course, if West had three trumps to the queen himself.

The passive diamond switch, which West could hardly expect to set up a trick for the defence, was a clear indication that the trumps were breaking 2–2. Holding queen and another trump, West would have good reason to give South the opportunity of taking a trump finesse.

Missing Easy Inferences

When an opponent gives you the opportunity to make a play that could not have been attempted without his assistance it is wise to suspect an ulterior motive.

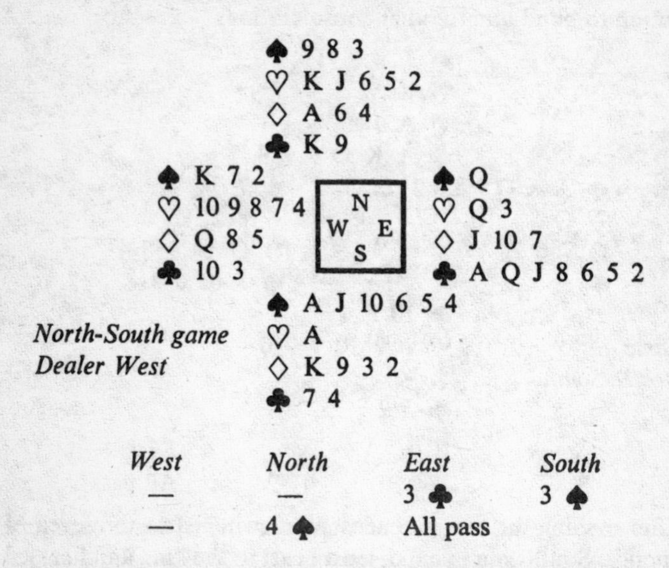

West	*North*	*East*	*South*
—	—	3 ♣	3 ♠
—	4 ♠	All pass	

West led the ten of clubs, and after cashing two tricks in the suit East returned the knave of diamonds. South won with the king in order to conserve dummy's entry, cashed the aces of hearts and spades, and continued with the knave of spades.

West took his king and returned the ten of hearts, and South seized the chance of a free finesse in the suit. The knave was covered by the queen, however, and South had to ruff. When West subsequently turned up with five cards in hearts South was unable to find a parking place for his second diamond loser and the contract had to go down.

South failed to draw an easy inference here. With a safe trump return available, West would not have led a heart if the finesse was working. The only possible reason for a heart lead was that West knew his partner's queen would fall. South should therefore have put up the king and called for the queen from East.

Missing Easy Inferences

The declarer was given the chance to make an impossible contract on the next hand, but he failed to take it.

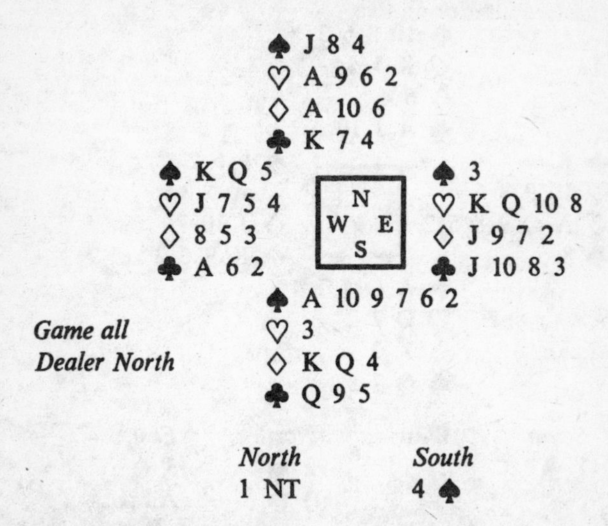

West unwisely led the two of clubs and the declarer captured East's ten with his queen. A heart was led to the ace and a spade finesse lost to the queen. West continued with the six of clubs and East's knave won the trick when dummy played low. East returned a club to his partner's ace, and West still had to score another trump trick which put the contract one down.

That was a good recovery by West after his initial lead had turned out poorly, but the declarer should not have been taken in. South should reason that West must know the whereabouts of the club nine from the play to the first round of the suit. To lead another club away from the knave would be a mistake so elementary as to be incredible.

The only honour card West could logically hold on this play was the ace. Possession of the ace would make it imperative for him to offer South an immediate alternative to the winning play. South should therefore have played dummy's king as his only chance of a second trick in the suit.

Missing Easy Inferences

Here is a hand on which the declarer drew a valid inference from the bidding but failed to make effective use of it.

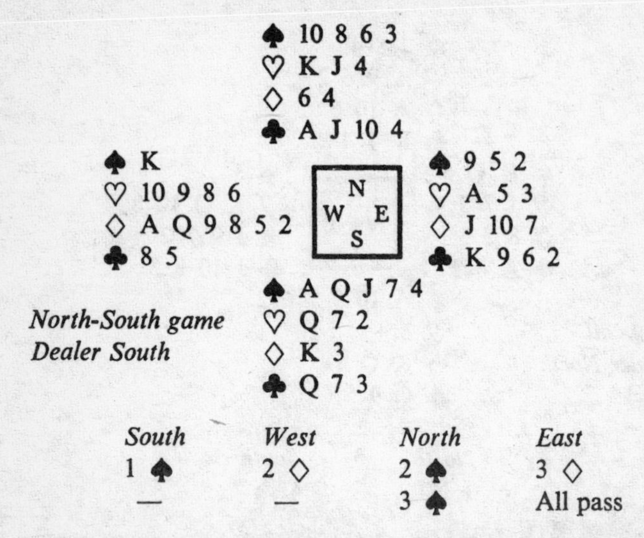

South	*West*	*North*	*East*
1 ♠	2 ◇	2 ♠	3 ◇
—	—	3 ♠	All pass

The lead of the ten of hearts was covered by the knave and won by the ace. East returned the knave of diamonds, and West cashed two tricks in the suit before getting off lead with another heart.

South reasoned that with both black kings East would have bid two no trumps rather than three diamonds. It seemed reasonable to test the clubs first, for if East produced the king of clubs South could play for a singleton king in trumps.

Winning the heart in hand, South led the three of clubs to dummy's ten, but West played the eight and East smoothly ducked. All appeared to be plain sailing, and South finessed trumps on the way back and lost to the bare king. He was subsequently shocked to find that there was a club loser after all.

South was working on the right lines, but he did not carry his line of thought to its logical conclusion. Once he had decided that East could not have both black kings, his first move should have been to cash the ace of spades. If the spade finesse is right there is never any need to take it.

Missing Easy Inferences

Inferences from the bidding can be invaluable to the defenders.

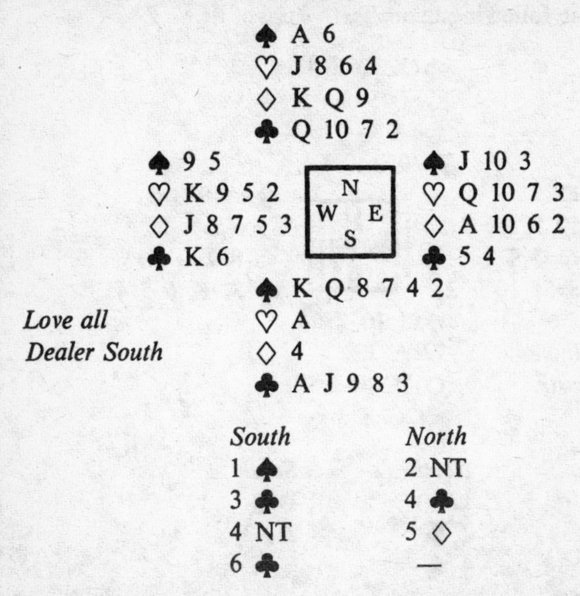

West led the two of hearts to the ten and ace. Entering dummy with the ace of spades, the declarer took a losing trump finesse to West's king. At this point West made the mistake of trying to cash the king of hearts. The declarer ruffed, drew the outstanding trumps, and discarded dummy's diamonds on his spades to land his slam.

It should have been clear to West that if the declarer had a heart loser he must also have a diamond loser. Otherwise he would have discarded his losing heart on dummy's diamonds before touching trumps.

West offered the excuse that he thought South might be void in diamonds, but this does not stand up when examined in the light of the bidding. Players who hold ace doubleton in one side suit and a void in the other do not, as a rule, use Blackwood. The clear inference from South's bid of four no trumps was that he held a singleton diamond.

Missing Easy Inferences

A defender with an ear to the bidding would not have gone astray on the following hand.

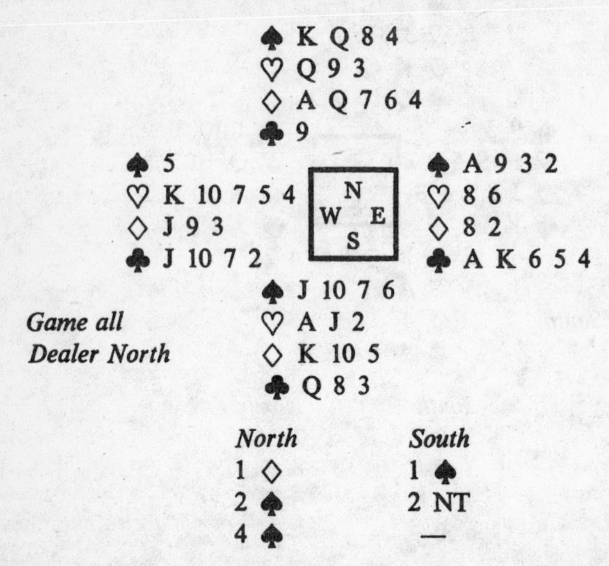

North	*South*
1 ◇	1 ♠
2 ♠	2 NT
4 ♠	—

The opening lead of the knave of clubs was won by the king and East switched to the eight of hearts. South played low and the king won the trick, and West led another heart in the hope that his partner could ruff. When East followed to the second round of hearts the declarer lost no time in forcing out the ace of spades and claiming his contract.

West failed to pick up a simple inference. South's rebid of two no trumps indicated a balanced hand, and yet he bid spades on the first round. Clearly South could not have four hearts, in that case, and East's eight could not be a singleton.

On the bidding East was marked with four cards in trumps, which makes a club return mandatory. This shortens dummy's trumps and causes the declarer to lose control. If he attempts to draw trumps, East will hold up until the third round and lead another club, while if South abandons trumps and plays on diamonds East will score one of his small trumps by ruffing.

Missing Easy Inferences

Defenders too often go wrong in situations like the following.

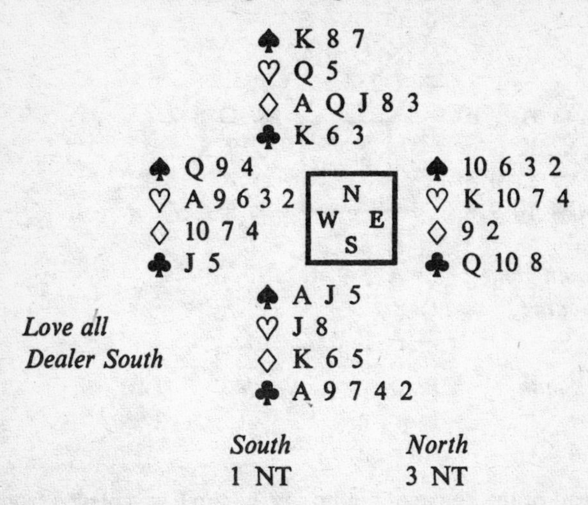

The opening lead was the three of hearts, and when the five was played from dummy East inserted the ten. The declarer then made cackling noises and ten tricks.

Although there are many occasions when it is right to finesse against a card on the table, this is not one of them. The play of the ten can be right only when declarer has the ace, but that is hardly possible here. If declarer had the ace of hearts he would not have played low in dummy. He would have taken his only chance of scoring the queen by playing it at once.

The play of the low card from the table is a clear indication that West has led from the ace. And in view of the strong dummy it should be clear to East that the declarer will have no shortage of tricks once he gains the lead.

As the only hope of defeating the contract, therefore, East should put up the king of hearts and attempt to take five tricks in the suit.

There is always an inference for the defenders to draw when the declarer adopts an unusual line of play. Any departure from normal practice should be given a long, hard look.

Missing Easy Inferences

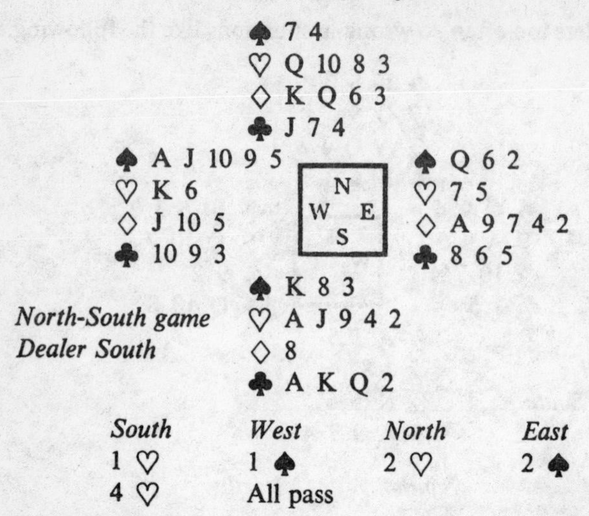

On the lead of the knave of diamonds the three was played from dummy and East encouraged with the seven. West continued with the ten of diamonds, which was covered with the queen and ace and ruffed by the declarer.

South entered dummy with the knave of clubs in order to take the trump finesse. West won and led a third diamond for South to ruff. After drawing the outstanding trumps South was able to discard one of dummy's losing spades on the fourth round of clubs and claim his contract.

East missed his opportunity at trick one. The unnatural play of a low diamond from dummy was highly suspicious. Why should the declarer fail to cover the knave? It could only be because he was terrified of allowing East to obtain the lead. If East draws the proper inference it is not hard for him to play the ace of diamonds on the first round and shoot back a spade to defeat the contract.

An unusual play by the declarer passed unnoticed on the following hand.

Missing Easy Inferences

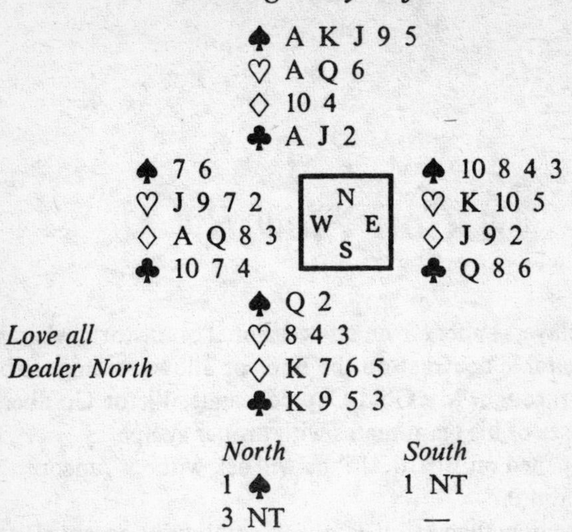

North	*South*
1 ♠	1 NT
3 NT	—

West led the two of hearts and the queen was captured by the king. East returned the ten of hearts to the ace, and the declarer played off three rounds of spades. South and West both discarded a diamond on the third spade, and South then threw West in with a heart lead. After cashing his fourth heart, on which dummy discarded a diamond and South a club, West was end-played, forced to concede the ninth trick either in clubs or diamonds.

East might have asked himself why South had departed from normal practice by risking his queen of hearts on the first trick. If South had had no problems he would surely have played the six of hearts in order to protect the queen. There were just two possible explanations. Either South had nine tricks on top and was trying for the tenth, in which case it would not matter what East returned, or South was anxious to avoid a switch to another suit. The only suit he could fear was diamonds, and on this reasoning East should have returned the knave of diamonds at trick two.

13

'A Cow Flew By'

THE best of players suffers from an occasional brainstorm when he puts an unbeatable contract on the floor or allows an impossible game to slip through. My Gold Cup colleague, Victor Goldberg, treats the lapses of his team-mates with proper sympathy.

'What happened on Board 31?' he will ask without rancour. 'A cow flew by, did it?'

This face-saving suggestion is always gratefully accepted, for there is no valid excuse that an expert can offer for his mistakes. He cannot plead inexperience, or lack of familiarity with the correct percentage or safety play, and his pride will not let him admit that any hand was too difficult for him. All he can do is to claim that a flying cow, or something equally improbable, distracted his attention at a critical moment.

Although a lapse of concentration is commonly known as the experts' error it is not, of course, confined to experts. All players need to maintain a high degree of concentration, especially in defence, if they are to play up to their own standards. The mistakes that really grieve us are the ones we are quite good enough to avoid. These are invariably brought about by a lack of proper attention.

Fatigue is often a factor, since a tired player tends to be a careless player. There is a big premium on physical and mental stamina in long championship matches. Playing something like sixty boards a day for ten days or a fortnight is enough to exhaust all but the very fittest, and for this reason bridge at the top is becoming more and more a young man's game. As a player leaves his half century behind his technique may become more assured, but he is progressively less able to maintain his concentration at the required pitch for long periods.

The best way of combating fatigue is to snatch a moment of relaxation between boards. That means deferring any discussion of the hands until after the session, which is a good thing from the point of view of partnership harmony as well. It is not difficult to train your concentration to ebb and flow in a regular cycle. Make a conscious effort to relax on the completion of each hand, and it will soon become second nature to end the period of rest with a tightening up of all the faculties of mind as you reach for your cards on the next board. A further opportunity for a short break presents itself when you are dummy. It is both unnecessary and unwise to subject yourself to the strain of mentally playing the hand card by card along with your partner. Relax instead and confine yourself to performing dummy's simple duties.

Members of a team of six engaged in serious competition should adopt and adhere to a rule prohibiting the pair sitting out from watching their team-mates in action. When you are personally involved in a match, watching can be an even greater strain than playing and is likely to detract from your performance in the sessions to come. Rest periods should be used for resting. Have a short nap, or take a bath, or stretch out with a book until such time as you are called back into the line-up.

It is easy to recognize the ambitious players at a championship event. They are the ones who avoid the late parties, going to bed at a reasonable hour in order to make sure they are fresh for the next day. They are sensible in their eating habits, avoiding large meals immediately before a session of play. And, however fond they may be of a drink, they realize that alcohol blunts the edge of concentration and do without until the day's play is over.

The hands in this chapter illustrate what can happen when experts lose their concentration. You have my assurance that the perpetrators of these horrors are all top-ranking players. Here is one of my own to begin with.

'A Cow Flew By'

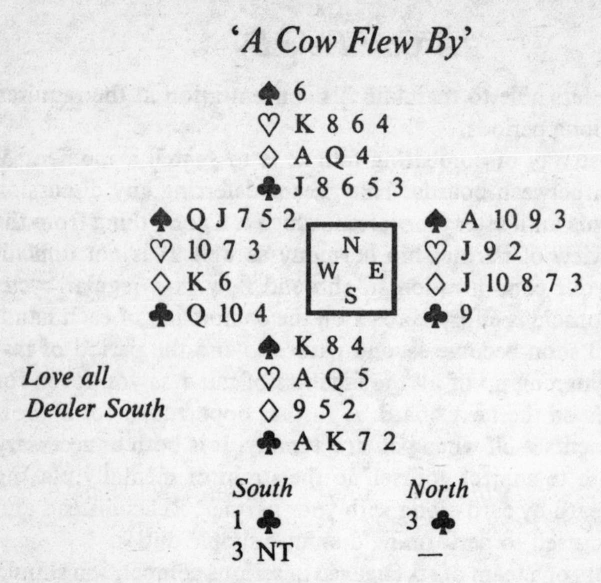

The five of spades was led to the ace and the three of spades returned. I held up the king until the third round, discarding the four and then the queen of diamonds from dummy. When the queen of clubs failed to drop I had no second string to my bow and the contract went one down.

With five top tricks in the other suits, four club tricks were all I needed for the contract, and of course I ought to have discarded a club from dummy on the third round of spades. When the clubs failed I would then have had the extra chance of the diamond finesse plus an even heart break and would have made this simple contract.

Why didn't I see it? Ask the cow.

A declarer paid the penalty for overlooking an elementary safety-play on this hand from the match between Britain and the Netherlands in the European Championships of 1969.

'A Cow Flew By'

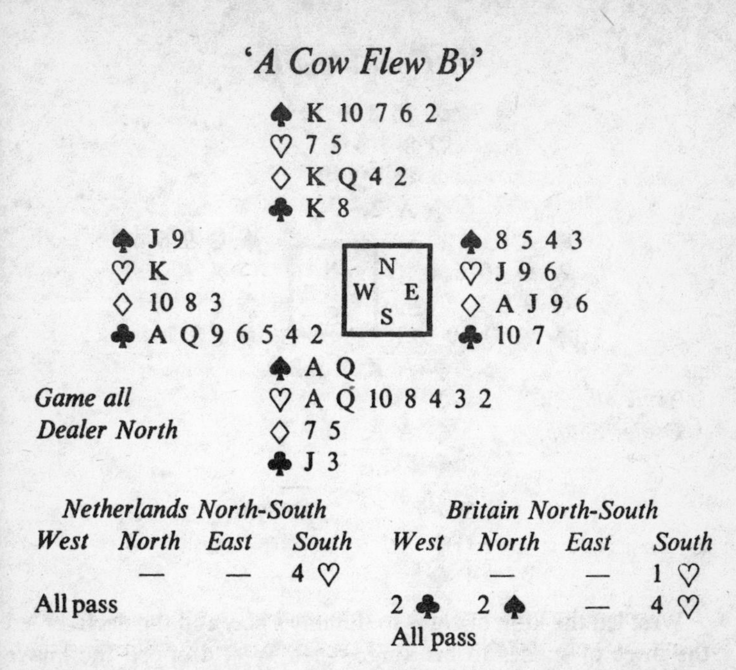

Netherlands North-South

West	*North*	*East*	*South*
	—	—	4 ♡
All pass			

Britain North-South

West	*North*	*East*	*South*
	—	—	1 ♡
2 ♣	2 ♠	—	4 ♡
All pass			

In both rooms the defence started off with the ace and another club. The Netherlands declarer then played like a beginner by finessing the queen of hearts and losing to the singleton king. On regaining the lead she tried to drop the knave of hearts and thus lost two trump tricks and the contract.

Only a massive lapse of concentration can explain this error. The British declarer was guilty of no such blind spot. Realizing that she could afford to lose one trump trick but not two, she played a heart to her ace at trick three. When the king dropped, she led a diamond to the queen and ace. Eventually she was able to take the marked finesse against the knave of hearts and make eleven tricks, giving Britain a surprise swing of 13 i.m.p.

The next hand comes from a Gold Cup match.

'A Cow Flew By'

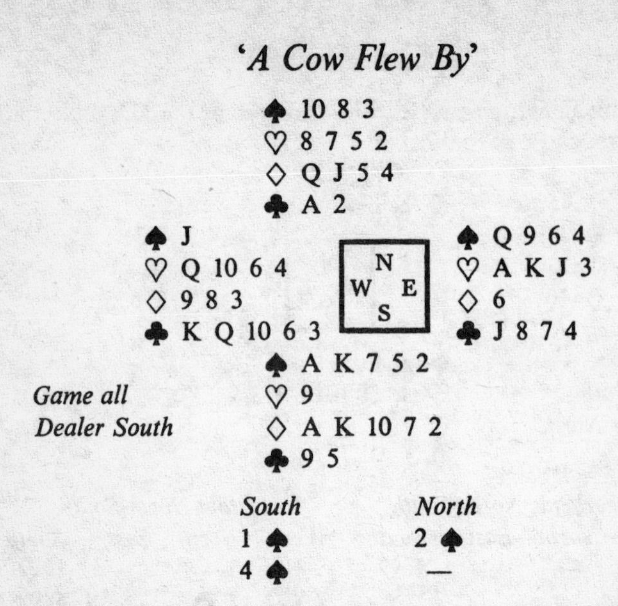

West led the king of clubs to dummy's ace, and the declarer led the three of spades to his king. When West dropped the knave South considered the implications of a 4–1 trump break, and his ears began to burn as he realized that he ought to have unblocked the eight of trumps from dummy. Perhaps it would not matter, he told himself. The diamonds could be 2–2.

But the diamonds were 3–1 and it did matter. South continued with a small spade to the ten and queen, and East switched to hearts. The declarer ruffed the second heart, led a diamond to the knave and ran the eight of spades. When he tried to return to hand in diamonds, however, East ruffed and cashed a club to defeat the contract.

In the other room the contract was the same and again West failed to find the killing heart lead. The declarer was careful to unblock in trumps and the contract was made.

That is how matches are won and lost. A player takes his eye off the ball for a fraction of a second and hands 12 i.m.p. to the opponents.

Even in expert circles there exist powerful taboos on the leading of singleton trumps. The following hand comes from the play-off match which determined the team to represent the U.S.A. in the 1970 Bermuda Bowl contest.

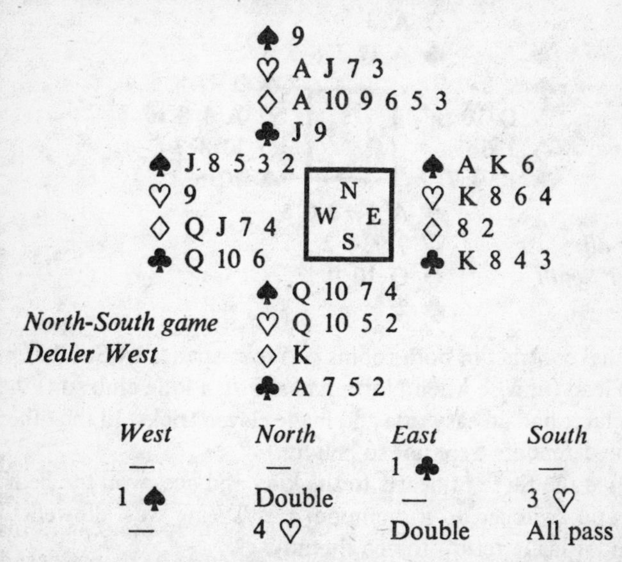

West	*North*	*East*	*South*
—	—	1 ♣	—
1 ♠	Double	—	3 ♡
—	4 ♡	Double	All pass

On the above bidding it should have been clear to West that the only way the declarer might arrive at ten tricks is by ruffing. A trump lead earns at least 500 and possibly 800 points, but West led the six of clubs and the prospect of a large penalty vanished.

The king of clubs was allowed to hold the first trick, and East still had the chance to inflict a one-trick defeat by switching to a trump himself. He cashed a high spade and returned a club, however, and the declarer made his contract on a cross-ruff.

In the other room North was the declarer in four hearts and again the trump lead was not found. East started with a high spade, and it was no longer possible to defeat the contract.

In the 1966 Bermuda Bowl contest the U.S.A. received an unexpected present of 13 i.m.p. on this hand when the Italian declarer had cow trouble.

'A Cow Flew By'

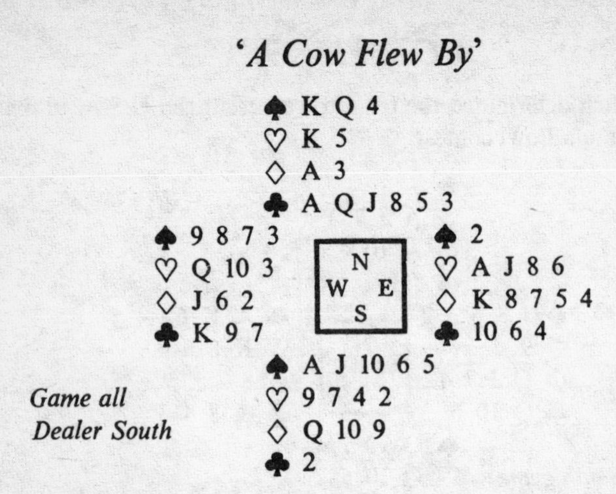

The final contract in both rooms was four spades by South. On a trump lead (unwise when North had shown a long club suit) the U.S. declarer had an easy ride and made eleven tricks. In the other room the defenders were not so helpful.

West led the three of hearts to the king and ace, won the heart return, and switched to a diamond. East's king was allowed to score and a heart return forced dummy.

Although the defenders have won three tricks, the Italian declarer is in no real trouble at this stage. All he has to do is cash the ace of diamonds, play ace of clubs and ruff a club, cash the queen of diamonds, ruff his last heart and claim the contract.

South was blind to the danger of a 4–1 trump break, however, and played ace and another club before cashing the ace of diamonds. When the fourth heart was led West discarded the king of clubs. South ruffed in dummy and returned to hand by overtaking the king of spades only to find that he had to lose a trump to West.

Counting in defence should be a matter of routine for an expert, but West nodded on the following hand.

'A Cow Flew By'

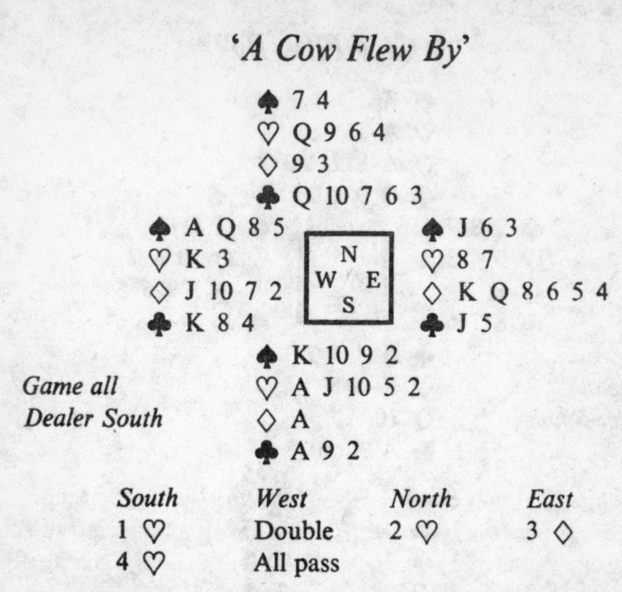

North: ♠ 7 4 ♡ Q 9 6 4 ◇ 9 3 ♣ Q 10 7 6 3

West: ♠ A Q 8 5 ♡ K 3 ◇ J 10 7 2 ♣ K 8 4

East: ♠ J 6 3 ♡ 8 7 ◇ K Q 8 6 5 4 ♣ J 5

South: ♠ K 10 9 2 ♡ A J 10 5 2 ◇ A ♣ A 9 2

Game all
Dealer South

South	*West*	*North*	*East*
1 ♡	Double	2 ♡	3 ◇
4 ♡	All pass		

The opening lead of the knave of diamonds went to the ace, and South, having no convenient entry to dummy, played out the ace and another heart. A second diamond lead was ruffed, and South led the two of clubs.

Not wishing to resolve the declarer's guess in the club suit, West played smoothly low, but South had no guess to make. He could not make the contract if East were able to gain the lead, so he played the queen of clubs and continued with the ace and another to end-play West.

If West had been functioning normally he would have realized that since South had only five hearts and one diamond he was marked with seven cards in the black suits. There was therefore not the slightest need to try for two defensive club tricks. West should have made certain of defeating the contract by taking his king of clubs on the first round and returning the suit, secure in the knowledge that he would have to score two spade tricks eventually.

An expert indulged in a spot of over-finessing on this hand from the U.S. International Trial of 1966.

'A Cow Flew By'

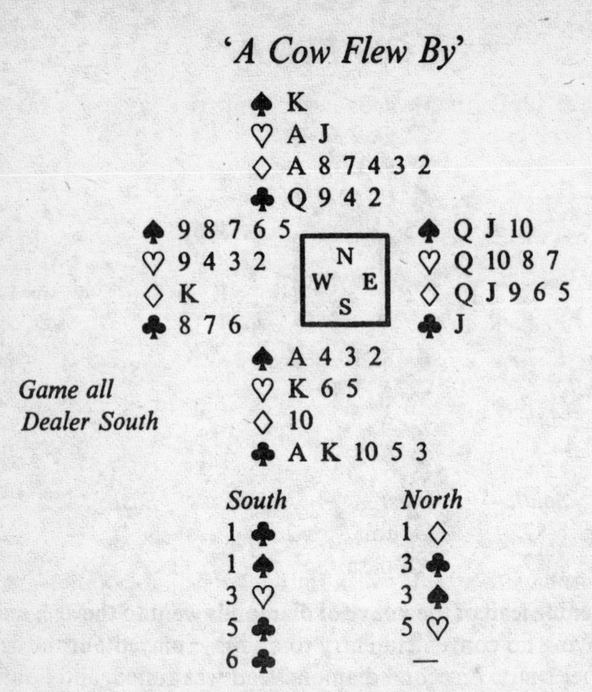

This is a very comfortable slam contract. The declarer has ten top winners and needs no more than two ruffs in dummy to produce a happy ending.

The lead of the two of hearts put temptation in the declarer's path, however, and South carelessly accepted the offer of a 'free' finesse. The knave of hearts was covered by the queen and South had to win with the king. Too late he realized that this play had removed a vital entry from his hand. With the diamonds breaking badly and the trumps 3–1, it was no longer possible to make the slam.

If South had been concentrating he would surely have realized that dummy's knave of hearts was a snare and a delusion. In a contract of seven clubs, needing to establish the diamond suit, it would be reasonable to play the knave of hearts, but it is unsound play in six.

Readiness to over-ruff the dummy is another defensive failing that is not confined to weak players. On this hand from a women's match in the 1961 European Championships the same cow made an appearance in both rooms.

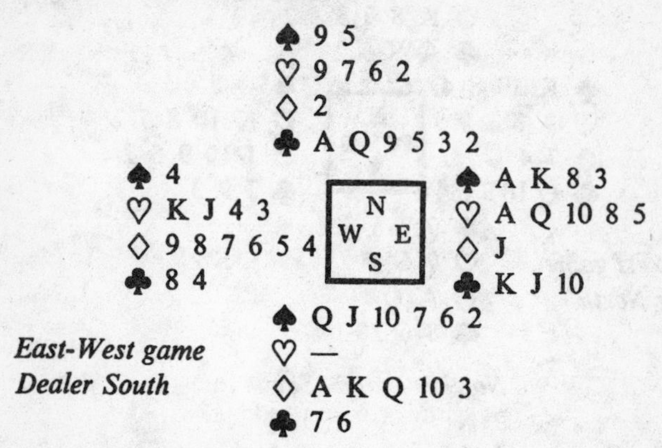

In both rooms South played in four spades doubled after East and West had bid up to four hearts. After ruffing the opening heart lead, the declarers cashed the ace of diamonds and continued with the three, ruffing in dummy with the nine of spades.

Both of the East players over-ruffed with the king of spades and subsequently found themselves unable to defeat the doubled contract.

It is almost incredible that two expert players should suffer from the identical blind spot, thus creating a flat board where there might have been a swing of 890 points. East should, of course, discard a club instead of over-ruffing. This play would make a difference of at least two tricks to the defence. When a trump is led East can win and punch the declarer with a heart return, and in the end South will be able to make no more than four trump tricks, one diamond and a diamond ruff, and perhaps two clubs.

The defence to the next hand is no more difficult, but again an expert had a blind spot and allowed an impossible contract to be made.

'A Cow Flew By'

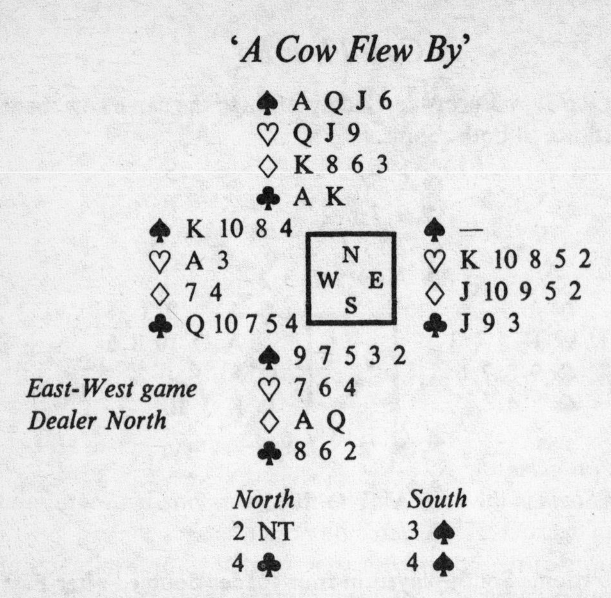

The opening lead was the ace of hearts on which East played the encouraging ten. West continued with a second heart to his partner's king, ruffed the third round, and put dummy on lead with a club.

There were no further tricks to be made by the defence, however. The declarer was able to enter his hand with the ace and queen of diamonds and finesse twice against the king of spades to make his contract.

Although West did not see it at the time, he was the first to point out his mistake in the post-mortem. In order to defeat the game all he had to do was to discard one of his diamonds on the third round of hearts. That simple play would have denied the declarer more than one entry to his hand, and West could not have been prevented from making two trump tricks.

This hand from the 1968 Olympiad shows the effects of fatigue on expert players. It occurred in the final between the U.S.A. and Italy after a fortnight of strenuous play.

'A Cow Flew By'

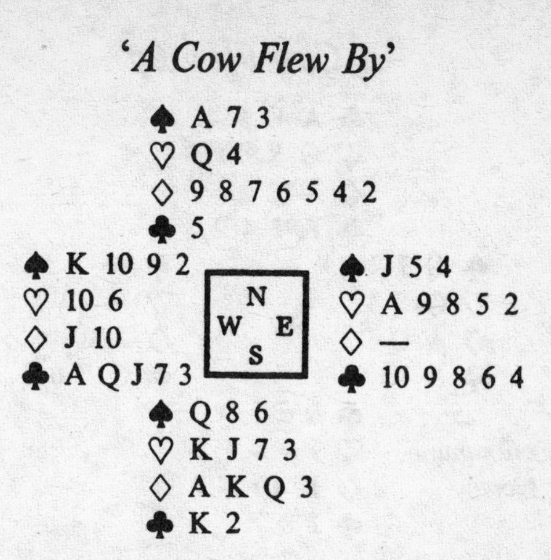

In both rooms the contract was five diamonds by South, and the Italian declarer was defeated on normal play.

Spectators in the open room were treated to an exhibition of confused play and weary defence. Winning the initial lead of the knave of diamonds, the U.S. declarer drew two further rounds of trumps and East handed him the contract by discarding two hearts.

Instead of attacking hearts next, the declarer, not to be outdone in generosity, led the singleton club from dummy and tried to steal a trick with his king. This play could have resulted in defeat if the ace of clubs and the king of spades had not been in the same hand. As the cards lay the declarer was safe enough. West was unable to attack spades with advantage from his side of the table, and the contract was made after all.

An even more striking example of befuddled play comes from the semi-final match between the U.S.A. and the Netherlands in the same event.

'A Cow Flew By'

	North	
	♠ A K 9 4 ♡ A K 10 6 4 ◇ — ♣ K 5 4 2	
West ♠ Q J 7 2 ♡ Q 5 3 ◇ A Q 9 ♣ A 10 9	N W E S	**East** ♠ 10 5 3 ♡ — ◇ J 8 7 6 5 4 ♣ Q 7 6 3
North-South game *Dealer East*	♠ 8 6 ♡ J 9 8 7 2 ◇ K 10 3 2 ♣ J 8	

West	*North*	*East*	*South*
		—	—
1 ♣	Double	2 ◇	2 ♡
3 ◇	4 ◇	5 ◇	Double
—	5 ♡	All pass	

This was the bidding with Holland North-South, and the seven of spades was led to dummy's king. The declarer cashed the ace of hearts, then played the ace of spades and ruffed a spade, West dropping the queen. A club was led to dummy's king and the club return won by the ace. West led his small heart to dummy's ten, and South ruffed a club in his hand and a diamond in dummy.

At this stage, with one trump left in his hand, South had the choice of trying to ruff dummy's last spade or the last club. No doubt influenced by the opening club bid and by the fall of the queen of spades, he attempted to ruff the club, but West over-ruffed and cashed the knave of spades to put the contract down.

Only battle fatigue can explain the declarer's error. When East covered the last club, South's ruff was a nonsense play which could not possibly gain. He had only to discard to make his contract. If West throws his spade dummy will be high. If not, South can ruff the losing spade in hand.

The lapse cost a vulnerable game swing, for in the other room South played in four hearts and made eleven tricks.

'A Cow Flew By'

The next hand is from a Gold Cup final.

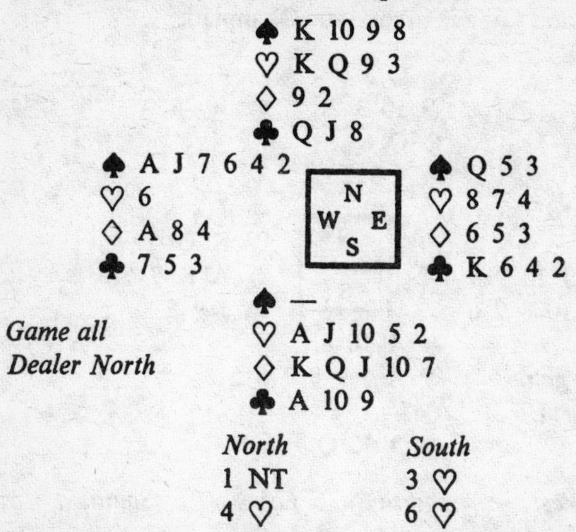

West led the ace of diamonds in order to have a look at dummy. East's three of diamonds offered no encouragement and it seemed that the clubs must be well placed for the declarer, so West concluded that the only faint hope for the defence lay in spades. Murmuring apologetically: 'I don't suppose this will stand up', he led the ace of spades.

He was right in that the ace of spades did not stand up. After drawing trumps and discarding clubs on his diamonds, South was able to ruff one club loser and discard the other on the king of spades.

West failed to appreciate that if South had a spade loser it could never disappear. A passive defence would leave the declarer with a two-way finessing position in clubs. The 3–1 trump break means that both club losers cannot be ruffed in dummy, and South can try for the twelfth trick either by a natural finesse through East or, after discarding clubs on his diamonds, by a ruffing finesse through West.

South might have guessed wrong if West had not solved his problem by trying to snatch the ace of spades.

'A Cow Flew By'

Here is an example of slovenly play from the match between the Netherlands and Canada in the 1968 Olympiad.

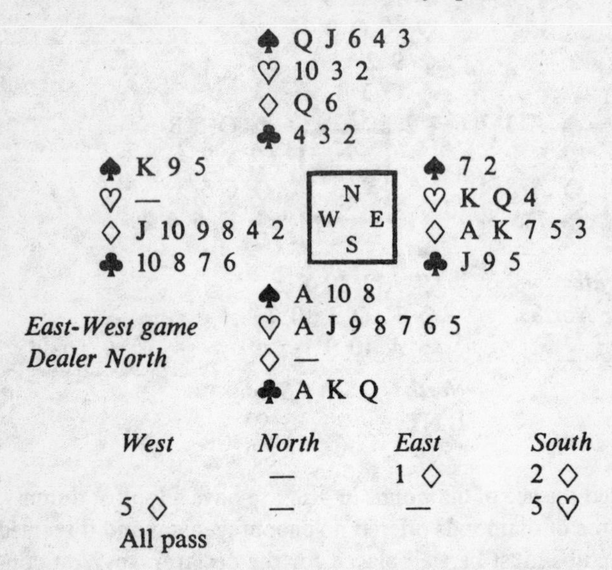

West	*North*	*East*	*South*
	—	1 ◇	2 ◇
5 ◇	—	—	5 ♡
All pass			

The above was the bidding when Canada held the North-South cards. The opening lead was the knave of diamonds, covered by the queen and king and ruffed by South. At this point the declarer completely ruined his chances by cashing the ace of trumps. He subsequently had to lose two hearts and a spade for a one-trick defeat.

The Canadian declarer is normally the most careful of card-players. Ninety-nine times out of a hundred he would have found the winning play of leading a small trump from hand at trick two. There is little risk in this play, for the danger of a first-round enemy ruff must be very remote. West's discard exposes the trump position, and South will realize that he must underlead his ace of spades in order to gain entry to dummy for a trump finesse.

Canada was fortunate to gain on the board when the Netherlands conceded 500 points in the other room in a contract of six spades doubled.

'A Cow Flew By'

A master player missed an elementary safety-play on the next hand.

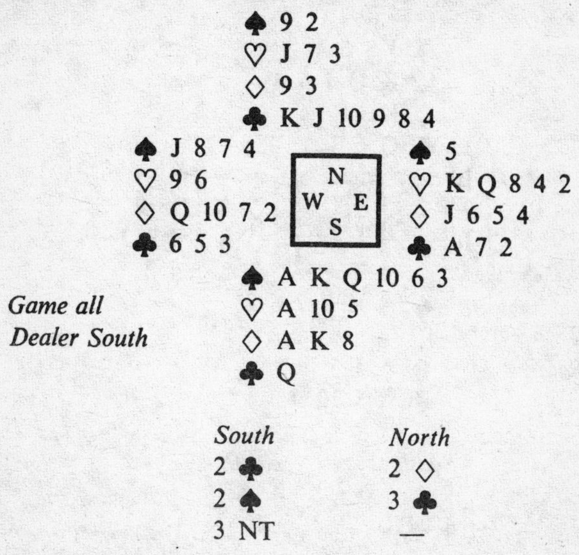

West led the two of diamonds to the knave and king, and the declarer's first move was to attempt to steal a club trick. East trusted his partner's three of clubs, however, and won his ace on the first round.

When the four of diamonds was returned, South took his ace and played out the spades from the top, but he had to concede the fourth round to the knave. West cashed two winning diamonds and led a heart, and the declarer was unable to avoid the loss of a heart trick.

South was quick to spot his own mistake. It was clear that the diamonds were 4–4, and after winning the ace of diamonds all he had to do to ensure his contract was to lead the ten of spades from hand. If West ducked South would have six tricks in the suit, while if West took his knave the nine of spades would provide access to the five winning clubs on the table.

After failing to find the winning defence on the following hand,

'A Cow Flew By'

West declared his intention of giving up the game. Fortunately he changed his mind and has since produced many fine defences.

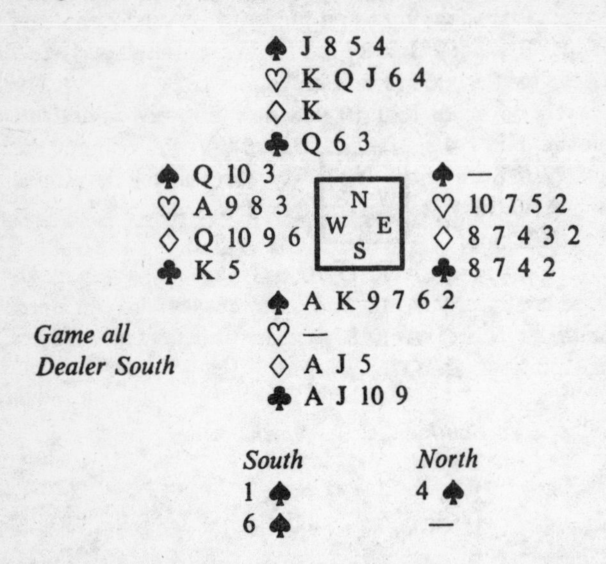

South	*North*
1 ♠	4 ♠
6 ♠	—

West managed to refrain from doubling and found a safe lead in the ten of diamonds, East playing the two under dummy's king. The declarer attacked trumps, playing out the ace, king and another while East discarded three more diamonds.

On winning the queen of spades West was again on the spot. It would clearly be foolish to attempt to cash the ace of hearts and a club lead was unthinkable. West therefore decided that the safest move would be to lead another diamond. But as the cards lay this was not good enough. South discarded two clubs from dummy on his diamonds and then played the ace and another club. When West's king appeared it was all over.

By discarding diamonds East had given his partner the right information. West knew that South could not have more than four diamonds and must therefore have at least three cards in hearts and clubs. It followed that the lead of a *small* heart could not give away the slam even if South had a singleton in the suit.

Eventually West would be bound to score the setting trick with his king of clubs.

For an expert, to whom counting ought to be second nature, this was not such a difficult defence to find. West himself was in no doubt about the magnitude of his blunder.

Master players do make frequent mistakes, not only in difficult situations but in easy ones as well. The experts who commit the fewest indiscretions are those with the most highly developed powers of concentration, and they are the players who win most of the major tournaments.

It is the same story at any level. The winners are those who make the fewest blunders in simple situations. Any player who can learn to cut his mistakes by half will find his game transported to a new level and his ambitions within his grasp.